SLIP

A novel by L. Ryan Storms

"[D]eftly balances magical realism with a sensitively observed portrait of a teenage girl struggling with debilitating panic attacks. A thoughtful and satisfying blend of magical realism and romance."
— *Kirkus Reviews*

"SLIP is sure to please YA readers with its compassionate exploration of mental health, first love, and supportive relationships. Its magical realism, seamless prose, and lovable characters elevate it from endearing to memorable and evocative."
— *IndieReader*

Published by RaineStorms Press, 2025.
The paperback edition has been catalogued as follows:
Name: Storms, L. Ryan, author
Title: Slip / by L. Ryan Storms
Description: Electronic file (eService)

Summary: A high school junior with crippling anxiety slips 9 minutes and 53 seconds into the past with each panic attack, and when a sandy-haired boy with hazel eyes and a dimple in one cheek tries to whisk her off her feet, she's caught between first love and paralyzing fear.

ISBN 979-8-9922827-0-2 (paperback)
ISBN 979-8-9922827-1-9 (ebook)

Subjects: YFH: Children's / Teenage fiction: Fantasy & magical realism | YFB: Children's /Teenage: general interest
BISAC: YOUNG ADULT FICTION / General
YOUNG ADULT FICTION / Magical Realism
YOUNG ADULT FICTION / Romance / General

www.lryanstorms.com

Cover art by AK Westerman
more at www.akorganicabstracts.com © 2025

For the anxious kids:
You're not alone

and

For Mom and Dad,
Who raised an anxious kid
with love, grace, and humor

CHAPTER ONE

Reader, I have no idea how old I am.

As someone who slips nine minutes and fifty-three seconds backwards through time with every panic attack, I figure I'm older than my birth certificate claims me to be. By five whole days.

Maybe six.

It feels like I repeated a lot more time than that. I think it should count for something.

They should let me get my driver's license a few days early, at the very least. Not that I plan on driving. I mean, I could slip while I'm driving, and then what? What if I "arrive" at my new location while I'm in the middle of making a left turn or something? No thanks. I'll stick to walking. Or running—I do a lot of that.

Still, I feel like I should get some sort of reward for the extra time I've put in. Let me tell you how much longer the school day is when you're called on in class (*especially* English class), experience a moment of pure terror, and then slip ten minutes backwards. An already eternal sixth period of Brit Lit now extends eons.

On the flip side, I now have time to prepare the correct answer when the teacher calls on me in version 1.2, which means all my teachers think I'm a very attentive student. That PJ, she's always so studious.

The only person who knows about my…affliction…is my best friend, Mariana Salvadore, and let me tell you, that was *not* an easy win. I never thought there'd be anyone who understood me or who would even take a minute to listen, but Mariana's been here for me for the last two years. Mom says she's the mac to my cheese, which is really actually super cheesy, and I'm not even being punny.

But Mariana? That girl is my rock. (And her avó makes the best queijadas, which is perfect for the times Mom works nights and I get to stay over for dinner.)

Of course, the story of how Mariana found out about my slipping into the past is worth diving into because once you see, you *see*.

Two years ago. Freshman year. Gym class.

I should mention I hate gym class. You'd think since I run cross-country, gym would be a no-brainer, right? Except that PE isn't about running. I think gym teachers like to create their own ideas of what's important in physical education. Who in the world actually plays badminton, anyway?

So Mariana and I are playing badminton, swinging the tweeter or the birdie or whatever it's called over the net to Josh McCall and Ellen Estrada when Mariana drops the news that her sophomore-year older brother (He's the middle one, not the one who works at the local garage.) got busted yesterday for vaping in the boys' bathroom. He's suspended for ten days, and her mama is beyond livid.

Mariana's mom can be a little scary. I don't even want to imagine what kinds of punishment Marco is currently facing, but ten days' suspension from Feris Alweather High is probably the least of his worries right now.

I'm not entirely shocked that Marco was caught doing something so dumb, but I definitely wasn't expecting to hear about the suspension part, so when Ellen drives the birdie across the net, I miss my next shot entirely. Josh and Ellen slap high-fives on the other side of the court while I check the gymnasium clock. Fifteen minutes left of badminton misery.

I pick up the birdie and hand it to Mariana to serve.

"That's not even the worst part," she says, plucking the plastic birdie from my fingers.

"How can this get worse for him?"

"He decided to sneak out the window, but my mom caught him." Mariana whacks the birdie over the net in a serve as she speaks. She says it so calmly I'm not even sure I heard it right.

"She must be ready to kill him!" I can only imagine the fury in Mariana's mom's head.

"Oh, but it gets better." She lunges to return the birdie back to the other side after Ellen hits it our way.

Then Mariana says words I should never have to hear. "He claims it's your fault."

"He *what?*"

"Yeah, he says he's distraught because you rejected him. He vaped to 'dull the pain,' he says."

Josh hits the birdie with entirely too much enthusiasm for high school gym class, and I dive for it, but I'm so distracted, I don't notice the birdie hitting the net and falling to the ground. It didn't even make it to our side. And yet, here I am, on the floor, my newly skinned knee starting to bleed, panic stirring my blood.

My heart starts to squeeze in my chest, that terrible feeling that always precedes a slip.

No, no, no.

I drop the badminton racket and start tapping the fingers of my right hand one by one against my right thumb. Tapping helps. It doesn't always stop a slip, but sometimes...

But it's not working this time. The pressure continues to build in my bloodstream, that awful release of adrenaline that signals something far worse. So I do the only thing I can.

I get off the gym floor and start running, my sneakers squeaking the whole way across the waxed surface. I don't stop even when I brush past Miss Fulton, our gym teacher. She's too surprised at my sudden sprint to say anything.

"Peej!" Mariana calls as I slam through the double doors that lead outside.

But I don't stop running. My feet pound the pavement of the path leading to the outside tennis courts where another gym class is taking place. If I can make it to the track, I might have a chance at—

"Guess what Marco did," Mariana says as we take our places on the court.

My heart thumps hard from the slip, pounding against my ribcage, threatening to escape my body. My brain takes a second to register the change from running outside to walking to our court in the gymnasium. No matter how many times it happens, it's still disorienting. I blink four times and give my head a shake.

How could Marco blame me for his issues? I mean, sure, he's been crushing on me since Mariana first invited me over to hang out a couple of months earlier, but now, suddenly, *I'm* his scapegoat for vaping in the bathroom and running away from home? Who does he think he is? He's never even asked for my phone number. How can he claim *I* rejected *him*? I mean, I *would* reject him, but that's not the point. He blames me for something I'm not remotely at fault for!

"Uh, hello? Earth to PJ. You okay? You look kind of pale."

That isn't how the original conversation went. The conversation started the same, but I first answered with a groan and "Oh no, what now?"

Because Marco was known for getting in trouble, and I figured he'd gotten caught sneaking out with friends after curfew or something. Then Mariana launched into what really happened, which, of course, ended with Marco blaming me and me running from the gym.

"Yeah," I finally answer. "I'm fine."

"Yo! You gonna talk all period, or can we get started?" Josh McCall yells from the other side of the court. I leer at him because it seems more appropriate for school than giving him the finger, which is what I actually want to do right now.

Breathe. Breathe.

The last thing I want to do is slip again. My heart rate is already beginning to slow, so I think the danger has passed, but I really don't want to repeat an extra ten minutes of badminton, let alone twenty.

I serve, sending the birdie soaring onto the other side of the court, and the game is underway. Again.

But Mariana's still giving me side-eye, most likely because I didn't respond to her juicy Marco-related gossip. To her credit, she says no more about it, and I manage to avoid having the conversation that Marco blames me for all his current screwed-upedness.

Later, in the locker room, Mariana tries again. Gym is last period, so I usually take my time getting changed, but today I rush, as if moving faster will somehow make my anxiety go away. Mariana can sense my unease.

"Okay," she says, her foot on the bench as she ties a shoe. "Spill it."

I finish brushing my hair and start pulling it into a ponytail.

"Spill what?" I drop the brush back into the side pouch on my gym bag.

"Whatever's up with you. You got all weird before when I mentioned Marco. You don't…like him, do you?"

"Oh my God! No! Mariana!" I can't help it. I hit her arm with the back of my hand. "Ew. You know better. He's your brother which, like, almost makes him my brother. Ew."

She laughs as she swats me away. "Yeah, but you've never looked like that before when I mentioned him. I had to ask."

The locker room starts to clear out, most of the girls eager to get home for the day. Mom's been working nights at the hospital for a year now, so no one's waiting at home for me. Now, my rush to get changed seems extra silly.

"Seriously, Peej. You okay? What's up?"

I sit on one of the beat-up wooden benches and fold my gym clothes before I stuff them back into the bag. There's really no reason to fold them. I have to take them home and wash them for the weekend anyway, but it gives my hands something to do.

How can I tell Mariana what's really bothering me? How can I expect her to believe me? *I* wouldn't believe me. I tried telling my mom more than once when I was younger. It didn't go over well, which is probably why I slipped a lot more when I was eight and why she wanted me to see a therapist. If she thought I was crazy, how can Mariana not think the same?

And yet. Not having anyone to talk to might drive me truly crazy.

"Fine," I say quietly. "I need to talk to you about something, but I'm terrified."

"Omigod, PJ, you can tell me anything."

Until this point, that's been mostly true. Mariana and I started hanging together at the beginning of freshman year, and I can hardly remember anything about ninth grade that doesn't involve her. When we aren't together in person, we're talking on the phone or texting late at night. But this…

I swallow.

"Peej…"

"Okay, just wait until the locker room clears out."

Mariana sits patiently beside me, obediently waiting until the last girl leaves the room and the slam of the door echoes shut behind her.

"Hey! Ellis, Salvadore, it's Friday. Let's get out of here." Miss

Fulton's voice echoes off the locker room walls even though she's nowhere in sight. She probably stuck her head in the door to yell for us.

"I just need a minute, Miss Fulton!" Mariana calls. "Sorry! My period came early. Taking care of business and all. PJ's waiting for me so we can walk home together. You don't have to wait for us."

"Alright, girls. Turn the lights out when you leave, please. And don't dawdle."

"Have a good weekend!" Mariana calls back.

"Your period?" I snort.

She shrugs. "It's almost the truth. It'll probably come tomorrow. I'm already getting crampy. So, everyone's gone. Spill it."

I take a deep breath. This seemed like a much better idea when I was first contemplating it. It doesn't seem so good now.

"PJ."

The way Mariana says my name makes me cringe. There's no going back. (Which is absurd because if I slip right now—and my heart *is* starting to pound again—I could totally go back and not tell her at all. Oddly, the thought doesn't comfort me.)

"I know what you were going to tell me before. About Marco."

"Did he text you? He's not supposed to have his phone!"

I shake my head. "I know because you told me."

Mariana looks confused for a moment, pushing her lips together as she tries to remember when she might have shared the news.

Before I lose my courage, I plow forward. "You're not going to remember telling me because that timeline no longer exists. Marco was caught vaping in the boys' bathroom and got suspended for ten days, but that's not even the worst of it because he tried to run away from home and says it's all because of me."

Mariana sits and stares at me for a moment.

"Is this…a joke? How did you know?"

I grind my forehead into my hands. "I told you. You told me this already, but I was so upset by Marco blaming me that I had a panic attack, and when I have a panic attack, well, sometimes I…slip."

"You what?"

"When I have a panic attack and I can't control it, I slip."

She stares at me, her eyes desperately hopeful that I'm joking with her. Oh God, I'm going to lose my best and only friend now, aren't I?

"You slip. What does that even mean, PJ?" She puts a hand to her abdomen and winces. She really is starting to get menstrual cramps.

I reach in my bag for ibuprofen. We're not supposed to have "drugs" in school, but I get awful cramps, and I don't need the school nurse monitoring my period every month.

"It means," I say as I shake two pills into her willing hand. "That I lose my grasp on reality and slip back in time ten minutes when I have a panic attack severe enough to trigger it."

She pauses in putting the pills to her lips. "I'm sorry. You what now?"

I hand her the water bottle from the side of her bag. "I slip. Back in time. And I'm the only one who knows it happened."

She gives me a look of disbelief but takes the water from my hand, nods once, and washes down the medicine. When she's done, she sets the water bottle on the bench beside us and folds her hands in her lap.

I wish I could tell what she's thinking.

I tap my foot nervously against the bench, waiting for her to respond. The pressure is building again. I really don't want to slip. Until today, it's been over a month since I last slipped. If I go twice in one day…

I need to hold. I check the time on my phone again. If I *do* slip, I need to make sure I wait another three minutes, or she won't remember this conversation at all.

"Tell me something I could never know." I grit my teeth together, trying hard to focus on staying in the moment.

"What?"

"Mariana, I'm about to do it again. I don't want to, but I think it's going to happen, and I can't do anything to stop it. If you tell me something now, I'll be able to convince you when we have this conversation in just a few minutes. I know how crazy this sounds, but I swear I'm telling you the truth. Just one thing. Tell me one thing."

She stands. I think she's angry.

"Please."

She must hear the despair in my voice. Another minute passes.

When she finally does speak, she doesn't look at me. She stares at the lockers, and her words come out in a rush. "When I was six, I broke Avó's favorite vase because I was throwing a ball around in the house even though I knew I wasn't supposed to, but the break wasn't all the way through. It was just a crack, so I turned the vase so no one could see. Then I blamed it on Marco when he ran through the living room a few minutes later and tripped over it because it wasn't right up against the wall where it should have been. Avó was furious, and Marco was grounded for a week. I never told anyone I broke it first."

I might have laughed, hearing that story any other time. Right now, I'm just focused on staying put for another thirty seconds. I could. I could. I—

"Hey! Ellis, Salvadore, it's Friday. Let's get out of here." Miss Fulton's voice echoes off the locker room walls. Again.

I close my eyes and will the spinning sensation to stop. Twice in one day. I hope fourteen isn't going to be like eight. When I was eight, I was so terrified of seeing the therapist Mom set me up with that I slipped sixteen times in a row. At eight, a hundred-sixty minutes might as well be a hundred-sixty hours. I don't think I can handle another year with that much slippage.

I open my mouth and echo Mariana's words softly in tandem, just loud enough so she can hear, but Miss Fulton can't.

"I just need a minute, Miss Fulton! Sorry! My period came early. Taking care of business and all. PJ's waiting for me so we can walk home together. You don't have to wait for us."

Mariana startles and looks at me, her dark eyes wide with confusion.

"Alright, girls. Turn the lights out when you leave, please. And don't dawdle."

"Have a good weekend!" Mariana's eyes don't leave mine. She waits until the slam of the door sounds, signaling Miss Fulton's departure. "How did you know exactly what I was going to say?"

I sigh, rub my temples, and then reach for the ibuprofen in my bag. I spill two into my palm and hand them to her wordlessly.

"I don't really have my period," she says, narrowing her eyes, but she takes the pills from me anyway.

"I know. But your cramps are starting, so take that and it'll help."

"Seriously, PJ. *What* is going on?"

"When you were six, you broke your avó's favorite vase with a ball, then blamed it on Marco when he ran through the living room and tripped over it. Marco was grounded for a week, and you never told anyone you broke it first."

The sound that comes from Mariana's lips is somewhere between a gasp and a squeak.

"I know this because you told it to me once already. Just like I know that yesterday Marco got caught vaping in the boys' bathroom, then tried to run away from home and blamed it all on me somehow."

Mariana takes a step back, pinning herself against the lockers, and stares hard at me. She makes the sign of the cross over her body, a sure sign she's freaked out since she only resorts to her mother's brand of religion when she's disturbed.

"Penelope Jane Ellis," she says. "You better start talking to me or, so help me, I'm taking you to confession with me before Mass this weekend."

"It's a long story," I say, my heart finally beginning to slow again. "Let's walk, and I'll tell you. I can't promise you'll believe me, but if you don't, I might throw myself from a bridge, so give it a try, okay?"

"That's not funny." But she washes the ibuprofen down with water, slings her bag over her shoulders, and we head for the doors.

And that's how Mariana Salvadore learned two years ago that her best friend was anything but normal. I count myself lucky she believed me at all. Not many would. She was even the one who helped me figure out my slips aren't ten minutes in length but are precisely nine minutes and fifty-three seconds. My little science-minded Mariana.

After that, though, she started calling me Slip more often than not, which was fine except the nickname caught Ethan Morrow's attention recently, and he's been trying to place its origin ever since.

I make a point of avoiding drama and complicated relationships in general, which is why when Ethan Morrow showed up in my life, I started slipping more days than not. It's eight all over again. Only now, it's eight plus Ethan Morrow.

And Ethan Morrow is a sandy-haired complication on two legs.

CHAPTER TWO

"So after you've got your base made, you'll want to apply your design elements, but you need a special paste to do it." Mr. Sandoz holds up his clay-covered hands, presumably to show us the paste, but all I can see is clay. So much clay. It is, after all, clay class.

"First thing you'll do is make a handful of hash marks on the surface of your base. Don't cut too deep or you'll end up with a hole and then you'll have to patch it or start over." He makes a mash of criss-cross marks on his clay cylinder with a sharp tool and holds it up again so we can see.

Then he dips his fingers in a bowl of liquid clay and applies it all over the marks. "This," he says, "is called slip."

Mariana turns to me, her mouth twisted into a smile barely containing outright laughter. "Slip," she says quietly before hiding her mouth behind a hand.

I roll my eyes. Great, now the nickname will evolve further. It's probably only a matter of time before Mariana calls me Paste. I vow never to respond to it. Slip, at least, is kind of funny in a desperate sort of way.

In a few minutes, Mr. Sandoz sets us free with our projects to decorate as desired. The tables in the art rooms are large, arranged so four students can use one table at the same time. Mariana and I sit across from each other. The seat next to me is empty because the slats underneath are broken, and the entire chair wobbles more than an amusement park ride. No one who values their life sits there, so it's been empty all semester.

But in the fourth chair sits sandy-haired, hazel-eyed, dimple-in-one-cheek Ethan Morrow. He's not really a new kid. I remember him from elementary school, but his parents split when we were in middle school, and he moved to California with his dad. I guess that didn't work out so hot because, well, because Ethan Morrow is sitting next to Mariana now, having started with our junior class at Feris Alweather earlier this year.

He's cute in a no-longer-a-kid-but-not-quite-a-man kind of way, and most of the time, I try to pretend he's not sitting at the table. It's not that I'm mean to him. I just don't start conversations when I don't know where they'll lead. With anyone. It's safer that way. I'm sure you'd do the same if *you* slipped every time you had a panic attack.

And most of the time, Ethan keeps to himself. He throws in his earbuds and pretends Mariana and I aren't at the table, too. A sort of unwritten truce, I guess. Besides, if he's listening to music, Mariana and I can talk freely, which is kind of nice.

Sometimes, I get paranoid and worry he's just got his buds in so he can listen in on our conversations, but then I think about the fact that Mariana and I are usually talking about whatever group assignment is due next in history or chemistry. Truly fascinating.

We don't talk about things like Marco, who's now a senior and still getting into trouble, but who at least is no longer blaming it on me. And we don't talk about things like slipping through time and how maybe it's genetic, and my dad (who I've never known and is nowhere to be seen) must be a secret time traveler, too. We don't mention how my generalized anxiety disorder probably stems from him since no one else in my small family has ever seemed to suffer from anxiety-related time travel. Or anxiety. Or time travel. No, those are conversations we reserve for munching on chips, listening to music, and scrolling through TikTok after school in Mariana's room.

I've actually been good for a couple of months straight, and I'm starting to hold out some hope I've finally outgrown my slippage problem. I've hardly had a single panic attack in the past six months, and Dr. Edmunds hooked me up with a great breathing app that helps me keep focused when I feel overwhelmed. She also has me keeping a diary. Can I still call it a diary if it's on my laptop? And then, of course, I still tap my fingers when I'm feeling overstressed, which is weird but helps.

All in all, things are moving in the right direction.

"So, Slip, huh?" Ethan says. His eyes don't leave his project except to dart to mine for an instant. Then they're back on his work as though he never glanced my way. Is he…smirking?

My pulse gives an off-beat leap.

"Only I'm allowed to call her that." Mariana points a clay-covered finger at him as though to emphasize her point. "You stick to PJ."

Ethan raises his brows but salutes her, leaving a thin streak of white clay across his forehead. I hold in a laugh, and my pulse settles again. At least until Ethan pulls his earbuds from his ears with his clean hand, apparently not interested in music today.

"Seriously, though, you call her Slip all the time. What's the deal with that? Where'd that come from?" He rolls a bit of clay between his fingers before fixing it to his cylinder. Is he making a skull and crossbones?

"She's terribly klutzy," Mariana answers before I get the chance.

Ethan sends a dubious glance my way. "PJ is our girls' cross-country star. Somehow, I doubt she's a klutz."

"Oh, no," I say earnestly as I dip my fingers in the shared bowl of slip to affix clay raindrops to my cylinder. It's harder than Mr. Sandoz made it look. My raindrops want to slide everywhere. Now I get why this stuff is called slip. "Mariana's absolutely right. If I'm not running, I'm walking into everything, constantly tripping over my own feet. Total klutz."

Ethan narrows his eyes like he senses we're leading him on. We are. I'm not klutzy. Not even a little, but I'm hardly a cross-country *star*. I just like to run. Keeping my feet moving makes for a calm brain.

"Hm."

"What about you, Morrow? Any nicknames we should know about?" Mariana asks.

Ethan shrugs.

"Okay, what's your middle name, then?" Mariana doesn't let it go, succeeding in turning the attention away from me and back to him, which is kind of one of her specialties.

"Me? Thomas."

She starts laughing.

Ethan's bottom lip curves in confusion. "Why is that funny?"

"Because it's the perfect setup."

"For?"

"T. Morrow."

I smile, but Ethan doesn't get it.

"Tomorrow," I say.

"Here today, gone T. Morrow!" Mariana throws a wrist to her forehead dramatically. I laugh. She's a goofball, but she's my goofball.

Ethan shakes his head. He's no longer asking about me, though, which is a relief.

"You're on the track team, aren't you?" Mariana asks.

He nods. "Yeah, but I can't do the long-distance stuff. Sprinting is my thing. You know what, though? I'll take running in California heat over running in PA humidity any day." Like any Pennsylvania native, he says Pee-Ay.

I shrug. "Humidity doesn't bother me."

"So why'd you come back to Pennsylvania anyway?" Mariana asks.

I'm a little surprised at the directness of the question, given his parents' divorce and all. I shoot Mariana a look. Ethan flusters, a shade of pink slowly creeping up his neck.

"My dad proposed to his girlfriend, and I'm about as much a fan of the new fiancée as she is of me. With the way they argue already, I figure they'll be divorced in two years. I don't need to be there for that drama." The disgust in his voice shows just how unhappy he is with his dad's decision. "Besides, I really missed cheesesteaks." He cocks a head to the side before adding, "And my mom."

I laugh in response, then successfully steer the conversation back to safer waters for all. "Hey, is that slide presentation on the Dust Bowl due Friday or Monday?"

"It was supposed to be Friday, but half the class is behind, so Mr. Elhab said we could take the weekend to finish it." Mariana follows my change in direction with ease, and, just like that, Ethan sticks his earbuds back in his ears, and we're back to our unspoken truce.

Later, when the final bell rings, I meet Mariana at her locker like I always do, but she scrunches her face. Something's up.

"What?" I ask.

She groans. "I forgot I'm supposed to tutor Tatum today. I have to stay and meet her. I'm sorry!"

I shrug. "I can wait if you want. I've got a ton of chemistry homework to do, and Mom's pulling a double shift because one of the other nurses couldn't make it in *again*. I don't know why she always picks up the extra shifts."

"Because she's the supervisor. Don't be mean to your mom. She's a saint, and I love her."

I roll my eyes. "Yeah, I know. Anyway…"

"Just walk home without me. This could be a while. Tatum says she flunked the last three chapter quizzes, so we're gonna start from the beginning."

I grimace.

"Gov?"

"Trig."

I pretend to gag. "Have fun with that. I'm out."

"I'm sorry! If I didn't need the service hours, I swear…"

"I know, NHS Prez. It's fine. I'll see you tomorrow. Same time, same place."

I leave Mariana and travel the mostly empty halls to the front entrance. Students at Feris Alweather don't mess around. It's been a whole six minutes since the final bell rang, and the school is a ghost town. It's like there's a competition to see who can make it from the door of their last class to the front door of the building in record time.

I never understood the rush. Sure, I want to get home as much as anyone else, but it's not like two minutes makes that much of a difference.

Anyhow, without Mariana, I can take the more direct route home, which will shave five minutes from my walk, but also get me back to a very empty house a whole five minutes earlier. I've been on Mom about getting a cat for company lately. I think I might have finally worn her down. I can feel it. The next time I ask, she's going to give a tired sigh and give in. There've just been too many double shifts lately, and I'm alone more often than not.

I'd ask for a dog if I thought I could get away with it, but dogs mean someone needs to be home to feed them and let them out and all. If I stayed late at school for even a day, I'd be stuck cleaning pee (or worse) off the floor. Cats are semi-autonomous, so theoretically, if Mom and I wanted to go away somewhere for a weekend or something, we still could.

Not that Mom and I go away much. I can't remember the last time Mom and I went anywhere that wasn't the dentist or clothes shopping for school. But if we had a cat, we *could* go to the Poconos or something for the weekend and not worry about the house being destroyed when we got back. We could probably even go to the Jersey shore for a couple of days. You know. If we wanted.

I'm so caught up on my walk home in the fantasy of owning a cat and going on vacation that I don't hear anyone behind me until someone gives a gentle tug on my ponytail.

I whip around, expecting Mariana with an excuse as to why Tatum canceled, but instead, I stand face to face with Ethan Morrow, and he's wearing a grin that makes the dimple in his left cheek stand out.

"Hey, Slip!"

"PJ," I remind him, my pulse speeding up as I realize Mariana's not here to rescue me from whatever Ethan wants. I glance around, looking for his friends. Why is Ethan here?

"Right, sorry. So, hey, I don't usually see you walking after school. You headed home?" He starts walking beside me, and I move forward again, keeping pace.

"I don't usually walk at this time," I answer. "Cross-country practice, you know. But Coach Burns is at a conference and couldn't find anyone to fill in, so she gave us the week off."

"Ah," he says as though I've unlocked the mysteries of the world for him. "It's probably not good for the stamina to take too long a break."

I view him from the corner of my eye, hating how my heart is thumping faster just talking to him. Why is my pulse racing? I have *no* reason to panic right now, and yet my entire circulatory system is thundering like the hooves of a racehorse just out of the gate.

"I'll run later," I reply. Maybe if I don't say a lot, it'll get awkward, and he'll take another route home.

"I have to get my run in later. You wanna go together? I'm right up on Park Street with my mom now. You live over on Lenox, right?"

I halt in my tracks and stare at him. Why does Ethan know where I live? Is he...did he...does he want to hang out with me? Like, a date? Wait, running isn't a date. Exercise isn't a date.

"Uh. Yeah. But, you know what? I might skip today entirely. My hamstrings were a little tight this morning." I make a show of stretching my legs a little as I start walking again. "Thinking about just soaking in the bath tonight instead."

Ethan flushes, and I realize I've just invoked the image of my naked body in a tub full of bubbles. He was probably picturing candles and all.

"I mean," I stutter. "I have a ton of chemistry homework, too, and I'm not even sure I'll finish it all, and I have to be home to...feed...the cat."

Oh God, that pressure. I've been so good for so long. My chest squeezes. Not now! I tap my fingers furiously against my thumb with my right hand while scrambling for my phone with my left. The breathing app. If I can get the breathing app open, maybe I can—

I slam into my body just as I'm leaving the front entrance of Feris Alweather, and for a second, my balance falters. I grab the door jamb to right myself and breathe hard.

None of it happened. No embarrassing conversation with Ethan Morrow and no invocation of nakedness.

I turn and take the way Mariana and I usually walk home, adding five minutes back to my travel time, but avoiding Ethan and the ridiculousness that ensued. Whatever it was.

I mean.

He couldn't have been asking me on a date. Not really. Right? Running isn't a date. It's getting sweaty and gross and breathing hard and...oh. Oh no. Now there are other images in my head that involve that kind of thing, and it's not two people practicing for cross-country.

I shake my head and pull myself out of thoughts of Ethan. I'll get home, log online, and search for a cat. Clearly, I need a cat to keep me company. Obviously, being alone too often has taken its toll on the fragile state of my mental health.

Then, once I've found the perfect shelter cat to print out and stick to the fridge door, I'll reheat the stir-fry from the freezer, start my chem homework, and—

I nearly jump out of my skin when there's a tug on my ponytail.

"Hey, Slip!"

I know exactly who it is before I turn this time, and yet the shock is just as great when I see Ethan Morrow standing in front of me, that stupid grin on his stupid face.

"PJ." My name comes out nearly a whisper.

"Right, sorry. So, hey, I don't usually see you walking after school. You headed home?"

I blink. What is Ethan doing here? He was supposed to walk the other direction.

I narrow my eyes. "Are you following me?"

"Uh. No?" And he looks genuinely confused, not at all embarrassed like he's being called out.

I shake my head. "Sorry, I gotta run."

I tighten the straps on my backpack with a tug, then start a light jog. But I haven't deterred him.

"So dedicated," he says, picking up speed and keeping pace beside me.

Despite its locked-down straps, my book bag thumps against my back a little with each step. So does Ethan's.

"Just trying to keep myself in shape for the meet at the end of the month," I say.

"Well, we should—"

I don't let him finish his sentence. I bolt.

I can't let him say it.

Ethan's taken by surprise, so I'm able to get a head start, but, sprinter that he is, he catches up a moment later.

"Hey! That's not fair. You didn't say go." He gives me a smile and races a pace ahead.

My pulse is still hammering, but at least this time there's no squeeze in my chest. Running usually keeps that from happening, which is why I joined the cross-country team to begin with and why I run four miles a day on the days I don't have practice.

I'm not going to slip this time, which means I'm going to have to give Ethan a whole different kind of slip. It doesn't take long for him to get winded, so I bolt ahead until he falls behind and eventually gives up, hands on his knees as he leans over and catches his breath.

"I won't let you win next time!" he calls from behind me.

There won't be a next time. I'll make sure of it.

By the time I unlock the front door to our tiny house, my back and book bag are covered in sweat, and my hands and face are clammy.

I drop my bag by the door, head straight for the kitchen sink, and shove my head under the faucet, letting cold water cool my neck. I take a few sips while I'm at it. When I've regained some sense of myself, I turn off the water. Mom would kill me if she knew how long I let it run.

I squeeze the extra water out of my ponytail before standing straight. Then I lean against the cabinets and slide to the black and white linoleum until my butt hits the floor. I rest my arms on my knees and drop my head against the cabinet behind me with a thunk. Droplets of water from my cheeks and chin fall to the front of my cotton t-shirt.

I finally let myself ponder the question I can't let go.

Ethan Morrow shouldn't have been behind me when I took my normal route home in version 1.2. So why had he?

CHAPTER THREE

Mariana doesn't answer my panic texts until almost nine-thirty. I sit at my desk, bent over my chemistry textbook—one of the few that's not online, trying to skim the text for the practical applications of magnesium hydroxide. I know it's here somewhere, but my brain doesn't want to translate the words on the page into any sort of meaningful information. I should make my life easy and just do an AI search, but AI is a notorious liar and I don't want to get caught taking the easy way out.

I'm still hung up on the fact that Ethan showed up on a different path in a different timeline. That's never happened before.

The phone vibrates in my hand. I answer and put it on speaker. It's not like there's anyone around to listen.

"Peeeeeeej! No! What's going on?"

I shake my head. "It's so dumb."

And just like that, the tears start flowing. I didn't even know I was going to cry.

"Hey, hey, breathe." Mariana's voice is the comfort I didn't know I needed. "Open the app. I'll wait. No, actually, I'll breathe with you. After all afternoon with Tatum, I could use it. She thinks SohCahToa sounds like the name of an indigenous people and would rather talk about that than how to calculate the length of a hypotenuse. So, yeah, let's breathe together 'cause I need it, too."

I know she's trying to make me smile, but I can't. I sniff and open the app on my phone, keeping Mariana's call connected in the background. A moment later, the calm, automated voice of a nameless lady Mariana and I have dubbed Susan speaks over the gentle sound of ocean waves.

"That's it, Susan. Tell me what I want to hear," Mariana says. I almost laugh.

I wipe a stray tear from my cheek, close my eyes, and focus on breathing in and out as Susan instructs me to do. After a few minutes, Susan releases us from our meditation and I close the app again.

I'm quiet for a moment, so Mariana takes the opportunity to be herself.

"One of these days, Susan's going to ask me to run off with her. I can feel it."

Laughter bubbles from my throat. I can't keep it in. Mariana is ridiculous when I need it the most.

"I hate to break it to you," I reply. "But I think Susan probably has a crush on Siri."

Mariana gasps. "Well, don't tell Alexa. She thinks she's Susan's one and only."

I wipe the tear stains from my face, feeling just a fraction lighter than I felt before Mariana's warm voice in my ear soothed my nerves.

"Alright, Slip. Let's hear it."

So I tell her. I relay everything that happened and how Ethan Morrow showed up in version 1.2 where he shouldn't have been. How the conversation led to the same place—or would have if I hadn't run away—and how he had kind of, sort of, maybe asked me on a date.

"Oh. Em. Gee. PJ! I knew something was up today when he started talking to you during clay class."

"Hey, can we focus on the issue, please?" I pick at a cuticle on my pinkie until it bleeds, then curse myself, grab a tissue, and wrap it around my finger. Mom's been on me about my cuticles forever.

"The issue is Ethan, no?"

"No. I mean, yes, but no. Mariana! Why was Ethan in version 1.2 when I took a different route home?"

She's silent for a moment. I think I hear her biting her thumbnail.

"Don't bite your nails," I scold, feeling only a little guilty as I stare at my own tissue-wrapped cuticle.

"This is why I prefer text."

"Don't stick your tongue out at me, either."

"Stop! That's just creepy. How'd you know?"

She's predictable. Maybe that's part of the reason why we're such good friends. It's easy to love someone who doesn't keep me guessing. Around Mariana, I don't slip. Not since that one time in gym class, after which we mutually staked our claim as each other's besties.

"Ethan," I say, bringing the conversation back to where I need it to be.

She huffs. "Maybe it was a fluke. Like, if it happened a lot—and it better not, because I don't want you slipping all over time, thank you—

maybe I would worry, but if it's just a one-time thing, it's probably chance. And you're sure he wasn't following you?"

"I'm telling you. He looked completely and utterly bewildered when I suggested it. Like, if he *had* been following me, I'd expect him to look guilty or something, but no. He really didn't. Just confused. And I know he lived in California and all, but I don't think he's that good of an actor."

"Bewildered, huh? Like that cute, confused face he makes?"

"Mari!"

"What! I'm not saying I like him or anything. I'm just saying he's cute. You'd have to be blind not to see it. You don't think he's cute?"

I search for a response, but fail to find one.

"Ha! See?" she gloats.

It's true. Ethan is adorable, but I'm not into adorable. I'm not into sun-kissed brown hair or hazel eyes or smiles with dimples because I'm not into anything. I'm into *not* slipping. That's it. That's all my life has ever been. A struggle not to slip.

I don't have time for boys.

Not even cute ones.

"You've been quiet for a hot minute there, PJ. You thinking about… things?"

"Look, even if he's cute, I don't have time for cute. I don't need cute. I need to focus, I need to breathe, I need to run, and I need to not slip. *And* right now I need to finish this chemistry homework so I can get some sleep. I'm always exhausted after I slip."

"Well, gee, I wonder why. I'm pretty sure human bodies aren't made to do what yours does. I kinda want to study your DNA and amino acids and stuff, but a one-person study doesn't make for good science."

"I'm going to pretend you didn't say that because that's super creepy, but, hey, before I hang up, what's magnesium hydroxide good for?"

"Heartburn. It's an antacid." She doesn't hesitate in her answer.

Why is she such a nerd? So much more reliable than AI.

"Thank you! That's the last question. I knew you'd know. Alright, I'm going to bed. See you tomorrow."

"Sweet dreams." The way Mariana sings those words leaves no doubt what—or who— she's hoping I'll dream about.

"Staaaaahp!" I reply.

She laughs, then hangs up.

I go to bed, and I do *not* dream of Ethan Morrow.

I'm not sure how I'm going to avoid Ethan the next day, especially since he's right there across the table in first period, but it turns out I don't have to avoid him because he's actually *not* here today. He's on an all-day field trip the photography class takes every year. Some nature hike somewhere just across the river in New Jersey.

I don't care where, really, so long as it gives me a chance to breathe and recover from our mortifying interaction yesterday. Not that it was mortifying for him. Not that he remembers the mortifying part of it. But I do, and seeing him first thing today might have made me slip again. As a result of his absence today, I'm unnaturally happy during first period. Relief will do that.

"Someone's chipper this morning," Mariana comments.

"Mmph," is all I reply.

And that's that. She smiles but says—or implies—no more about Ethan, and we go the rest of the day pretending yesterday never happened at all.

When I get home, I spot Mom's note on the fridge. She used to just text me, but I forgot to put my phone on silent in school once, and then *she* had to explain to Mr. Burgess why she was texting me during an algebra quiz in the middle of the school day. I was mortified, but Mom might actually have been forever scarred. After that day, sticky notes became a regular thing in our house.

I take in her familiar handwriting. Can handwriting sound like a person's voice? I swear hers does. She's working night shift on Thursday but has off on Saturday, which means after she catches up on sleep on Friday night, we can do something together over the weekend.

Sure. If none of her staff call in sick.

I know she works hard. I try not to be angry she's not around, but it's difficult when I see other kids with two parents who work normal hours, and other families who seem to live much more normal lives than we do.

Sometimes I wonder if I would still slip if she worked normal hours and I had a dad. Then I mentally kick myself for wanting something different. Mom is amazing, and she's always been there for me.

Just not physically.

At least not since I was old enough to know not to burn down the house. Before that, I just spent a whole lot of time with Mrs. Koehler next door. Nice lady, baked amazing brownies, but her choice of television left a lot to be desired. For my own sanity, I usually brought along my tablet and vegged on YouTube for three hours. Can't say I regret growing out of needing a sitter.

I swap my school clothes for a light t-shirt that says "*I run like a girl, try to keep up*" and a pair of slinky shorts that highlight my runner's thighs, pull my hair into another ponytail, and lace up my sneakers. Then, I grab my phone from the kitchen counter and slip it into the armband pouch Mom got me to make sure I always had my phone when I'm out on a run. You know, just in case I get abducted.

I pull the front door shut behind me and stand on the porch, stretching my arm and leg muscles, warming up my core. I'm aiming for six miles today. I think I can do it in an hour, but I've never really tried before. The cross-country courses don't usually go more than three to three-and-a-half miles, so on the days I'm not running for the team, I try to push a little harder. (Of course, the cross-country courses are measured in kilometers, not miles, but that's not how I track it on my own time because I'm an American, for crying out loud.)

I'm about two miles in, just starting to set my pace, my breathing slowing into a deep, easy rhythm, my legs feeling like they could take me a thousand miles if I ask them, when I reach the local park and merge onto the loop around the lake. A couple of laps around the half-mile loop is good for adding in the extra mile to my normal run, and the paved path makes for easy footing.

The paved path also makes for lots of young kids on bikes and skateboards. My eye catches on a little girl who can't be more than four. She peddles as fast as she can, her training wheels taking her down the path far in front of her father, who stops to talk with a couple of guys along the way.

He calls to her just as I near, warning her not to go too far without him, but the girl is all smiles. She probably doesn't even hear him. Her first bike, I bet. Mom got one like it for me when I was about five, but even then, I preferred my own two feet. I smile and wave at the little girl, trading the path for grass so she won't have to go around me.

"I like your helmet," I say. Red curls trail from the back of the pink plastic dome.

"It's pink! It matches my new bike." She smiles back at me, stops peddling for a second, then rings the bell on her handlebars.

She's so cute. I want to lean down and smoosh her cheeks, but her dad would probably frown on that (not to mention it's a creeper kind of move), so I keep my pace. In another minute, I'm a quarter of the way around the lake. The sun is shining and a light breeze rustles the leaves of the massive oaks and maples surrounding the lake. It feels like one of those days where nothing in the world could possibly go wrong.

And then Ethan rounds the corner up ahead, jogging with earbuds in his ears, eyes down, focused on the path in front of him.

I'm starting to wonder if the universe is conspiring against me. If I dart off the path and into the surrounding woods, I could avoid him, but all he has to do is look up, and I'll be caught anyway. Better to stand my ground and keep moving forward. Maybe he's in "the zone" and won't see me.

A girl can hope.

But the grin that emerges when he looks up and recognizes me can't be avoided. He slows as though we might stop to chat.

I don't stop, but I give him a nod. (See? I'm not completely without manners.) Then I breeze past him. It doesn't take long for him to turn around and catch up.

And now we're running together even though I vowed I wouldn't run with him.

At least he doesn't try to talk.

We're at the far end of the lake when I see a commotion on the opposite shoreline. People run, racing to the water's edge, a few of them actually wading into the water, which is really weird. No one swims in this algae-filled mess except for the ducks and the occasional overzealous Labrador retriever.

I turn my attention back to the path and increase my pace just to get back to that spot to see what's going on.

"Oh, shit," Ethan says.

I peer around him and follow his gaze.

They're pulling a body from the water. Oh, God. They're pulling a tiny body with a hot pink helmet. What happened?

My blood starts to race, and I stop in my tracks. Suddenly, I don't want to reach that side of the lake. The little girl who just smiled at me, who rang her little bicycle bell and proudly showed off her helmet…is receiving CPR. I don't want to see it, don't want to know.

Ethan stops beside me and puts a hand on my shoulder. I think I've started hyperventilating.

"Hey, PJ," he says as he steps between me and the sight I can't tear my eyes away from. He puts another hand to my other shoulder, then stoops down a little so his eyes are even with mine and I'm forced to look at them. They're more green than hazel in the sunlight.

Why am I noticing Ethan's eyes?

"Hey, look here. Look here, PJ. It's okay." His voice is calm and controlled and his eyes bore into mine, examining them as though he can somehow find a way to climb inside my head and speak directly to my brain.

"I just…I just passed her."

"I know. Listen, there are sirens already. I hear them. Do you hear them? Help is coming. She's going to be okay."

"Okay," I choke. But the crowd grows around her, voices shouting for help to hurry.

My hands start trembling at my sides. Automatically, I begin to tap with the fingers of my right hand. I don't want to slip. I don't want to see this happen again. I don't—

When I'm thrown back into my body, I'm still hyperventilating, but I'm no longer in the park. I'm two blocks away. My eyes dart from left to right, looking for Ethan, who isn't here. Not that he should be. But something about the way his hands gripped my shoulders a moment ago has me feeling like they're still there.

I bend over, put my hands on my knees, and focus on slowing my breathing, calming my heart. I have to get a grip. I need to get ahold of myself so I don't keep slipping. I can't. I can't do it again.

I can't see that little girl again.

I stand upright, take a quick glance at the time on my phone at my arm. I don't know what time it was when she rode her bike into the lake. I don't know when she stopped breathing or how long I was in the park before it happened.

But I can't just let it happen again. I won't.

I take three deep breaths, and then I sprint like it's the 400-meter dash, and I'm coming in second.

I make it to the park, pause for a moment, and scan the loop around the lake as far as I can see. Right away, I spot Ethan on the far end of the lake. He hasn't seen me yet. There's the old couple holding hands, the kids playing frisbee in the field to the side of the lake, and…there—the group of guys talking.

Where is she? Where is she?

I scan the path, but now I'm running again. Her dad is there. Gray shirt, red ball cap. He's in the group, which means she's just ahead, or she *was* until she steered herself down the dirt path the boys my age take when they come to fish the lake. I rip at the velcro band that holds my phone to my arm and throw it to the ground, never missing a stride.

I race to the water's edge and leap in, gasping as the cold water hits my skin. It's not freezing, but it's still a shock. The lake is waist-high here, and there's a pink training wheel visible at the surface of the water. It's still turning. I plunge beneath the water, my hands grabbing for purchase on the bike that will lead me to wherever the girl is. My probing fingers locate the problem in seconds.

She fell over the handlebars, and the bike pinned her to the muck at the bottom of the lake. Still beneath the water's surface, I toss the bike to the side, grab her shirt, and heave upward with everything I've got. It doesn't take much. She can't weigh more than thirty pounds.

She reaches for me, her fists forming tiny death grips on my shirt. She's not yet unconscious. She's alive. My heart beats with the rhythm of those two words. *She's alive. She's alive.* We break the surface together as I gain my footing, greeted by hands that pull us from the water. My diving into the lake gained us an audience.

Ethan's there, as well as the little girl's father, who's already taking the coughing, sobbing child from my arms.

"Kayleigh! Kayleigh! What were you doing? What were you thinking? Oh my God, Kayleigh." He hugs the girl tight, tears openly streaming down his face, then he kneels and puts her on the ground so she can stand. His voice is choked with near grief. "Do you know what could have happened?"

"I'm sorry, Daddy," she sobs. "I didn't know how to stop. I went down the hill." The last part is said with a sob between each word.

He undoes the latch of her helmet and tosses it on the ground, then he holds her tight and kisses the top of her head again and again. Someone nearby pulls off a windbreaker and drapes it around the little girl's shoulders. Her father pulls back just enough to wrap her tightly in it. Then he hugs her all over again.

I can still see her lifeless body being pulled from the lake.

It didn't happen. That version of events never happened. The evidence is in front of me, but my brain still hasn't quite embraced the truth of it. For once, nine minutes and fifty-three seconds mattered. I choke back a sob of my own.

Wordlessly, Ethan holds out a hand. I grab it, and he pulls me up the muddy bank. My soaked clothes hang from my frame. Once my feet are on dry land, I squeeze the extra water from my t-shirt and my ponytail while Ethan helps another guy drag the bike from the water and pull it up the soggy bank back to the paved path.

When Kayleigh's dad finally stops profusely thanking me, he gathers the little pig-tailed girl in his arms again and hoists her to his hip, one forearm holding the girl tightly to him. They head for home, one of the men from his group walking the little bike beside him, the hot pink helmet swinging from the handlebars.

I shiver.

"You okay, Supergirl?" These are the first words Ethan speaks directly to me in this version of events. His eyes are serious, like he's worried I actually might fall apart.

I give a quick nod, but I'm still a bit breathless, and I can't fight the image of a dead child receiving CPR in my head. The picture of her alive in her father's embrace is slowly replacing the former image as a reality, but I think her death might always be with me. I've never seen death before, certainly not up close.

"How did you get there in time?" Ethan asks, his face filled with genuine curiosity.

"I don't know," I lie. I squeeze my ponytail again, a few reluctant droplets falling to my shirtfront. "I just got to the park, and this pink blur caught my eye. It just...didn't look right."

"Yeah, well, you came flying across that path like you were trying to break the speed of light. Color me impressed, Slip."

I shrug, ignoring the nickname. "Just getting my run in."

I trudge up the muddied path back to the pavement, my sneakers squelching with each step. I hope the lake water won't make them stink. Mom won't be thrilled if I need a new pair of trainers, even if I ruined them to keep a kid from drowning. Actually? That's not true. Saving a child might be the only thing that would make needing to purchase a new pair of expensive sneakers forgivable.

"Running like a girl, huh?"

"What?"

"Your shirt." He points.

I look down. "Oh, yeah."

I shake my head. My pulse is still pounding, and I'm starting to feel chilled from being soaked to the bone.

"You're a hero," Ethan says, his words leaving no room for argument.

But I'm not a hero. I don't want to be a hero. I just want to go home, so I change the conversation.

"You weren't in school today."

He brightens a little. Internally, I groan. Now, it seems like I noticed.

"Come on," he says. "You need to get home and get some dry clothes."

I nod, and because he's Ethan and his mom's house is a block and a half from my house, he walks me home. He doesn't make conversation, which should be weird, but somehow isn't. Or maybe I'm just so exhausted that I don't notice it's weird. I don't know. Either way, I'm just relieved to escape having to talk.

We're at my front porch when I realize I don't have my phone. I close my eyes.

"Oh no."

"What's up? Are you locked out?"

I sigh, look up to the sky, and drop my shoulders. "My phone is at the lake. I had it on my armband. When I realized I was jumping into the lake, I took it off and threw it on the ground. I forgot about it…after." I don't elaborate on after what.

"I'll go back for it," Ethan says.

I sigh again and turn back toward the sidewalk. "No, I'll get it. I'm the idiot who—"

"—saved a little girl's life. The least I can do for you is grab your phone. Go inside, get a hot shower and some dry clothes. I'll bring it

back. You don't even have to talk to me. I'll put it in the mailbox."
Ethan's words shock me into compliance.

I bite my bottom lip, then nod as he turns to leave.

"Ethan," I call, and he glances over his shoulder. "Thank you."

Ethan gives a crooked grin, the kind of grin boys in YA novels are always giving, the kind of dimple-evoking grin that makes the main character's heart flutter a little.

But my heart isn't fluttering because of Ethan's smile. It's just from adrenaline.

CHAPTER FOUR

"What do you want to do tonight?"

Usually, when Mom asks this question, the answer is to make popcorn and watch a movie, but she's actually done it. She's taken an entire Saturday off, and, as it's Friday evening, I feel like we're in need of more than just a movie.

"We could...go away for the night?" I say. "Like a cabin or something? That's not too expensive, right?"

She narrows her eyes, thinking. Then she shakes her head, her thick, not-as-dark-as-it-once-was hair swinging at her shoulders with the movement. It's rare I see her hair loose and not pulled back in clips. It's rare she's not in scrubs. Is she...wearing makeup?

"I've got a better idea. Pack a bag and prepare to be spoiled."

She is. She's definitely wearing mascara and a little bit of blush. Maybe light lipstick?

I plant my hands on the kitchen island. "Wait. Where are we going? You've already got something planned, don't you? What is it?"

She sticks her tongue between her teeth, and her eyes light when she speaks a single word. "Theater."

I practically leap. I love theater. Books and movies and podcasts and theater. Storytelling come to life. Life and living in a way that won't send me hurtling backwards through time with panic attacks. Living vicariously through characters who embrace danger and mystery, adventure and love.

I take a moment. Where did she get the extra money for theater tickets? And why do I need to pack a bag to see a show?

I grin at her. "Why am I packing a bag? Where else are we going?"

"Hotel and spa."

"Mom! This sounds like an expensive date. Are you sure you don't want to save this for your boyfriend?"

Mom doesn't have a boyfriend. I think she should get one, but she insists there's no time, so Mom continues to work too many hours and not have a boyfriend. She also says thirty-six-year-olds shouldn't have boyfriends. I think she's wrong.

She puts one arm around my shoulders. "There's no one better to spoil than my favorite daughter."

I regard her through narrowed eyes. "I'm your only daughter."

She responds by tapping a finger on my nose as though I'm five. "Ah, well then, that does make for an easy choice."

I grab Mom's hand and squeeze, concerned about how many hours she'll need to work to pay off a night at a spa, a show, and a hotel.

"Seriously. We don't have to go out," I say.

"PJ, I work too much. You know I work too much. I know I work too much. We deserve to spend some time away, some time together."

"But—"

She puts a finger to my lips to stop me from arguing.

"No buts. We're going. Now pack your bag, and let's get out of here. Show starts at eight. Hotel afterward. Spa tomorrow morning at ten."

I don't offer any more arguments.

Instead, I throw a bag together in record time, then get changed into a light pink sweater dress and black leggings. I pair them with sparkly black flats, throw on sheer pink lip gloss and a little blush, and pull my dark hair into a messy braid. Hmm. I'm kind of cute when I put some effort into my appearance.

I snort at my reflection.

"Don't get cocky," I tell the girl in front of me.

For a second, I wonder if this is what I'd wear if I went on a date with Ethan. My pulse gives an offbeat leap with the thought.

Clay class Ethan was back to normal the rest of this week. He didn't try to draw me into conversation. He didn't ask anything more about my nickname, and, other than when he told Mariana about my heroic act at the park (which she already knew from me), he kept his earbuds in.

It left me feeling oddly dissatisfied. After the few days where I seemed to run into him everywhere, I started to feel like maybe I'd just see him all the time around the neighborhood, no matter where I went. But I ran every afternoon this week and never encountered him again. I mean, I also slipped each time I saw him outside of school, too. I suppose I should be grateful for the reprieve.

I scowl at the mirror and vow to stop thinking about Ethan.

I shouldn't be thinking about him anyway.

Then I'm down the stairs, my bag is in the car, and Mom and I are on our way to the theater an hour and a half away. It's not Broadway, but that's okay by me. Spending time with Mom is something I don't get enough of.

I watch her as she navigates the traffic on the highway. She looks relaxed. The worry lines normally etched between her brows whenever one of the desk nurses calls with a problem or when she's planning out the month's finances? No sign of them now. It's good to know she can still relax. I worry about her sometimes—that she's working too hard, too long, just to take care of the two of us. Maybe I should look for a job to help out. Most kids my age are working after school. I could probably pick something up part-time at the library.

"What's on your mind, Pigeon?"

I groan. "Not Pigeon!"

When I was three, I liked to point at the different birds in the yard, and mom would name them one by one. Cardinal, robin, finch, sparrow, etc. When she got to pigeon, I got all excited because I thought she said PJ. "Pigeon" stuck through most of elementary school.

She laughs.

"Pigeon is cute. I miss cute." She glances at me before turning her eyes back to the road again. "How'd you get to be a junior already? Seems like yesterday I was changing diapers. I swear all I did was blink."

"Oh, no. Mom, can we not?"

"What?"

"Talk about diapers."

She laughs again. It's a good sound, my mom's laugh. Mariana says I inherited her laugh, but I don't hear it.

"Alright, I'll let Pigeon go…for now. Tell me what's going on in school. How was your last meet?"

I shrug as I watch the outside world pass by the window. "Meet was fine. Didn't have practice all week 'cause Burns is out at a conference, but I clocked my miles anyway."

"That's my girl."

We fall into silence again, and Mom switches on the radio. Like cave people, we still use the FM radio. I could just plug my phone into the car's audio system, but Mom insists that takes the fun out of guessing what song might be next. Unsurprisingly, we listen to the local eighties and nineties station. It could be worse. She could like disco.

My phone buzzes in the bag on my lap, and I pull it out to glance at the screen. It's Mariana.

I stare at her last words. "E" can only mean Ethan. Why would Ethan ask about me? My throat suddenly feels dry, and I cough to clear it. When was Ethan talking to Mariana?

Mom glances my way.

"Everything okay?"

"Yeah, just Mariana," I answer quickly—maybe a little too quickly.

She pretends to try to glance at my phone, but her eyes never actually leave the road, so I'm not worried she's seen anything I'd rather she didn't.

I laugh a little nervously. "It's really just Mariana, Mom."

"Sure, Mariana today. A boy tomorrow. You just wait."

I cringe. The words sound too much like Mariana's when she decided to change Ethan's name into T. Morrow. *Why* does everything remind me of Ethan lately?

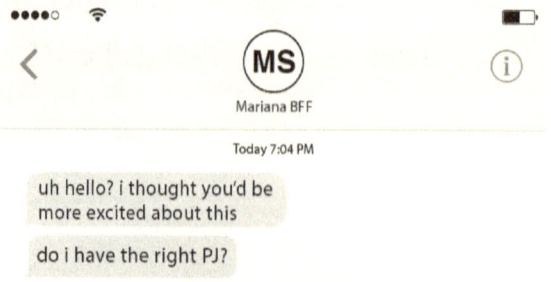

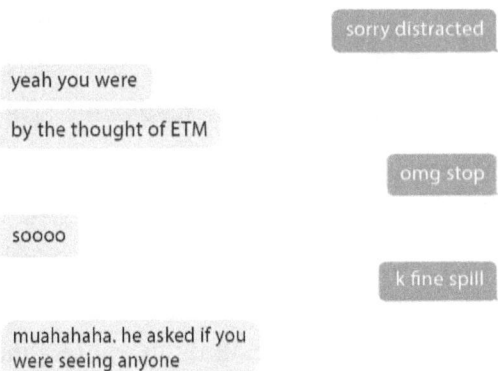

I hold the phone to my stomach. Ethan Morrow wants to know if I have a boyfriend. There's really only one reason a guy would ask that question. My heart is in my throat. I might throw up. Pressure starts to build in my veins, and what was exciting five seconds ago is now exceptionally terrifying.

I don't want to slip here and now. Not when I'm supposed to be enjoying time away with Mom. I tap out a quick "gtg," turn off my notifications, and shove the phone back in my bag.

I don't want to hear anything more about Ethan right now.

"Oo, I love this song!" Mom turns up the radio and starts belting out U2. "Come on," she says, giving my shoulder a shove. "Sing with me, Pidge!"

I give her an embarrassed glance, but I oblige because singing is better than slipping. And singing, like running, requires breath and control. At times like this, I desperately wish I could tell Mom about my issues, my anxiety, and my tendency to slip into the past.

I wish I could confess and have her believe me. And I wish her response to my confession was a giant hug—her gathering me in her arms and helping me find a way to stop having panic attacks once and for all…or, at the very least, to help me stop slipping. But telling her about slipping long ago didn't go well for me.

I try not to resent her for it, but sometimes it's hard not to feel isolated in a way no one else in this world can understand, and while I know that's not Mom's fault, I wish things were different. I wish she, like Mariana, knew what my life was really like. That it's not school and boys that have me on edge, that it's my anxiety itself that makes me anxious—and that slipping thing I do when I'm at my worst.

Mom's been concerned about my anxiety as long as I can remember. Since well before my kindergarten days, she was the first person to support me and try to ease me through panic attacks I can't even remember. And like the concerned parent she is, she's tried to balance being supportive while also letting me figure out my needs. As I've gotten older, I've taken to masking my anxiety around her so she doesn't feel the pressure to take responsibility for something she can't fix. It's probably not a healthy way to cope, but it seems like the path of least resistance.

In a few moments, the tightness in my chest has relented, and I loose a sigh of relief. I vow to leave my phone in my bag until we're safely back home again. Mariana will understand, and Ethan can wait.

Right now, it's me and Mom doing the kinds of things girls do with their moms, living our best lives.

Without Ethan Morrow.

I don't want to return home. The last twenty-four hours have been some of the best of my life. Mom and I stayed up late after the musical on Friday, ordered room service, and watched old movies on television. Most people prefer HBO in the hotel, but not me and Mom. Give us Turner Classic Movies any day. We're old romantics, she and I.

An Affair to Remember is one of my favorites, and after Deborah Kerr's character gets hit by a car while looking up at the Empire State

Building, where Cary Grant is waiting to meet her after six months of not being together, I always think it might be the one time ever that going back in time nine minutes and fifty-three seconds could be helpful.

But I guess that's not entirely true.

My mind flashes back to Kayleigh. Little Kayleigh, whose life I actually *did* save. When nine minutes and fifty-three seconds made an enormous difference. For once.

When I talked to Mariana that night, she tried to convince me this was my superpower, and this was why I had been given the curse—er, gift—of slipping.

"Maybe this is it, Slip! This is what you're meant to do. You just need to find more people to save." Her voice was full of excitement, as though I was about to become the friendly neighborhood Spiderman.

I had to remind her that slipping to save someone's life would require me witnessing something terrible happening first and then getting panicked about it enough to slip, which is not exactly something I can do at will. I mean, how would I even go about finding and witnessing awful events to begin with, especially with less than ten minutes to work with? And what would happen if I didn't slip?

No. The slip that allowed me to save that girl was an amazing stroke of luck. I'm relieved she's alive, and I hope I can get over the trauma of seeing her little body pulled from the lake the first time, but I'm no superhero. Just a girl who gets caught in her own anxious life and has a penchant for losing track of time.

After an amazing massage Mom splurged on for the two of us Saturday morning, I pull on a pair of jeans, turn my shirt right side out, and slip it on again. Real life is about to come crashing in and I'm not sure I'm really ready to go back to worrying about chemistry homework and cross-country meets and Ethan Morrow asking if I'm single.

"Is this what it's like to be an adult?" I flop into the cush gray chair in the corner of the massage room. "Theater and hotels and massages whenever you want?"

Mom laughs and shakes her head.

"Dream on, kiddo." Her button-down shirt hangs open, a practical black cotton bra peeking out, as she leans over to tousle my hair. "But I'm glad we did this. We deserve the break, and it's nice to spend time with you. I don't get enough of that."

I rest my head on the striped chenille pillow behind me. It *was* nice. I didn't know my body could feel this relaxed. Sure, lying naked on a table under a blanket was definitely weird, but I quickly forgot about the awkwardness once the lady started rubbing out knots in muscles I didn't know I had. (Also? I kept my underwear on. Mom said I could if I was more comfortable that way. And Mom was on the table right next to me, so it's not like I was alone with anyone. That *might* be weird.)

"I wish we could hang out more, but I get it. Back to the grind tomorrow. You're pulling a double again, aren't you?"

She finishes buttoning her shirt, then leans over, takes my face in her hands, and kisses my forehead.

"You're worth it. We're worth it. I know I work a lot of hours, but I do it because I love you."

I don't need to hear her say the words to know it's true. I just wish it weren't necessary. She easily looks twenty-six instead of her thirty-six years right now, and I'm sure it's from having a whole day and a half without having to work a shift at the hospital and worry about super ill patients who might stop breathing at any minute.

Mom makes one last surprise stop before we get home—The Cookie Crumble, my favorite bakery. She orders two small fruit tarts with custard centers, half a dozen mini-cannolis, and two pieces of flourless chocolate cake. We sit on a bench outside the bakery and indulge in a sugar-filled late "lunch," but Mom says it's okay because it includes our fruit and dairy for the day, so it's healthy. Putting a hand to my stuffed stomach, I'm infinitely glad for my runner's metabolism.

In fact, I'm happy and relaxed almost all the way home. It's the park that does it—seeing the lake and the people walking around it. My mind is immediately transported back to Tuesday. Kayleigh. And Ethan. My dessert-lunch twists in my stomach, and suddenly I wish maybe I hadn't eaten all of it.

I should check my messages from Mariana. Guilt tugs at my conscience as I think about leaving her hanging yesterday. Still. I don't want to look at my phone, so I hold off until we get home. I even manage to avoid a peek until I'm unpacked, seated on the bed, and have done two rounds of breathing with Susan.

Finally, I open my text threads.

There are twenty-three unread messages.

Fourteen are from the kids in my group project for German IV class. I answer those first, apologizing (in German) for not being around. Then I add my two cents as to how we should tackle the project and who should be responsible for which sections. Within a few minutes, the group is talking again and we've got a tactic. We agree not to text again until Monday because no one needs to be thinking about German class on a Saturday afternoon.

I take a breath and switch back to the text menu. There are four from Mariana and five from a number I don't recognize. Probably spam. I hit Mariana's name.

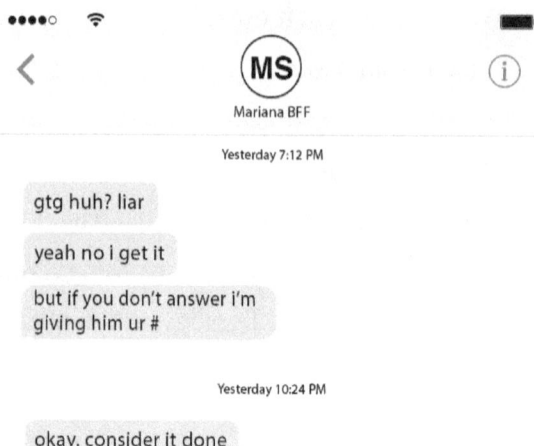

Mariana is full of it. She wouldn't. Then I think of the other text, the unknown number.

I throw the phone to the bed as though it's been dipped in acid, and I clutch the ties of my hoodie, drawing the hood shut around my face, leaving only the tip of my nose and lips exposed.

She wouldn't.

But I know Mariana.

I loosen the drawstring again, push the hood down off the back of my head, and reach for the phone to turn it over. Closing my eyes, I scrunch up my face and click on the unknown text. Then I peek with one eye.

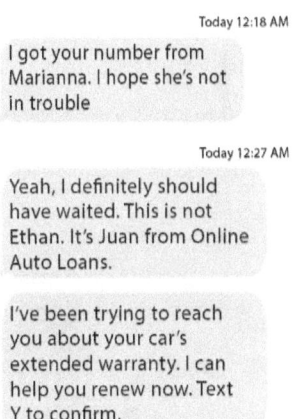

Today 12:18 AM

I got your number from Marianna. I hope she's not in trouble

Today 12:27 AM

Yeah, I definitely should have waited. This is not Ethan. It's Juan from Online Auto Loans.

I've been trying to reach you about your car's extended warranty. I can help you renew now. Text Y to confirm.

I give a soundless laugh as I read the last text. Then I stare at the string of texts and the times they came through. Ethan was waiting for me to reply. I don't know how to feel about that.

On one hand, I kind of like the idea that he was holding his phone on a Friday night, staring at the screen, willing me to answer. On the other hand, he was thinking about me for almost an hour (or texting in between video game rounds, maybe?), and that's...a lot to process.

I hesitate, my fingers hovering over the keyboard screen of the phone, then I reply.

●●●●○ 🛜

‹ **Unknown** ⓘ
(Maybe Ethan)

Today 4:27 PM

hi. Mariana spells her name with one n. i don't have a car. or a license. how's ur Saturday?

I bite my bottom lip and wait. While I'm waiting, I add Ethan's number to my contacts. Other than one of the kids in my German group and Mariana's brothers, he's the only boy on the list. Mom was right.

"Mariana today, a boy tomorrow." Literally. When I return to the text, the three little dots start to jump almost immediately.

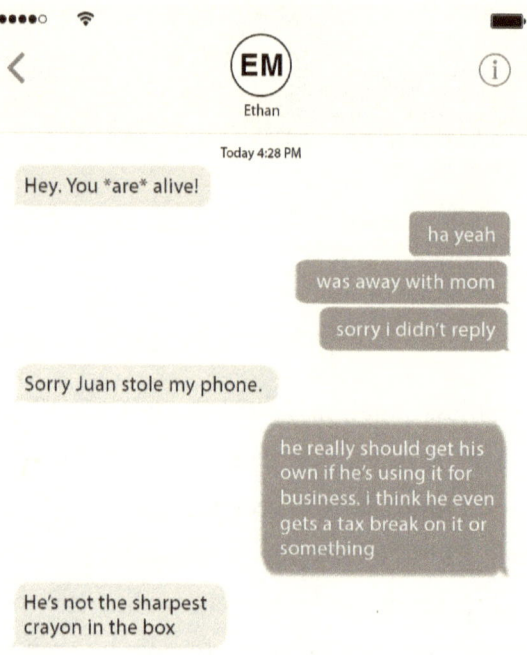

I laugh, then think for a moment. Why are Ethan and I texting? What are we even texting about?

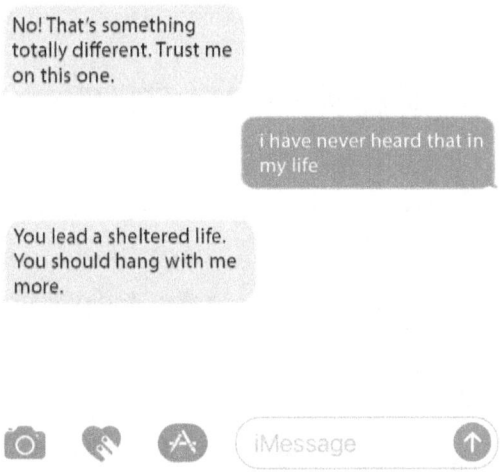

And there it is. My breath catches in my throat. I do not have the kind of life that will lend itself to dating. I don't. I should tell Ethan I'm not interested. I should tell him I don't want to hang with him. I should tell him never to text me again. It's safer that way.

I close my eyes, grip the phone tight in my hand, and type one word.

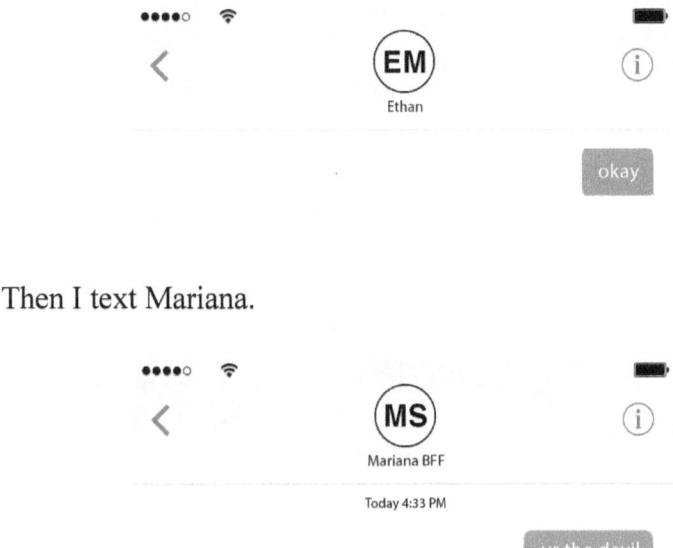

Then I text Mariana.

CHAPTER FIVE

When I open my locker on Monday morning, a note falls out onto the floor. If I was wearing boots, I might have missed it, but it hits the top of my foot. Since I'm wearing my red flats today with a white sweater (which might be a mistake for clay class; I'll have to be careful) and a pair of gray leggings, I feel the thump.

I shove my backpack into the locker and reach down for the folded piece of paper. My name is written on the outside in blue marker. Curious. I glance up and down the hallway before opening it, as though that might give me a clue as to who's written me a note.

Then I unfold it.

> *Thought this was more fun than a text. Scavenger hunt.*
> *Your first period clue can be found, but only if you turn*
> *up the heat.*

A scavenger hunt? There's no doubt in my mind this is Ethan's handiwork. We texted most of Saturday afternoon and evening—a combination of awkward and sweet. He never actually asked me on a date like I expected him to, despite the number of times he hinted at one, though we *did* discuss scavenger hunts. Apparently, Ethan and his dad are geocaching fanatics, which is basically a scavenger hunt with GPS, which means this ridiculous note can only be from one person. Is a scavenger hunt during school hours his idea of a date? I'm perplexed.

After homeroom, I head to the clay room. Normally, I'd be thinking about my current project and how the heck I'm going to finish it before Mr. Sandoz wants to fire up the kiln this week, but today, I'm thinking of Ethan, which, if I'm not careful, is going to become a very bad habit.

I slide into my seat across from Mariana, who gives me the kind of smirk that says she's well aware of the kind of imp she really is. I turn to Ethan, who has his earbuds in. He's already got his clay project out even though the first period bell hasn't yet rung, and he looks like he's making a point to not look at me.

As I haven't even gotten my project out yet, I ball up a bit of Mariana's clay and throw it at his head. He winces from surprise when it hits him and bounces harmlessly to the table, then looks up, grins, and pulls out his earbuds.

"Slip!" he says.

"PJ," Mariana and I respond simultaneously.

He shrugs. "I had to try."

"What's this?" I hold up the handwritten note from my locker.

Ethan squints his eyes and pretends to inspect the paper while making no effort to take it. "Hmm," he says. "Looks like someone's sending you on a scavenger hunt."

I raise an eyebrow. "Someone?"

He shrugs, but he doesn't put his earbuds back in.

"Intriguing," Mariana says. "So, where are you going to look first?"

I shake my head but smile. "First, I'm going to get my clay project and get it finished or I'll have a big fat zero for a grade."

Turns out, I don't have to look very hard to find my next clue. When I go into the back room to pull out my project, there's another folded note tucked by the kiln's temperature dial. It's not in plain sight, but since the kiln is the only hot place in the whole clay room, it was the obvious place to look.

I carry the note and my project back to the table.

"Hmm, what'd you find there?" Mariana looks on with interest.

She's not looking at my clay project, which is still unfinished and wrapped in damp paper towels. No, her gaze is on the paper I slowly unfold. I narrow my eyes at her and scrunch my mouth to one side.

"You know all about this, don't you?"

Briefly, I wonder if Ethan had this planned out with Mariana before he even texted me. She seems unsurprised by today's turn of events.

She smiles. "Moi? Non! Je suis le diable!"

"I have only a vague idea of what you just said," I mutter as I shake my head again.

> *I'm not a big fan of period four, but you'll have to be if you want your next clue.*

I peer at Ethan over the top of the paper. First period is our only shared class. Mariana is definitely involved in the shenanigans.

Fourth period is gym class for me, and it doesn't take me long to find a clue stuck to the side of the bleachers. Mariana has gym third period, so I'm not surprised. I mull this over. If Mariana is participating by helping to hide these clues, she's on Ethan's "side," which means she trusts him…and wants me to do the same. I'm half-elated and half-ill all at once. If my heart keeps like this, I'm concerned I'll start slipping daily.

For a moment, I worry Mari might have told him my secret, but no, she wouldn't dare. She might share my phone number, but she'd never tell anyone the one thing that separates me from everyone else in the entire world. If there's one thing I trust Mariana with, it's my life, and my secret *is* my life.

I can't unfold the note until I'm back in the locker room, so the suspense eats at me while we play kickball in the gymnasium. (At least I'm better at kickball than I am at badminton.)

One more clue to find. Beneath the raven's wing, the final note will sing.

I shake my head. He didn't list a period this time, and Feris Alweather's mascot is a raven, so there are ravens literally everywhere—murals, statues, flags through the halls and the classrooms. But if I have to look beneath a wing, I'm thinking Ethan is sending me outside to the courtyard where there's a giant raven with outspread wings.

Every year, some of the seniors climb on the wings and dress it up in a ridiculous costume for Senior Week. Last year, they transformed it into Ironman, and someone even went so far as to stick a glowing orb to its chest. The janitor wasn't thrilled, and if you look closely, the adhesive from the orb is still just visible even after all his scrubbing.

Next year, I hope to turn the raven into a giant chicken, but I'll have to enlist a few people to make papier-mâché feathers with me because there's no way I'll be able to make that many by hand myself. Mostly, I just think the courtyard raven would look hilarious with a giant comb and big, red waddles... And no one has ever turned him into another kind of bird before, let alone something as ridiculous as a chicken.

The rest of the day seems to take forever, partly because Mariana, who shares almost all my classes, smirks at me and refuses to spill the tea, but mostly because I wait impatiently until the final bell so I can check out the raven in the courtyard. It's got to be there, this "final clue" of his.

So when the last bell rings, I race to the courtyard like every other student who wants to leave school behind for the day. I've got five whole minutes before I need to get to cross-country practice, but I've been thinking about this all day. There's no way I'm going to let this wait until after practice. I'll go bananas.

Mariana follows, probably to gauge my reaction because that's what friends are for. I hovered over her when Henry Judge asked her to homecoming last year, too. (She said yes, but nothing serious ever came of it. I think her brains intimidated him.) It's fun when you know something your friend doesn't—especially where boys are concerned. Plus, since we walk home together, Mariana isn't going to leave without me, so I guess her motives aren't entirely in my interests alone. She'll hang out in the yearbook room doing yearbook-y stuff until I'm done running.

I scour the area beneath the raven's wings three times, but I cannot find even the slightest hint of where anyone could possibly hide a note, and I've got to get to practice. Frustration is an understatement.

Mariana presses her lips together and shrugs. "Maybe it's by a different raven?"

"Do you know how many ravens there are in this school? It'll take forever to find the right one. Unless…" I shoot her a pleading look.

"Uh oh. I don't like when you look at me like that."

The two of us head for the school again. I need to get my butt to the locker room before Coach Burns starts to wonder whether I've quit the team.

"All I'm saying is you *could* maybe do a preliminary search while I'm at practice…"

"You know, I have commitments, too."

"Look, you pretty much *are* the yearbook committee. No one else stays late every day like you do, so it's not like you'll be missed. Just check a few ravens for me. Please?" I let my shoulders drop and give her wide eyes and a help-me-out pout. It works. She laughs.

"Okay, fine. I'll hit up a few areas while you're at practice. Meet you by the locker room after. I'll wait outside. Four?"

"Yes, perfect! You're the best, Mari!"

She laughs over her shoulder as she walks away. "Remember it."

I can't stop grinning. Why am I grinning?

Coach Burns runs us twice as hard as normal, but that's to be expected. Whenever she misses even a day of practice, she wants to make sure we haven't slacked. This isn't a problem for me since I run every day anyway, but it seems like a few of my teammates might have taken last week off entirely. I almost feel sorry for them.

By the time Coach Burns releases us, we've toured four different neighborhoods around the school, and I'm drenched in sweat. It's been an unseasonably warm autumn. I could rinse off in the locker room showers and change back into my leggings and sweater, but I'll die if I have to get into anything warmer than a t-shirt and shorts right now, and I don't have soap or shampoo. So even though I'm a sweaty mess, this is how it's going to be.

It's fine, though. I'll shower and change the minute I get home. Even *I* don't want to be around me when I'm like this. At least my deodorant is still working…

Mariana is just on the other side of the locker room door, as promised, but she makes a face when I emerge.

"Hey, you know they have showers in there, right?"

"Haha. Be glad I don't wrap you in a big, sweaty bestie hug."

She holds out both hands and skirts backwards. "No, thank you!"

"She ran us hard today, but I'm not wasting time with a shower. I mean, I'm sweaty, but I don't stink, right?" When she doesn't answer immediately, I panic a little. "Right?!"

Mariana tentatively leans forward as though she's afraid to smell me. "Mari!"

After a moment of uncertainty, she finally tilts her head to the side.

"No, you don't stink. You mostly smell like deodorant…and damp."

"Damp? What does that mean? How can I *smell* damp?"

"Just…you know. Damp."

I sniff my armpits. "But not smelly?"

"You smell like roses, PJ," she deadpans.

"Don't mess with me! I don't want to be ostracized. The gossip squad will start rumors that I don't know what soap is, that I run twenty-five miles a week and shower once a month."

In response, she cracks an evil grin, revealing perfect teeth, like scaring me senseless was her intention all along.

"You're too easy to rile," she says. "You smell fine. You're tolerable, at least."

I let out a huff. "Did you find the last note?"

With the change in subject, Mariana visibly deflates. "No. But I know where *not* to look now."

"Super helpful, thanks. I guess he didn't have you hide this one."

"Alright, here's my thought." Mariana starts holding up fingers as she names off places to look. "There's the raven flag hanging in the lobby, the fountain on the second floor with the raven in the middle, the hallway with the raven tile mosaic, and the band room, which has a huge raven painted on one wall. Is Ethan in band? The last note singing thing makes me think band and chorus, you know?"

I shrug. "I don't think so. Is it weird that I don't know if he's musical?"

"Not really. He's only been back in town a couple of months at best. Okay, so let's start in the band room if it's still open."

At four-fifteen, we shouldn't really be hanging out at the school. The teachers have mostly gone for the day, and anyone still here might kick us out or threaten to call our parents. (Mom would probably laugh, but still…)

We check the band room, but the doors are locked since all the instruments are in there, waiting for use tomorrow morning when the bando kids arrive way earlier for practice than anyone should ever have to report to school.

Mariana cups her hands and presses her face to the glass to peer through the door window into the darkened room. While she's looking, I check my phone. There's a text from mom saying she'll be home at seven tonight, but nothing from Ethan, so I tap out a quick message.

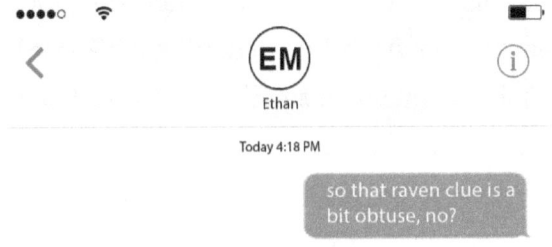

"Can't see a thing," Mariana says. She heaves a sigh as she pulls away from the glass.

I shove my phone in my bag. "C'mon. Let's go to the fountain. I feel like it wouldn't be below Ethan's sense of humor to stick a note in the middle of the fountain and make me wade through the water to get it."

"I mean, you *do* need a bath."

I press my lips together, give her *a look*, and push forward to the fountain. I can't see anything out of the norm in the center where a stainless steel raven sits in the middle of a pool made up of a few thousand tiles of varying shades of blue.

"What are you waiting for?"

I turn to look at her. She gestures to the fountain and lifts her eyebrows.

Oh.

She wants me to climb in.

"I don't see anything there, do you?"

"No, but that doesn't mean he hasn't taped it somewhere! Where's your sense of adventure?"

I roll my head back to look at the ceiling and drop my book bag to the floor.

"I can't believe I'm doing this."

Then I untie my sneakers, slip off my still-damp socks, and wiggle my toes. If a teacher walks by *now*, I really am dead meat. Detention at the least. Mom might not laugh at that.

I dip my toes into the water. It's shockingly cold, or maybe I'm still overheated from my run. Actually, if I don't think about how many boys probably spit in this fountain on a daily basis, it feels kind of nice.

I wade to the center, the water sloshing around my calves. There's nothing anywhere near this raven except a wad of chewed gum stuck beneath one wing, which seems kind of absurd. Wading into the fountain is a lot of work to get rid of gum. Seems like a trash can would make more sense, given there're at least two in every classroom. I turn to tell Mariana there's nothing here, and I just start to speak when I realize she's holding up her phone. Oh my God, is she filming?

Words forgotten, I screech.

"Don't you DARE!"

She wiggles her eyebrows and grins. "That's blackmail material in case I ever need it."

She might as well grow a pair of horns. She really is the devil. Now there's video evidence of me, sweaty and gross from practice, barefoot in the middle of the school fountain like an absolute idiot.

And she has Ethan's number.

I groan, then wade back to the edge of the fountain.

"If that ever goes anywhere, I'll make sure the entire yearbook staff knows exactly who overflowed the girls' toilet in the science hall bathroom freshman year.

She gasps. "You wouldn't!"

I smile my most angelic smile. "I would. Take care that video never leaves your phone."

She holds the phone to her chest like I've personally threatened to throw it in the fountain, which…is an idea worth considering, but I don't actually hate my best friend, even if she *is* the devil.

I sit at the fountain's edge and finish putting my socks and sneakers back on. Then I stand, pull my book bag off the floor, and check my phone. Nothing from Ethan, but he *did* read my message a minute after I sent it.

So why didn't he answer?

"Come on, mosaic next," Mariana says.

School has been out for almost two hours. We need to get the heck out of here, but I think I'll lose my mind if I don't find the last note. I text Ethan again.

"He's reading these! Why isn't he responding?" I follow Mariana down the hall, shoving my phone in my bag when it's clear he's not going to respond.

"Because he's obviously enjoying your discomfort. You didn't tell him you climbed in the fountain, did you? Cause I'd only mention that if he'd actually hidden it there…" She takes one look at my face.

"Oh no, you did."

"I did."

When we reach the tile mosaic raven by the art room, I groan. "I'm an idiot!"

"I've always thought you above-average in the intelligence department, but I can reassess if you'd care to enlighten me," Mariana says.

I point.

The tile mosaic is a raven, wings outspread, beak wide open with a rainbow of mosaic music notes indicating birdsong, which is kind of ironic given that ravens don't produce any sort of musical sound. They're pretty much crows on steroids.

But the note is there, taped to a tile the same color, folded in the same shape as the tile it's stuck to.

"How could I not have realized? He *said* it in the last note. Beneath the raven's wing, the final note will sing. Sing. *Sing.*" It seems so obvious now that we're standing here in front of a bunch of musical notes.

"Are you going to keep me here in suspense? Open the note!"

You'd think these notes were written for Mariana. Blood rushes through my veins with the anticipation. It's not unlike when I slip and I *really* don't want to slip right now. (As if there's ever a time when I *want* to…)

I unfold the note and read.

> *Congratulations! A reward awaits the finder. Slip—I mean skip—on over to the clay room.*

"What are we waiting for!" Mariana squeals as she grabs my hand. We race around the corner to the clay room, which is just the other side of the art room since the two rooms are connected by the back kiln room. Then Mariana skids to a stop, and my breath catches.

Ethan sits in the doorway of the clay room, doodling on a sketchpad. He looks up when he hears us arrive, a lopsided, dimpled grin on his face...

"Hey. You found me."

"Oh, shoot!" Mariana puts a hand to her forehead. "I'm supposed to sit for the neighbor's dog. I should have let him out an hour ago! I gotta go!"

I stare at her. It's the worst excuse I've ever heard, but she's already running down the hall and, in a few seconds, it's just me and Ethan standing at the doorway to the clay room.

Now I really wish I'd taken a moment to shower and change back into my non-grubby clothes. My damp hair hangs in a limp ponytail down my back. I resist the urge to take it out and fluff it with my fingers. It wouldn't matter. After sweating like I did, my hair won't cooperate until I get shampoo and conditioner in it anyway.

"So, hey," he says again.

I realize I haven't spoken yet. My heart starts to thump against my ribcage. I should say something.

"You sent me on a scavenger hunt to meet you outside the clay room?"

"Um, yeah?"

"Why didn't you just text me to meet you here? You wouldn't have had to wait so long." Ethan must have been sitting here since the last bell rang almost two hours ago.

He gives a guilty grin. "I guess I thought the raven one would be easier to figure out than it was. It's okay. Mr. Sandoz left an hour ago. Figured this was a safe enough place to hang out without Mr. Schellenberger coming by."

Mr. Schellenberger is the principal no one wants to meet during school, let alone after hours. Then Ethan shrugs, tosses his sketchpad into his backpack, and stands. I'm very conscious of exactly how tall Ethan is. I'm not short, but Ethan stands a head taller than me. And he's standing close. Suddenly, I'm very, *very* conscious of the fact that I haven't showered after my run. I pray my deodorant is doing its job like I thought it was, that Mariana hasn't lied about detecting body odor.

"I thought we might get ice cream as a reward for solving the scavenger hunt. My dad and I always go for ice cream after we find a cache. It seemed like a good tradition to carry on. It's kind of late, but… what do you think? You look like a mint chocolate chip kind of girl."

"Cookie dough, actually," I manage. My voice is weak.

He planned a scavenger hunt to ask me on a date, and he actually looks nervous. But he's not the one on the verge of slipping; I am. I breathe out slowly and tap my fingers. I can stay. I can stay. I can do this.

My heart is in my throat, that hateful pressure building. Maybe if I say "yes" fast enough, I can avoid—

I'm in the fountain. Again.

This time, I don't make it to the raven at the center. I know the last note isn't there. I wade back to the edge of the fountain and climb out before Mariana can even manage to start filming.

"Hey, you okay?" she asks, her brows drawn in concern. "You got quiet on me really fast. Like, total vibe change."

I drag my eyes to hers and swallow past the lump in my throat. It's hard to meet her eyes after a slip, mostly because she usually realizes what's happened pretty quickly. This time is no exception.

"Oh, Slip. I'm sorry. Come on," she helps me out of the fountain, holding one arm like I'm a porcelain doll who might break into a thousand pieces if she lets go.

I sit at the fountain's edge, dry my feet with my damp socks, then put my socks and shoes on again. I don't speak. I don't know if I can.

A boy asks me on a date and goes to elaborate lengths to ask me for ice cream (ice cream!), and I can't even say yes without losing control and slipping. How can I expect to ever be in a relationship? I can't. Not with him, not with anyone. I should know better. I can't believe I started to think maybe Ethan was a possibility. I can't have this.

I'm safer leading a boring life with my boring routine—a routine that doesn't include Ethan Morrow sending me on scavenger hunts or asking me out for ice cream.

"You wanna talk?" Mariana asks.

I shake my head and utter a low, "No."

Frustrated tears burn my eyes. I won't cry. I refuse.

I pull out my phone and stare at it. I'm tempted to not text at all, but I can't leave him waiting outside the clay room forever. I may be a disappointment, but I'm not unnecessarily cruel.

EM
Ethan

Today 4:18 PM

so that raven clue is a bit obtuse, no?

i'm not gonna finish this hunt - sorry, M's not feeling well. taking her home

"Moi? *I'm* not feeling well?" Mariana says from over my shoulder.

I hate using her as an excuse, but I don't want to seem like a self-centered jerk, either. I shove the phone back in my bag before I can see his response. I don't want to know.

"I'm going home." It takes everything I've got not to burst into tears.

CHAPTER SIX

I try not to look at Ethan the next morning, but it's difficult. It's hard not to stare at his sandy hair and the dimple missing from his cheek. It's hard not to notice his hazel eyes—disappointed eyes. He's watching Mariana now, probably thinking about asking her if she's feeling better, so I spare him the effort.

"How are your cramps?" I ask, using the period excuse we've used so many times before.

Mariana holds my glance with an unamused stare but plays along. "Better today. Thanks for taking me home. Sorry if I screwed things up." She gives Ethan a reconciliatory smile, a sheepish grin that says she knows she's responsible for his messed-up plans.

She's a saint.

"You know, if you still have the last clue hidden, I bet PJ is still up for finding it today," she offers.

Did I say saint? I mean devil. Mariana is the devil.

I widen my eyes at her and press my lips together, desperately trying to convey my reluctance to such an idea. She knows. We texted last night when I finally gained control of myself and could think about Ethan without feeling like I was going to slip again. She knows I don't want to get to the last clue. She—

"I have track practice after school today, so maybe another time," Ethan says.

Is it me, or does he look upset?

Of course he's upset. I'd be upset, too, if I went out of my way to set up an adorably complex scheme to ask a girl out on a first date, and then she stood me up because her best friend had pretend cramps.

I texted Mariana last night, but I *didn't* text Ethan. I couldn't bring myself to open his texts. I didn't want to make excuses. I didn't want to have to lie again.

I hate that he's mad, but in a way, it makes things easier. Maybe if he's mad, he'll forget about me and move on. I rub a spot at the base of my throat with the hand that isn't clay-covered, trying to brush away the lump that's taken residence there.

"Ethan." Jenny McGinnis saunters to our table and sits in the rickety death-trap seat across from Ethan. Her hands are suspiciously clean for this class, and she bats her salon-enhanced eyelashes in Ethan's direction. "Are you still up for taking headshots this weekend?"

I wish I could tune out her words. Jenny. And Ethan. Ethan taking photos of Jenny. Ethan's camera trained on Jenny, who will probably be wearing skimpy clothing that makes her boobs look big. No doubt she'll be working those doe eyes as hard as she can on the photographer behind the lens.

I'm not jealous.

This is good.

This will help Ethan forget about any plans he might have wanted to make with me faster.

"Yeah," he says, but he locks gazes with me, and I quickly turn my attention back to my project—a dragon this time. My raindrop-covered cylinder is in the kiln, probably well on its way to exploding thanks to an air bubble I didn't fully wedge out of the clay. It would be my luck.

"Yay! I'm so excited. So, what should I wear? Or should I bring a change of clothing?"

I pray to the clay class gods that her seat collapses. I force my will upon the loose wooden slats beneath the chair to finally break free of their constraints.

"Uh, whatever you want, I guess. I mean, I'm yours for the day. You said you wanted to shoot in a few locations, right?"

I'm yours for the day?

I'm going to throw up. He's doing this on purpose.

"PJ, did your mom give you the okay to sleep over on Friday night?" Mariana asks, momentarily focusing my attention on her.

We didn't talk about a sleepover on Friday, so Mom couldn't have possibly given me the okay to stay at Mariana's. I'm not sure where she's going with this.

"Uh, yeah," I say, mostly because I don't know what else to say.

Jenny clears her throat and leans forward in the chair to get closer to Ethan. The chair creaks beneath her with the shift in weight.

Break. BREAK. So help me…if there's any justice in this world, that chair will break right now.

"I'm really looking forward to this, Ethan. You're such an amazing photographer. I can't wait to see how you spin these photos. We can start at the lake. Like noon?" Jenny says.

"Actually, the best lighting will be the morning or evening, so probably more like eight? Nine?" Ethan's not looking at her while he talks. His attention is fixed on the piece of clay he rolls back and forth between his palms. He twists it.

Is he…making a noose?

"You're really going to make me get up early on a Saturday?" Jenny narrows her eyes at him, pretending like she's contemplating. I'm pretty sure Jenny doesn't have more than three brain cells, so I hope she's not thinking too hard. She'll burn one of them up and only have two to use for the rest of the year.

"I mean, we could wait until the afternoon, but then you're only going to get a couple of good daylight hours," Ethan begins. "If that's what—"

"No! I'm just kidding. Nine is fine. That way we can have all day.

Tell you what. I'll treat you to lunch since I'm taking up your whole Saturday."

Way to backpedal, Jenny.

Ethan shrugs. "Okay," he says.

"Great. It's a date!"

Ethan's eyes fly open in alarm at the word, but Jenny's already pushing out of her chair—the traitorous death chair that *didn't* break—and heading back to her own table.

I slink lower in my own seat and focus on transforming the clay dragon sculpture in front of me into an incense holder. Right now, I feel like fire. What's a dragon without fire?

I actually do sleep over at Mariana's on Friday. We sit in her room, watch movies, eat cinnamon and brown sugar Pop-Tarts, and pretend Ethan Morrow doesn't exist.

I scroll through the local animal shelter's adoptable cats on my phone, checking out the available kittens and fantasizing about taking them all home, while Mariana scrolls through summer programs at colleges I couldn't even dream of getting into. (And, to be honest, who wants to spend their summer going to school? Mariana, I guess.)

"Awww, look at this one!" I collapse on Mariana's bed and turn the phone to show her a tiny tan puffball with bright blue eyes.

"He's so cute! Have you convinced your mom yet?"

I shake my head and continue scrolling. "Not yet, but I'm close. I think if I—oh, wait, check this one out. I *need* him." I turn the phone again.

"I *love* tuxedo cats! That one's already two, though. Didn't you want a kitten?"

"Yeah, but his nose is a *heart*, Mari! I would die if I had a cat with a heart for a nose."

"You're hopeless."

This is true.

I close the shelter app with a sigh and click my texts. It's time. I've left Ethan's messages unread all week. I'm a monster.

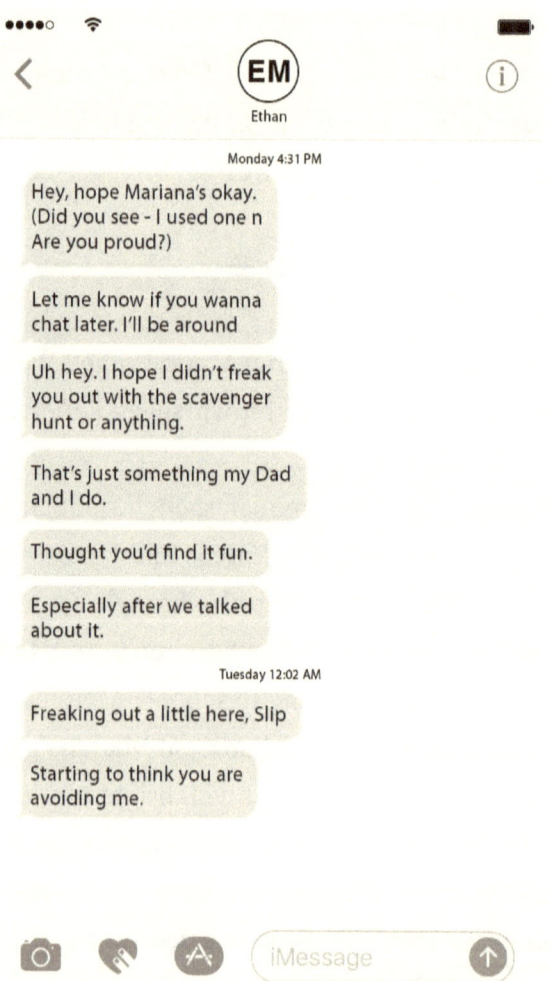

Ethan

Monday 4:31 PM

Hey, hope Mariana's okay.
(Did you see - I used one n
Are you proud?)

Let me know if you wanna
chat later. I'll be around

Uh hey. I hope I didn't freak
you out with the scavenger
hunt or anything.

That's just something my Dad
and I do.

Thought you'd find it fun.

Especially after we talked
about it.

Tuesday 12:02 AM

Freaking out a little here, Slip

Starting to think you are
avoiding me.

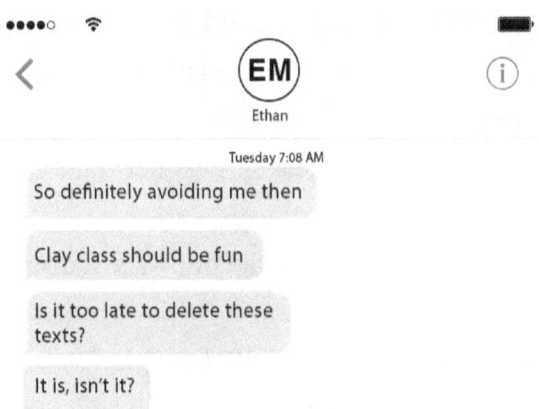

EM
Ethan

Tuesday 7:08 AM

So definitely avoiding me then

Clay class should be fun

Is it too late to delete these texts?

It is, isn't it?

I bite my lip. I want to respond. He's gone all week without a word from me. Earbuds back in during clay class, pretending I didn't leave him unread, the two of us both pretending it's Mariana who put a kink in his plans on Monday.

My thumb sits ready to type a response, but the truth is—I don't know how to respond. What excuse can I possibly give that would make my behavior this week okay? And I don't want to tell him we're okay because we're not okay. *I'm* not okay. I'll never be okay, and he's better off without me. It's early enough in whatever this is (I can't even call it a relationship because it's not) that he can move on and pretend none of this ever happened. No harm, no foul.

I switch to the thread with Mom and text her good night. I've never not said good night to Mom, even when she's working the night shift. There's always at least a text or a quick phone call. Tonight, she texts back quickly, so I know she's at the desk, which means no one's called out.

Her reply is almost always a string of moons (that align closely with the phase of the moon outside—a quarter waxing tonight), hearts of varying colors, and snoring faces. It's her quick way of saying she loves me and goodnight without having to pull her attention away from the job. On the nights when Mom has to fill in, she doesn't get a moment off her feet. I often don't get a response until long after I'm asleep, but she always responds.

On Saturday morning, Mariana springs her trap. Undoubtedly, this is what she planned all along.

"Yoga in the park!" she says as she throws a squishy, purple, rolled yoga mat at me. I let it hit the floor.

"I am not doing yoga in a park full of people."

"Relax, it's ten a.m. How many people will be in the park?"

I count on my fingers. "Uh, let's see, all the regular joggers, the parents with kids who get them up at the crack of dawn, the kids who fish, and—oh, I know—Ethan Morrow and Jenny McGinnis."

"Oh, that's right. They did say they were going to be there today, didn't they?"

I lean my head to one side and glare at Mariana. She knows darn well Ethan is taking photos of Jenny at the lake today.

Mariana picks the mat off the floor, shoves it into my arms, and drags me out the door by the hand. I could resist. I know I could say no and really mean it. But there's a part of me that actually wants to ruin Jenny's photoshoot, and there's definitely a part of me that wants to distract Ethan even though I can't have him. I'm mostly mad at myself and at the circumstances, but somehow, it feels less unfair if Ethan's as frustrated as I am.

There are a few dozen people scattered around the park. Unsurprising, given the beautiful, cool, sunny day. Autumn has finally arrived. Even the trees agree. Tipped yellow and orange, they're just starting to lose their deep summer green.

It doesn't take long to spot Ethan and Jenny. Jenny climbs out on a large rock just off the shoreline and does her best to pose like a supermodel, leaning back on her hands, her wide-necked sweater draped artfully off one shoulder, almost-white hair (courtesy of many rounds of bleach) falling down her back in beachy waves.

"I thought she wanted headshots," Mariana says as she stares.

"I don't think Ethan's looking at her head," I reply, stating the obvious.

Mariana laughs and pushes my shoulder. "Are we jealous, my little Slip?"

I shrug.

"I can't have him, but that doesn't mean I want to watch *her* throw herself at him."

"Alright, well, let's get our yoga on. If we're lucky, we can photobomb and mess up all her shots."

I laugh, but I don't really want to mess up Jenny's photos because they're Ethan's photos, too. And she'll take it out on him if he somehow doesn't notice two idiots doing sun salutations on the other side of the lake.

Yoga actually does feel good, even if I can't get my mind clear the way you're supposed to. I don't know how anyone manages not to let thoughts slip through. I've got at least half a dozen.

Warrior pose is stupid. Warriors don't pose. Don't fall over, don't fall over.

Ew, I think that old guy just checked out Mariana's chest. This is why we don't do yoga in the park.

Did Jenny fall in the lake yet?

I peek over my shoulder. She's off the rock and sitting on a picnic table now. Her feet are no longer bare but are clad in thigh-high black boots with a heel that has to be at least four inches. How can she be comfortable in those?

I close my eyes and refocus on yoga. Mariana has us doing chair pose now, then a lunge into something new. I follow along.

Should I text him? Is it wrong to lead him on if nothing can happen?

Who's to say I'm leading him on? Is it leading him on if I just want a friend? Can't boys and girls just be friends? Can I not have more than one friend in my life?

Not that I need more than one. I'm so grateful for Mariana. God, please don't think I don't love Mariana. She's a gift. I'm thankful. Please don't take her from me. Ever.

Ow, that hurt. Acorn. Why did I just step on an acorn? Stupid oak trees.

I look up at the tree in question and kick the acorn off my mat.

"Come on, Slip. Triangle pose. Open wide, reach for the sky. Feel that stretch all down your side. Deepen your breathing. Really fall into the pose."

I lift an eyebrow. "When did you get certified as a yoga instructor?"

"Took a six-week online course." She grins.

"You're so full of it." I roll my eyes but fall into triangle pose and run with it. It does feel good. I close my eyes and deepen the stretch, for one brief moment focusing on my breath, hearing and feeling the breath moving in and out of my body, pushing the stretch deeper as I lean. It's as close to relaxed as I've ever been.

"Hey."

My eyes fly open. My balance dissolves, and I fall backwards onto my butt. My heart lurches in my chest. Why is Ethan here? Ethan should be on the other side of the lake, where he was standing only a few moments ago.

"Hi," I squeak out.

Ethan cringes and holds out a hand to help me up. "Sorry," he says. "I didn't mean to scare you."

I take his hand and pull myself off the mat. His fingers are warm despite the cool morning. I kind of don't want to let them go, but I probably should, so I reclaim my hand to brush grass and dirt from my leggings.

"Hey, Ethan," Mariana says. Effortlessly, she transitions into another warrior pose, her arms stretched forward like a superhero. He nods in her direction.

"I thought you were…" My words trail off, so I point to where he and Jenny were taking photos only a few minutes earlier. I don't see any sign of her.

"We were. I mean, we are. She's changing in the restroom, so I figured I'd come say hi since I spotted the two of you doing your Zen thing up here in the grass. So, anyway, hi." Ethan gives an awkward smile. His camera hangs from his neck by a cushioned strap, and he holds it in one hand. I wonder if he knows he's cradling it, one thumb caressing the side of the camera as he talks.

Why am I looking at Ethan's hands?

I snap my eyes back to his, but that's a mistake, too.

I really should say *something*.

He looks down. "So you, uh, saw my texts?"

I wind a stray lock of hair back toward my ponytail and hope it stays. It doesn't. I tuck it behind my ear.

"Yeah, I'm…sorry about that."

"She's had so many issues with that phone this week, I swear," Mariana says without breaking pose. I gape at her, but she continues. "I texted her six times, but not a single one showed up! Then, all six came through while she was at my house last night. Bling, bling, bling— notifications like crazy. You getting a new phone soon or what, Slip?"

"Oh." Ethan takes a step back as though he needs to process this information. The hurt and confusion on his face melt away.

What am I supposed to say *now*? I wasn't planning to lie to him. But if I counter Mariana's story, she'll look like a lying fool, and I don't want that either.

I shrug. "I'm sorry," I say again.

"Hey, it's okay. I guess…I'm just glad that means you weren't ghosting me." He chuckles.

I laugh, too, but it's a nervous laugh.

"Ethan!"

Ethan turns. Jenny stands on the paved path near the lake in a slinky sapphire dress that glitters when the sun catches it. I can only assume she bought it for homecoming. Her hands are on her hips, then she waves impatiently at him.

"Guess I should get back to it," he says with a roll of his eyes.

"Yeah." At least I'm safe from further conversation.

"Text you later?" He asks permission, though whether he's asking if he can text me or if I'll answer, I'm not sure.

"Okay," I say.

He grins and then starts down the grassy hillside, but he takes only three steps before he pauses and turns with his camera in hand.

"PJ!" He snaps a photo before I can protest, then smiles as though he knows he got away with something he shouldn't have.

I shake my head. "I reserve the right to delete that," I call.

He walks backwards the last few feet to where Jenny stands and lifts his shoulders in a shrug. Jenny's face is red. If humans could produce steam, I'm pretty sure there'd be some coming out of her ears.

"No way!" Ethan calls back. "My camera, my rules."

I scowl, but Mariana laughs from downward dog.

She looks at me upside down from between her legs, her curly black ponytail spilling onto the mat beneath her. "I know why you don't want to encourage him. Like, I get it. But that boy is smitten with you, and you're just as smitten with him. The two of you should just kiss already. Maybe then you'll stop slipping every time you're alone with him."

My ears burn with the thought.

Kissing.

Kissing Ethan.

I've never kissed anyone. I mean, once in kindergarten, I kissed Joey Hobbs on the playground, but I'm pretty sure that doesn't count.

"Don't you slip on me now." It's like Mariana can see the gears turning in my head. "I'm just about done here. I don't need ten more minutes of yoga. Back to your mat, Slip. Downward dog, then child's pose, then corpse."

Corpse. How very appropriate.

CHAPTER SEVEN

I stare at the picture on my phone. The photo Ethan took of me is one of the best I've ever seen. Maybe it's because I wasn't ready for him to take it. I had no chance to mask my expression or flash a smile. It's just me. I don't know how he did it, but he captured *me* in a photo.

I like it.

The photo? Or me?

I pull a knee up and lean on it. Mariana and I left the park after we finished our yoga, and I headed home shortly after. I've been sitting in my room most of the day, barely making progress on the history assignment I'm supposed to complete this weekend. I put it aside for a while and attempted chemistry, but my brain doesn't seem to want to work on that either. No, my brain appears to be occupied with a different kind of chemistry.

I laugh out loud. There is literally *no* way I will ever let Ethan see—
or hear—me burp.

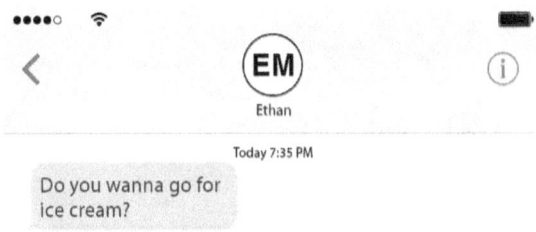

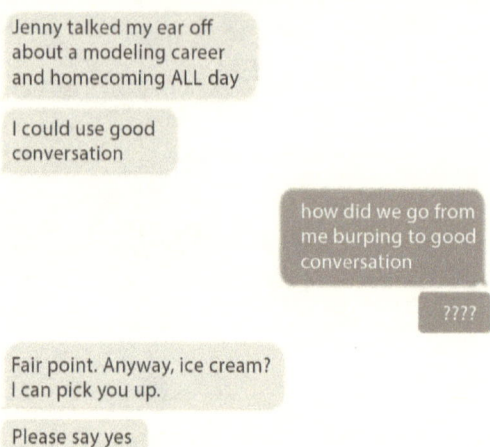

Jenny talked my ear off about a modeling career and homecoming ALL day

I could use good conversation

how did we go from me burping to good conversation

????

Fair point. Anyway, ice cream? I can pick you up.

Please say yes

If I say yes, Ethan and I will be alone. I mean, obviously there will be other people getting ice cream, but we'll be on the actual date he asked me on in the first version of the scavenger hunt. The one where I slipped, then ran away so he couldn't ask me for ice cream.

My heart pounds. The pressure is already there. It's building. I tap my fingers against my thumb and breathe like I'm back in the park, doing yoga. I breathe like my only goal in life is to make Susan proud.

Slowly, the pressure subsides. The feeling like I'm about to lose control dissipates, and I'm left staring at Ethan's last text. Mariana would tell me to go for it. She'd probably grab the phone and text a "yes" for me. I hold my breath and type a response.

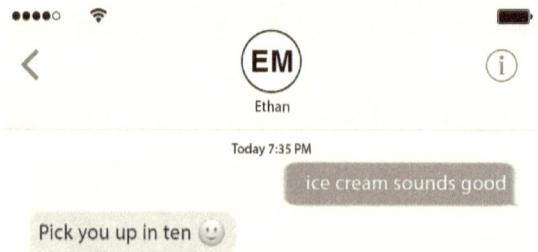

EM

Ethan

Today 7:35 PM

ice cream sounds good

Pick you up in ten 😊

I suppress a scream by shoving my knuckles into my mouth. I can't believe I'm doing this. My heart starts hammering again, but it's a good hammering—the excitement of doing something I want to do. This is good. I text Mariana.

I have eight minutes left to change into something nicer than a sweatshirt and my yoga pants. I've never thrown so many clothes from my closet onto my bed at one time. I don't want to seem like I'm trying too hard because of a date.

Oh. Em. Gee. A date.

Focus. Clothes.

But I also don't want to look like I'm a slob, either. Gotta find something that balances. In the end, I pick the pink sweater dress and leggings I wore to the show with Mom last weekend—the very same outfit I thought about wearing on a date with Ethan Morrow.

And now I'm going on a date with Ethan Morrow.

I know I should stop saying it, but the more I repeat the words to myself, the more they'll seem normal, right?

I put on a little blush and lip gloss again because, without them, I look like a ghost, then brush my hair out and leave it down. I rarely leave it down. I kinda…look like a proper girl this way. Huh.

I glance out the window. No Ethan yet, but Mom will be home soon, and I should probably let her know where I'm going. I don't *think* she'll say no, but I bite my bottom lip. *Mariana today, a boy tomorrow.* She really wasn't wrong.

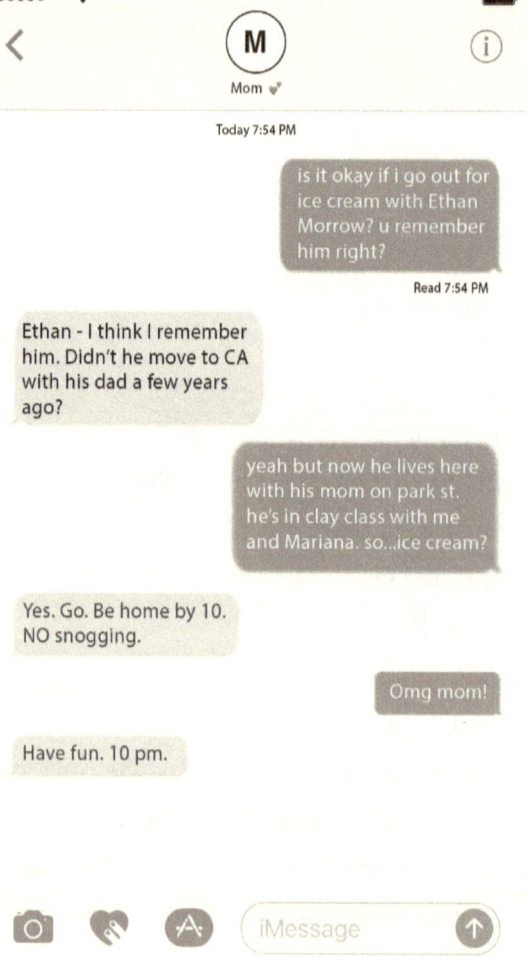

I do *not* respond again. My mom just used the word "snogging." Has she been reading her British novels again? No one on this side of the Atlantic uses that word. No one. And now it's going to be stuck in my brain for the rest of the night. Thank you, Mom.

Of course, that was probably her intention.

I'm at the front door before Ethan pulls up. I don't give him the opportunity to get out of the car and ring the doorbell. That just feels like it would be too formal. And weird. I can only handle so much weird tonight. I pull the front door shut behind me and bound to the car before he has a chance to turn off the engine or get out and hold open the car door for me.

Ethan seems like a door-holding kind of boy, and I really don't want that kind of extra attention right now, so it's best if I just pretend this date (say it, PJ—date) is just two friends hanging out and getting ice cream together.

Ethan wears a light green polo shirt and khaki shorts even though it's barely fifty degrees.

"You know it's October, right?" I point to his legs as he shifts the car into reverse and backs out of the driveway.

He laughs, and I'm rewarded with that dimple I like so much.

"Yeah, but we're going for ice cream. I'm holding onto every last scrap of summer I can, shorts and all."

He turns from our development onto a main road that leads to a nineteen-fifties ice cream parlor that's straight out of a movie with its checkered floors and outdoor tables. Ethan drives well. Not that I expected him not to, but he drives like my mom, which is safe, cautious—in a good way. No macho squealing tires or revving engine.

"So, Jenny McGinnis, huh?"

He groans. "Don't remind me. I cannot believe I said yes to photographing her, but I wanted to add to my portfolio, and she needed photos for her modeling portfolio, and it just… seemed like a good idea at the time?"

"That sure was a long *date*."

"I swear, we were *not* on a date."

I laugh despite my leaping pulse. It's okay. This is okay. *I'm* okay.

"Did *she* know that?"

He screws up his face. "She definitely knew it by the end of the day."

"Uh oh…hope you got lunch out of it first."

"Fast food, if that counts."

I don't have a reply, so I look out the window at the streetlights and the houses rolling past in the dark.

"If it makes you feel any better, your one photo came out a thousand times better than her six hundred eighty-four."

"Six hundred eighty-four!"

"Yeah, I'm probably going to delete about six hundred fifty of them. She is *not* a natural when it comes to the camera."

"Well, that won't work out well for the modeling career she has in mind."

"Right? I didn't have the heart to tell her."

There's really not much more to say about Jenny, so we fall silent, but the ice cream place comes into sight, so we're saved from making conversation. At least the inside of the car is dark, so he can't see the desperation I feel must be visible on my face.

How is it possible to be so incredibly comfortable *and* so incredibly uncomfortable with someone at the same time? In some ways, hanging with Ethan outside of school feels just the same as our texts, which always seem to flow, but in other ways, it's entirely alien, and I feel like my brain is turning circles to think of something intelligent to say. He did say he was looking for intelligent conversation, right?

Why is it so difficult to think of something smart right now? I'm no

Mariana, but I still get good grades in school. I know how to construct basic sentences and hold an intellectual conversation. At the moment, though, I somehow just can't figure out how.

Ethan parks in a spot close to the building, and we walk to the front window to order. I've never been so conscious of my hands at my sides before. I wish I'd worn a light jacket with pockets. Pockets are a good place to put hands.

The ice cream parlor is nearly abandoned, but that's hardly a surprise. It's October, and the sun is already down. Most people aren't crazy enough to encourage the chill already in the air by eating something cold, but here we are. There's a family with three kids sitting at one of the tables and a couple of kids from our school just leaving. I swallow and wonder if this will start gossip about me and Ethan. I don't think I'm popular enough for gossip, but...

When we approach the window to order, Ethan looks at me before scanning the ice cream flavors posted on the wall behind the counter.

"Hmm, don't tell me. I'm gonna guess. I think you're a..." He squints his eyes at me and purses his lips. "Cookie dough kind of girl."

My lips part. A bolt of surprise shoots from my head to my toes. He didn't say cookie dough last time. He didn't know. He thought I was a mint chocolate chip kind of girl last time. His exact words. How...how did he remember?

He couldn't have.

"PJ?"

"Yeah," I say, coming to, realizing he's staring at me, and I'm buried in my own thoughts. "Cookie dough sounds good. In a cup. Hot fudge?"

"Heck, yeah, hot fudge."

He turns to the girl behind the counter. "Two cups of cookie dough, hot fudge, and whipped cream, please." Then he looks back at me. "Wait, you want whipped cream? I should have asked."

"Heck, yeah, whipped cream." I smile.

He smiles back, then dips into his wallet to pay for the ice cream. I brought my purse, and I offer to cover my share, but he shakes his head.

"No way. This is my treat. You've saved me from a day spent exclusively in the company of Jenny McGinnis, the most talkative upcoming model Feris Alweather has to offer modeling agencies everywhere."

I accept my cookie dough sundae with thanks and immediately lick a bit of hot fudge that drips down the edge of the cup. It's divine. Of course, I could eat a vat of just hot fudge and be satisfied, so...

We eat our ice cream at one of the tables and watch the family with the three small kids as the mom and dad wrangle them into finishing the last of their cones. There's a significant amount of melted ice cream both on their table and the concrete around them. I don't recall ever being that messy when I was little.

My mind turns back to Ethan and his cookie dough comment.

Why? How? He couldn't have remembered that cookie dough was my favorite ice cream flavor. He thought mint chocolate chip in his version of events last time. And yet, *somehow*, he chose cookie dough now.

With a spoonful of ice cream and fudge to my mouth, I pause.

"What made you say cookie dough?" I finally ask. The best way to get any answer is to ask, right?

He spoons a giant mass of whipped cream into his mouth and shrugs. "I dunno. The first thought that popped into my head was mint chocolate chip. And then, I swear, it's like I could just hear your voice."

"My voice?"

"Yeah. Crazy right? 'Cookie dough, actually.' Like, I heard that, but in your voice."

I almost drop my spoon, fumble to recover it, and get whipped cream on my sweater in the process. At least it wasn't fudge. I wipe it off and lick my finger.

Ethan remembered words from a time he never experienced. My heart is starting to do its thing and I fight to stay present. I fight *hard* because I do not want to slip now. I want to know more.

"Anyway, is it really cookie dough, or are you just humoring me?"

"It really is."

"Okay, so what else should I know? We've got your favorite ice cream flavor. What about...favorite season?"

The conversation forces me to stay focused on the moment. "Autumn," I say. "October is my favorite month. You pretend it's still summer at the beginning of the month, but by the end, there's no denying everything's changed."

He looks down at his clothes. "You wouldn't be referring to me pretending it's still summer, would you, by any chance?"

I laugh. "Are you freezing yet?"

He fights a shiver and laughs. "Probably should have worn pants."

I agree, but Ethan also has tan, muscular calves from running, lightly covered in gold hair. I probably shouldn't be looking at Ethan's legs, but he's the one who wore shorts.

"Why do you like running?" he asks.

Because it's kept me from hurling myself backwards through time nine minutes and fifty-three seconds on more than a few occasions.

I suck my spoon and think for a moment.

"It clears my mind. If my feet are running, my mind can't."

"Hm."

"What?"

"That just feels like a really honest answer."

Not nearly as honest as I could have been, which makes me feel a little guilty, but it's not exactly like I could tell him the real answer.

He'd think me a nutcase. And aren't I? Mariana would answer that with "Aren't we all?" and she'd be right, but still.

"Well, what about you? Why do you like running?"

He pauses for a long moment before answering. I suppose he's trying to find an answer that will be half as honest as he thinks mine was.

"I think I just feel free from expectations when I'm running, you know? Like, not at a meet or anything. There are definitely expectations *there*, but like when I'm just running for the sake of running. No one expects me to be anywhere or act a certain way or perform for them. It's just…me, you know?" Then he gets sheepish and runs a hand over his face. "That sounds stupid."

"No," I say. "Not at all. I get it."

I lean back into the bench and look up. The stars are starting to come out, though I can't see many of them beyond the bright lights of the parking lot. Ethan follows my gaze and then grabs my hand. Touching his hand, holding his hand, makes my breath catch a little. He takes both our empty ice cream cups and tosses them in the trash, then leads me across the street to a field knee-high with grass.

The one thing about October is that the air is finally free of humidity, which makes for crystal clear views of the sky. I don't care how many times I look up, I'll never tire of looking at the night's sky. I follow in Ethan's footsteps as he stomps down a bit of grass we can sit in. He's got to be freezing by now, but if he is, he's not showing it.

"Guess I should have asked first. Do you want to stargaze before I take you home? I mean, you were looking up, and the look on your face, I just thought…" He's suddenly nervous. The thought is oddly comforting, and it's doubly cute that he used the word "stargaze," which I think most kids our age would agree is an old-time, cringe-worthy phrase. I think we're supposed to "watch the stars" or "look up" or something. "Gaze" seems so intimate, but it's just another weird Ethan quirk I'm starting to like.

"Yeah," I answer, my voice a little breathless. "I love the stars."

I sit on the flattened grass, my back facing the ice cream parlor across the street, and hug my knees as I look up into the twinkling sky. When I was six, my grandparents got me a telescope for my birthday. It wasn't a fancy one, and I couldn't use it on stars, but I'd sit and stare at the moon's craters almost every night for two months straight. I finally stopped when Mom said she was starting to worry I'd burn out my retinas from the light of the moon. (That's enough to make any six-year-old panic.) But I never stopped looking up. There's just something about—

"There's just something about the vastness up there." Ethan steals the words from my brain.

I look back to him, meeting his eyes in the dark, which suddenly seems a thousand times more intimate than it did a minute ago.

"I was about to say the same thing."

"There's so much light pollution outside of L.A., you can hardly ever see the stars. I kind of forgot what they looked like for a few years." Ethan turns his gaze upward again.

I'm relieved when his eyes are no longer trained on me. My heart is starting to do its thing, and I'm loving this moment so much I don't want to spoil it.

"Do you miss your dad?" If I turn the attention to him, maybe my pulse will settle.

He gives a sort of noncommittal sound that could mean yes or no.

"I mean, I miss how we used to get along, but even that started to become strained before he started seeing Lindsay. I don't…want to put blame on anyone, but getting older, I think it's become clearer to see why my parents got a divorce. I still love my dad. I just…" He doesn't finish. I don't push him. "It's good to be back with Mom."

I nod. "Hey, there's the International Space Station."

Convenient of it to swoop overhead at this particular moment. It's the perfect time to change the conversation.

He squints. "Where?"

I don't even think. I put my head next to his so we're touching and try to line up my finger with his line of sight.

"That light? That thing's moving!"

"Five miles a second."

He startles and looks at me, and suddenly, I'm hyper aware that our faces are inches apart.

"Why do you know that?" He speaks the words, but he's looking at my lips. I tap my fingers against my thumb and breathe.

"Science project. Last year." I barely get the words out.

"Hey," he says softly. "Do you remember third grade?"

"Yeah."

Okay, this is good. Third grade. I can calm myself on memories of Miss Beldorf's class and the silly things we all did in the classroom and on the playground. We were eight. There were a lot of silly things. I breathe.

"Remember they gave all the boys yellow roses to give to the girls on Valentine's Day?"

I nod.

"Kyle Hoffert got your name, so I traded with him so I could give you my rose."

I almost can't breathe. I remember very well because I was so freaked out by getting a flower from Ethan (though it wouldn't have mattered *who* gave it to me back then) that I slipped three times in a row and convinced the teacher I was sick and needed to go to the nurse. In version 1.4, I got sent home sick and never received a flower.

So while I remember getting a yellow rose from Ethan Morrow eight years ago in version 1.1, *he* shouldn't remember giving it to me.

My pulse hammers in my veins. I can't slip now. I need to know more.

"Then you went home sick that day, and I was crushed I didn't get to give you your flower first. I ended up giving it to Miss Beldorf."

I close my eyes and let out a breath. Ethan doesn't remember. He just remembers trading names with Kyle Hoffert. That's all.

"Funny thing, though. I feel like I must have had a dream where I gave you the rose because I have this image in my head of handing it to you. Like a really vivid image of standing in front of your desk. You were in the front right corner, right, by the pencil sharpener? I remember that. I stood there, and I handed it to you, and then…I guess I woke up." He laughs. "Weird, right?"

I can't breathe.

Ethan remembers version 1.1.

Ethan remembers—

I'm thrown back into myself, sitting on a table outside the ice cream parlor, my ice cream cup still streaked with bits of fudge but otherwise empty in my hand. I draw a shaky breath.

"That just feels like a really honest answer."

I shrug. It's the only response I can give right now. I don't trust my voice.

"Do you want to know what I like about it?"

"Sure." But my mind is elsewhere. My mind is on Ethan nine minutes from now. Ethan in the dark with the stars. Ethan who remembers version 1.1 from a slip in third grade.

"I think I just feel free from expectations when I'm running, you know? Like, not at a meet or anything. There are definitely expectations *there*, but like when I'm just running just for the sake of running. No one expects me to be anywhere or act a certain way or perform for them. It's just… me, you know?" He runs a hand over his face. "That sounds stupid."

"No," I say, finally regaining my composure. "Not at all."

I do not look up at the stars.

"Hey, this was a lot of fun," I say. "But I should probably get home if you don't mind. My mom's gonna be home soon and she just worked a twelve-hour shift. I don't want to come in after she's asleep."

"Oh, yeah. Sure. Your mom's a nurse, right? She works a lot?"

"Yeah, sixty hours a week, usually. Sometimes more." Talking about my mom seems safer than talking about stars and yellow roses and third grade. "But she's awesome at what she does. There's no one I'd trust more with my life."

"That's a lot of hours to be alone," Ethan says.

I shrug in response. Ethan collects our empty cups and throws them in the trash as we walk to the car. He doesn't take my hand this time, though he does open the car door for me, and I let him. My fingers still tingle from the last time he held them.

We ride home in silence. Maybe he's grown tired of carrying the conversation as I have suddenly become a spectacularly bad conversationalist. When we get to my house, I open the door before he can think to get out and open it for me, before he can try to walk me to the door.

"Thank you," I say. "I had a good time."

And it's true. I did. Right up until I slipped. Right up until I ruined it all.

"Me, too. We should do it again, yeah? I'll wear pants next time."

Then I'm forced to laugh because Ethan makes it sound like he wasn't wearing anything on his lower half tonight.

"Sounds good."

I step out of the car. Ethan waits until I'm in the front door, then flashes the headlights once before pulling away.

Mom is on the couch with a glass of red wine in hand, watching a Netflix documentary. There's an octopus on the screen when she pauses it to turn and look my way. Wild Saturday night. She really should be dating. *She* wouldn't slip on a guy in the middle of a date.

"Home already? It's barely nine!"

I shrug. I seem to do that a lot lately. "Doesn't take long to get ice cream."

"Bad date? Guess I don't need to ask if there was any snogging."

I cringe and shake my head. She definitely doesn't need to ask about snogging. There will never be snogging. I can't stay in one place long enough for Ethan to want to snog me. Kiss. Kiss. I can't stay in one place long enough to be kissed.

"Do you want to sit a while? I can put something else on if you want to watch a movie together."

I contemplate. I really want to go to my room and sob into my pillow. Or call Mariana and wallow in her sympathy. But suddenly, I want Mom more than ever. I nod my head, then grab the fuzzy throw blanket from the back of the couch, throw it around my shoulders, and plop beside her.

"Whoa! Easy," she says, setting down her wine on the end table. "You okay, kiddo?"

I curl my legs beneath me and rest my head on her shoulder. "Yeah." I breathe in the smell of her freshly shampooed hair. "Just tired."

"Hm." Her reply tells me she doesn't believe me for a minute, but she won't press me for answers I'm not ready to give.

Instead, she puts an arm around me, snuggles me close like I'm five again, and kisses the top of my head before pressing play on the remote.

If this is how all my dates end, I'll be the crazy lady who lives alone with her thirty cats someday. For sure.

CHAPTER EIGHT

When Mom eventually heads to bed, I tromp to my room to text Mariana. The only reason she hasn't texted me during the past few hours is because she thinks I'm still on a date with Ethan, and she doesn't want to interrupt. I already dread the conversation that's about to happen.

I kind of like watching Mom's animal documentaries, where I don't have to think about anything at all. It's a nice escape. I wonder if that's why she watches them so often. Does she need an escape from real life, too? Does watching wildlife's fight for survival make her problems seem small by comparison?

I sigh and pick up my phone.

The phone rings thirty seconds later. I pull my head out of my arms to answer it. I sit at my desk, my knees pulled to my chest. I'm not crying, but I feel like crying.

"Don't tell me you slipped again!" Mariana wails when I put the phone to my ear.

"Worse." My voice is barely a whisper.

It's not that I'm worried Mom will hear. She's probably already asleep. I just...don't want to say it out loud.

"PJ, you're scaring me. Did you breathe with Susan?"

I hang my head. "I know you're being funny, but Mari, I can't right now. I can't."

Then I burst into quiet sobs. I don't want to. I didn't think I was going to. I thought watching television for two hours had taken the sting of tonight's slip out of me. Apparently not.

"Damn. I'm sorry, Peej. Are you okay?"

In between sobs, I mumble something that might be "I'm okay," but Mariana is patient and waits for me to get the tears out of my system. She fills my ear with stories of her day, and how Marco started working at the garage with Luis, and how Luis finally trusts him enough to put him on more than just rotating tires. She doesn't expect me to find this interesting or anything. Like any bestie, she knows that if she talks, it gives me a chance to calm down enough so I can stop crying.

It works. When I'm finally breathing normally again and the tears have stopped flowing down my face (*and* after I've blown my nose half a dozen times), Mariana grows silent and waits.

"I did slip," I say. "But it's worse than that. Ethan remembers version 1.1."

"*What!* He knew you slipped?"

I rub my eyes. They're swollen now. Fantastic. I'll look like a troll in the morning.

"No, not *this* time. He didn't know I slipped tonight. He remembers a slip from third grade."

"What? Hold up. I'm going to need you to back this up and explain from the beginning."

"Yeah, so remember in third grade…no, wait, you weren't in our school yet, were you?"

"Nope. Didn't move here until fifth. But go on, please. My student enrollment status is of no importance here."

"Okay, so in third grade, the teachers gave all the boys these yellow roses to give to the girls on Valentine's Day, right? They had them draw names so it wasn't like giving to anyone you liked or anything. Only, I was so freaked out when Ethan gave me my rose that I slipped three times in a row until I finally got ahold of myself and convinced the teacher I wasn't feeling well and had to go to the nurse. So I *never* actually got a rose in the final version of the events."

"Okay."

"But Ethan remembers giving me a rose. He said it was like a dream or something."

Mariana gives a small gasp, then grows silent for a moment. "Are we sure he didn't *actually* dream it? I mean, that would explain a lot."

"Not only does he remember giving it to me, but he remembers beforehand when he traded names with another kid in our class so he could give me a rose, which happened even in the version that played out. He just didn't actually get to give it to me because I went home sick."

"Aww! That's *so* cute! He was crushing on you back then, too!"

"Mariana!"

"What?"

"Focus."

She sighs.

"Ethan remembers giving me the rose. He knows it didn't actually happen, but he *remembers* it. HOW?"

"Do you think he's, like, your meant-to-be?"

I bang my head on my desk. It hurts, but the pain almost feels good compared to the thoughts in my brain.

"No," I say. "That's impossible. There's no such thing."

But a part of me almost hopes. If meant-to-be people exist, then maybe I won't always be alone. Maybe I *could* actually venture to let someone in. The thought is so tempting, but when I pull myself back to reality, a weight on my chest makes it almost impossible to breathe.

"He remembered a slip from the other day, too. The day he sent me on the scavenger hunt? Well, I mean, he didn't exactly remember it, but when he asked me to go out for ice cream that first time, he said I seemed like a mint chocolate chip kind of girl, but then I told him cookie dough's my favorite."

"Okay. And?"

"And when we got ice cream today, he turned to me, and he got this weird look on his face. Then, out of nowhere, he said I looked like a cookie dough kind of girl."

"Well, as long as you don't look like cookie dough."

"Mariana."

"Yeah, yeah, I know. Focus. So, he somehow remembered your favorite flavor."

"Uh-huh."

"PJ, this is worth investigating."

"Please." I don't want to know how Mariana thinks we can possibly *investigate* this.

"No, really. I mean it. This has never happened before, right?"

"Never."

"So don't you want to know what makes Ethan remember things when others can't? Don't you want to know what makes him special? I mean, PJ, this is *big*. And also? I'm a little jealous. If anyone gets to remember things about you, it should be me. I mean, I'm the only one who knows, right? I'm the one who's been by your side through thick and thin, right? This isn't fair."

I give a pathetic laugh. "There is absolutely *nothing* to be jealous of," I say.

"Says the girl who can remember things about people they never remember telling her."

She can't see me, but I roll my eyes. "I promised you I would always tell you anything that you said or did if a slip involved you. It's not my fault I rarely slip around you. What can I say? You keep me grounded."

It's true. I made the promise to Mariana shortly after the incident in ninth grade gym class. She was mortified by the thought I might know something she didn't remember telling me. And I've been true to my word. Anytime Mariana's been involved in a slip, which is hardly ever, I relay every word of what's happened.

"So what do you want me to do?" I ask.

"I think you should hang out with Ethan. Like, a lot."

"Mari, really."

"What? I'm being serious. I think you need to hang out with Ethan a whole bunch. At best, you'll eventually be comfortable enough that you'll stop slipping, right? And at worst, you'll have a panic attack every day and slip. A lot. But you've slipped before. You know it won't kill you. You know you're going to survive."

The very thought of slipping once a day sends my heart into a palpitating mess.

"You can't tell me figuring this out isn't worth a few slips."

"Says the girl who doesn't actually have to do the slipping."

"Look, I'm not saying it's easy or that it will be entirely pleasant, but don't you want to know what makes Ethan different? You like him, right?"

I close my eyes and rub a temple. I like Ethan more than I care to admit. I don't want to like him, but there's something about his smile that hits deep in my chest. I can't explain it. It's like when he smiles at me, he's sharing a part of himself he doesn't share with anyone else, and I know that sounds stupid. It's ridiculous to think he doesn't smile at anyone else. He does. He's a nice guy. He smiles a lot. So I have no reason to feel his smiles toward me mean anything more or less than when he smiles at anyone else.

And he appears at the strangest of times, usually when I least expect it. He shows up when I don't think I'm going to have to interact with anyone, when I've finally let my guard down. Maybe that's the real reason I slip with him. He's so genuine that it's impossible not to let him through the safety barriers I try to keep in place.

"PJ."

"Hmm?"

"You've been quiet a long time. It's a simple question. Do you like him or not?"

I sigh and fight the knot in my throat. "I do. I mean, I think I do."

"Then you know what you have to do."

I'm silent for another long moment.

"Dammit, Mariana."

Ethan doesn't give me a chance to text him first. When I wake up Sunday morning, he's already texted me three times.

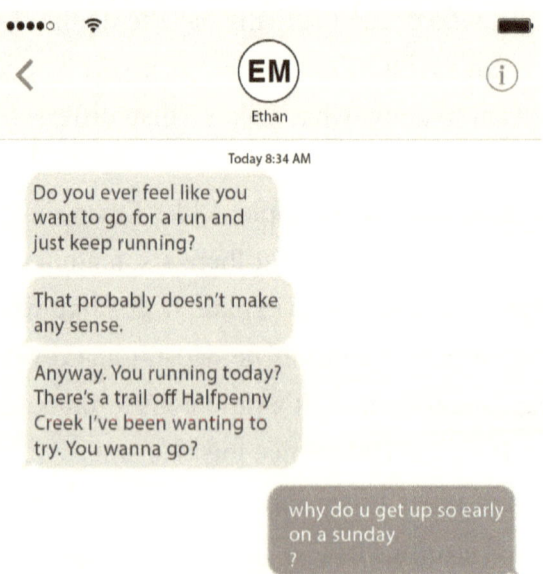

The three dots start jumping immediately. It's nine-thirty, and I haven't even rolled out of bed yet. I just picked up my phone to check messages, scroll social media, and generally wake myself up. My eyes don't feel as swollen as I thought they'd be.

It's not like I should be tired. I got plenty of sleep last night. But when your dreams are filled with threats of slipping, and you wake up with a racing pulse, wondering if you *did* actually slip, the night can seem pretty long.

Actually, I could go for a run this morning. My legs are itching to go. But do I want to run with a boy who might make the course three times longer than normal if I slip? *You know what you have to do.* Mariana's words ring in my ears. I growl even though there's no one here to hear me.

By the time Ethan shows up at my house in a pair of shorts, sneakers, and a t-shirt featuring a band that was popular in the twentieth century, I'm ready to go. I stare at the logo on his shirt. If my mom didn't listen to them, I'm pretty sure her parents did. I think the station Mom listens to still plays a lot of their songs.

Seeing my stare, he looks down and then grins.

"Aerosmith," he says.

"I know." A partial truth. I mostly knew.

"Classic."

"If you say so." I start stretching on the front porch, loosening muscles for a long run, calming a heart that's already galloping at the sight of Ethan Morrow. Stupid heart.

Ethan is probably already warmed up from his jog to my house, but he shakes out his legs and does a little hop from foot to foot to keep his muscles warm.

"You okay?" I ask him.

"Yeah," he says. "Why wouldn't I be?"

"Well, you started your text to me this morning by talking about running away, so…" I trail off, unsure whether he was serious or not in his text. I'm not crazy. There was something underlying the words in that text; something's bugging him.

He pauses a moment before answering, and when he finally does speak, he's intentionally vague. "I didn't say I was going to run away."

"Seriously. You okay?" I pause in my stretching and tug the sleeve of his shirt so he'll look at me.

His eyes are guarded, hesitant. Mariana's always been there for me. I feel like Ethan doesn't have a Mariana of his own, so maybe I can fill the role. I'm surprised to find I *want* to hear his problems. Usually, the thought of adding other people's troubles to my own has me running in terror. But things with Ethan are different.

Still, I can tell he's not sure if he wants to share this side of himself and his life. I sense it in him the same way I know whenever Mariana's had an interaction with the racist drunk who sometimes shows up at Bluestone Lake to fish. No matter how much she knows he's a jerk who isn't worth her time and that she'll still be the first Latina President of the United States someday, his slurs hit some core part of Mariana deeply.

Ethan looks that same way now.

"Ethan," I say when he doesn't answer right away.

He licks his lips. "Mom and I had a fight."

"Oh."

I find I don't actually know what to say to that. Mom and I rarely fight. I can't remember the last time we had an argument that was about more than just dishes or laundry.

He waves a hand. "It's nothing. Really."

"So why do you want to run away?"

"I don't. I just... My dad called yesterday, and I didn't feel like talking to him, so I didn't answer. So then he texted my mom about it, and I got lectured about how important it is to maintain a relationship with him. Like I can't let one call go to voicemail without getting in trouble." He runs a hand through his hair, frustrated, but at least he's letting out his emotion instead of keeping it all bottled inside. I know what *that's* like.

"I'm sorry."

"It wouldn't have even been a big deal, but now Mom thinks I'm dodging him. She asked if the only reason I moved back here was to avoid him."

"Is it?" I ask.

"No! I mean, it's probably not bad for us to have a break from each other, especially with Lindsay—his fiancée—in the picture. But it doesn't mean that's the only reason I moved back here."

"Did you tell your mom that?"

"No. I mean, yeah. I told her I wanted to come back because I missed her. I missed home. I missed..." For a minute, I think Ethan is about to tell me he missed me, but then he finishes, "...everything here."

"And?"

He shrugs. "And then I left the house to run with you. It'll be okay. I know it will. I just…I don't want my mom to get it in her head that I should be in California."

I nod. I don't like the thought of Ethan going back to California, either. "You should probably give your dad a call."

He sighs. "I will. Later. When I get home." He gives a hesitant smile and adds, "Thanks."

I frown in confusion. "For what?"

"For pulling it out of me. I guess I needed that more than I thought."

Before I know what I'm doing, I take a risk and grab his hand. My heart leaps in my throat at the contact, but I squeeze, relishing his hand in mine. "You can talk to me anytime, Ethan. I mean that. I know you only just got back to the area a few months ago, and I know it's not a 'guy-thing' to want to open up, which is dumb, by the way, but…well, I'm here if you want to talk."

His smile grows wide, genuine. He squeezes my hand back. "Thanks, PJ. That means a lot." He pauses to clear his throat as though to indicate the topic is closed. "Okay. Let's get running."

It feels weird to see Ethan barely twelve hours from the last time I saw him. I mean, I like it, but it still feels weird. Given the briskness of the morning, I'm glad I opted to wear capri leggings. I'll warm up fast enough, but at least I won't be chilled before I do.

Even so, I don't miss the subtle glance Ethan directs toward my butt—which, I might add, looks spectacularly good in this particular pair of spandex capris. But maybe he was just looking at the porch railing behind me.

We start slow and steady to warm up. I follow his lead, heading to the trailhead at Halfpenny Creek. I love the name of the creek, but I've never stopped to take the trail that runs its length before crossing over the creek and into the next county. I've always wanted to. This is kind of exciting.

By the time we make the trailhead, I've just hit my stride, the sweet spot that feels like I could run for days. I love this feeling. I love the breeze against my skin, my ponytail swinging at my back, and the smell of autumn air in my nostrils.

I also love that when we're running, neither of us feels the need to talk. It's just sunshine, birdsong, and feet on the ground. Sure, I'm getting a little sweaty, but Ethan has seen me far worse at cross-country meets. It's strange to think about how many times Ethan's been right in front of me, but all I saw was another kid from school. I certainly didn't see him as…whatever I see him as now.

I glance at him. Sweat drips down his temples, but his breathing is slow and even. He's in the zone. All thoughts of the fight with his mom and the worries about his dad's fiancée are gone from his head. It's what I love most about running.

The trail starts out in great shape. It's clearly well-used and well-loved by many. But about a mile in, everything changes. The path splits. We take the path that sticks close to the creek, but it's littered with fallen tree branches, overgrown bushes, and trash. Why is there so much trash on this trail? Ethan must be thinking the same thing.

"I bet all this junk's from that flood last month." We slow our pace to accommodate for the now uneven terrain of the path.

Finally, Ethan stops and puts his hands on his knees. I gain a few more steps before I pause to wait.

"You're a long-distance runner," he says. "This is nothing for you, I bet."

"I wouldn't say it's nothing." The distance isn't a problem, but I'm not thrilled about possibly twisting an ankle on the debris all over the trail. "This trail would be a lot easier if someone cleaned it up, though."

Ethan looks up and stands straight. He takes in our surroundings like he's really examining them, like someone's going to test him on it later.

"Why don't we?" he says.

"What? Like, now?" I'm all for cleaning up the area, but I'm not about to go touching trash with my bare hands, and we have nowhere to put it anyway.

"No, like we can do it for our community service hours. You, me, and I bet we can grab a few more people to help out. We'd get credits toward graduation and clean up a trail while we're at it."

The idea has merit. We all need forty hours of community service in order to graduate. Why not spend it outdoors? If we got a group together (not that I'd ask anyone except Mariana to join us), it might even be fun.

"That's actually a good idea," I say with mock surprise, as though I couldn't imagine Ethan thinking up something so brilliant. "So you're an environmentalist now, too?"

"Hey, look, you save kids from drowning. I've gotta find some way to keep up."

I blanch a little with his reply. I still don't want to think about what happened to that little girl in version 1.1.

She's alive.

"So when do you want to do this thing?" I ask. "And who do you want to ask to join us? And do we need to, like, clear it with the township or get permission from someone?"

"That's a lot of questions. We'll figure it out," he replies. "You ready to head back?"

I hold out a hand to the trash-strewn trail in front of us. "It's probably for the best. I don't see any point in trying to go on, not if the rest of the trail looks like this."

With that, we turn and head back the way we came, leaping over some of the same fallen logs again. Ethan clears one with a foot to spare, and I almost laugh.

"What is this, hurdles?" I call.

"Maybe we keep the fallen logs when we clear all this, and then we can advertise it as a Feris Alweather track trail with built-in hurdles," he calls back. He laughs as he runs ahead.

In a few quick sprints, I've caught up. Running with Ethan turns out to be fun. I don't slip when I'm running, not even with Ethan. I smile.

I'm still smiling when I walk in the door. And when I get in the shower. And when I get dressed. And even when I sit down to tackle my German assignment.

When my phone rings with an unknown number, I let it go to voicemail, instead focusing on translating *Rumpelstilzchen* word by word for Frau Elle's class on Monday. But then my phone dings with the voicemail chime. No one ever leaves an actual message, so I dial into the voicemail to listen.

"Hello, my name is Angela Stevens, and I'm a reporter with WRHF. I'm looking to get in touch with PJ Ellis. You're not an easy person to track down, but I heard about the events that happened at the lake at Bluestone Park last week, involving you saving the life of a little girl by the name of Kayleigh Owens. Mr. and Mrs. Owens contacted me, and I'd like to run a story about this spectacular act of heroism. If you can, please call—"

I end the call. The memory of Kayleigh Owens's dead body is still too fresh in my mind. Who could have told them my name? No one there knew me. No one could have—

But there was one person there that day who knew me—who knows me. And only one person who has my phone number.

Ethan.

Suddenly, I'm not smiling anymore.

CHAPTER NINE

I'm so angry I don't even know who to text first. Ethan or Mariana? Do I tell him off immediately? (Because I am *really* mad.) Why would he give out my phone number when he knows I haven't wanted to talk about what happened at the lake—when he knows I've done my best to pretend it didn't even happen? Or do I talk to Mari, who will calm me down before I give Ethan a piece of my mind?

Unable to sit any longer, I stand and pace my room. I dial Mariana. I'm too angry for a text right now. The phone rings twice before she answers.

"No, I already helped Avó and Mamãe fold all the clothes. It's *your* turn, Marco! Just go put all the clean sheets back on the beds. It's not that hard. Even you can figure that out!" I'm not sure Mariana meant to answer the phone when she did, but after yelling at Marco, she plows on, this time talking to me. "Bestie, what's up? Have you got another date with Mr. Morrow lined up yet?"

"Funny, I just got back from a run with him."

"Omigod! Nicely done, imp! I didn't think you had it in you to plan two dates in less than twenty-four hours. Crafty!"

"Oh, and it was great, too, right up until I found out he gave my number to a reporter."

"He WHAT?"

"Yeah. I just got a call from a reporter about my heroic act at the lake last week. There was only one person there that day who had my number."

"That jerk!" I can always count on Mariana to be on my side. "What the hell?"

"So I had to either call you or text him, and I'm so angry, I could kick something right now."

"Hm. Probably a good thing you don't have a cat."

"*Mariana!*"

"Just saying."

"I just. I can't. *Why* would he do such a thing? He knew I didn't want to make a big deal of it."

There's silence on the other end of the line for a second. "Did he?"

"He did."

"Did you tell him you didn't want to be contacted?"

"He *knew*. Trust me. He did, alright? I didn't even want to talk about it that day, let alone afterwards."

"Okay, but why wouldn't he tell you if he gave out your number? Like, why wouldn't he say, 'Hey, I hope you don't mind. I gave your number to a reporter who wants to do a story 'cause you saved a life, and that's really awesome?'" Mariana lowers her voice an octave to mimic Ethan, and she sounds so stupid that she *almost* gets a snort out of me.

"Probably because he knew I'd be mad."

"Yeah, but if that's the case, he knew you'd find out when the reporter contacted you anyway, so doesn't it make sense for him to have just said something when you guys went for ice cream last night or on your run this morning?"

I'm silent for a moment. "Well, if it wasn't him, then who would have given my number out? Who else *had* my number?"

"PJ, you told me yourself that there were a bunch of people there that day. Hear me out here. Isn't it maybe just slightly possible that there was someone else who saw it happen and knew your number?"

"I guess. The reporter said the Owens—that's the girl's parents—contacted her to begin with."

"Whoa. Hold up. Did you just say the Owens contacted the reporter?"

"Yeah."

"Um, hello. So it wasn't Ethan."

I sigh. "Mari. The Owens don't have my number. That means the reporter got it from someone else."

"Look, I know this is a wild idea, but…why don't you call the reporter back and ask where she got your number?"

I could do that, but then I'd have to talk to a reporter, and I'd rather drink a gallon of grape soda than talk on the phone with someone I don't know. (And grape-flavored anything should never be allowed to exist.)

"I'm coming over, and you're calling her."

"What? No. Mari—"

The line is already dead. Knowing Mariana, she'll be knocking at the door in exactly four minutes, as that's how long it takes to ride a bike from her house to mine. And she won't wait for me to answer the door. She'll knock, then walk in. It's what she does.

Instead, I hear her voice twenty minutes later.

"Hello! I'm here," she yells as she slams the front door behind her.

"Up here," I call.

Mom is working (yes, even on Sunday), so it's just me in the house. Mariana bounds up the stairs. It's easy to tell she shares a house with two older brothers. She sounds like an elephant coming up the stairs.

"Sorry," she says as she breezes into my room. "Avó made me vacuum the house before I was allowed to leave." Then she practically sings, "It's chore day!"

I shrug. Mom makes me do the same sometimes, so I can't fault her for taking so long to get here. Besides, it's not like I'm in a rush to jump on the phone with a reporter.

Mariana slips off her shoes and throws them against my closet door haphazardly, where they blend right in with the pile of my shoes already there. Then she jumps on my bed and settles with crossed legs.

"Okay, let me hear the message."

I roll my eyes but pull up my voicemail and put it through to speaker.

"Hello, my name is Angela Stevens, and I'm a reporter with WRHF. I'm looking to get in touch with PJ Ellis. You're not an easy person to track down, but I heard about the events that happened at the lake at Bluestone Park last week, involving you saving the life of a little girl by the name of Kayleigh Owens. Mr. and Mrs. Owens contacted me, and I'd like to run a story about this spectacular act of heroism. If you can, please call—"

I hang up again.

"Okay, nowhere in there does it say that she got your number from Ethan."

"Mari."

"Give me the phone." She extends her arm, holding her palm out.

"What? No!"

"Look, I can call her, or you can call her. Which do you want it to be?" Her dark eyes bore into mine, one black eyebrow raised as if challenging me to disobey.

I hand her the phone, but I glare at her for a long moment first. She dials into the voicemail and listens to the whole message, then jots down the number on her phone so she can remember to dial it on *my* phone.

She puts the phone on speaker and then dials. When the line begins to ring, I bite my lip.

"Angela Stevens, WRHF," a voice on the other end says.

"Hi, Ms. Stevens. This is PJ Ellis." My eyes grow wide. What is she doing? "I got your message, and I'm happy to speak with you about the incident, but I wonder if you might be able to tell me how you got my number. I'm not listed anywhere, and my mom might be a little upset if my number is just out there for anyone to find. I'm sixteen, you know."

I'm shaking my head and mouthing *no* as hard as I can, but Mariana ignores me. What is she doing? Why would she commit to speaking with the reporter? My heart pounds hard now, so fast I feel like I could slip any moment.

"Oh, sure. That information isn't confidential. It was another student by the name of Maggie Burak."

Maggie Burak—

I slam so hard into my own body it takes me a moment to recover. Thank goodness I'm sitting. What the heck was Mariana thinking? Why would she—

And then Mariana walks in my front door.

"Hello! I'm here."

"Up here," I call.

She stomps up the stairs with all the elegance of an elephant for the second time.

"Sorry," she says as she breezes into my room. "Avó made me vacuum the house before I was allowed to leave. It's chore day!" She even sings the last line in the very same tune.

"You're a jerk, you know that?" I say, standing from my desk chair.

She looks confused for only a moment, but something on my face must give it away.

"I made you slip!"

"Yeah, you did! You called the reporter and told her I was going to give her the story."

She brightens as she kicks off her shoes and adds them to my pile.

"Oh, good! That's exactly what I was planning to do. Now I don't have to."

"You're awful!"

"Please tell me you got a name. If it didn't work, I'll feel bad I made you slip for nothing."

"Yeah, it worked."

"And?" She looks at me impatiently, hands on her hips, head cocked.

"Apparently, Maggie Burak was at the park that day and saw the whole thing. She talked to the reporter."

"Oh, good! So, not Ethan! Wait, how does Maggie have your number? Are you cheating on me, bestie?"

I roll my eyes, then shove her so she falls onto my bed. She resists only momentarily before letting herself be pushed over. Then she sits up, crosses her legs, and rests her arms on her thighs. She's still waiting for a response.

"Relax. She's in my German group."

She laughs. "Oh. Okay, then. As long as I'm not being replaced."

Now it's my turn to laugh, though it sounds a little desperate. "As if anyone could measure up to you.."

"So," she prompts.

"Yeah?"

"You gonna call that reporter back?"

I throw a pillow at her. She laughs and dodges, but it still hits her before falling to the floor.

"Seriously, though. Ethan. Can we get back to Ethan?"

I groan as I slide against the wall and fall to the floor. "Ugh! I'm an idiot."

Mariana rolls onto her stomach to lean over the edge of the bed so she can see me.

"No, you're not. You're just a normal girl with normal boy problems."

"Did you...really...just call me normal?"

"Well, okay, you're a mostly-normal girl with normal boy problems."

"Yeah, but what if I'd gone off on him? I was going to, you know. I was ready to text him first. I just happened to call you before I let loose on him."

"Proof that you should always talk to me first. I will be your conscience and your guide and will help you successfully navigate this tricky thing we call…life."

"You're so dramatic."

She sticks out her tongue. I wish I had another pillow to throw at her.

As if on cue, my phone pings. It's Ethan.

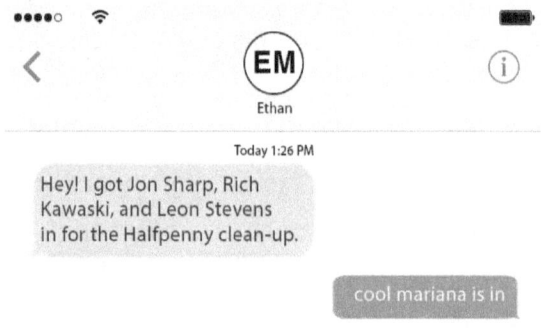

I have not actually asked Mariana yet, but I'll have no problem strong-arming her into a trail cleanup. She's all about combating pollution and climate change. This is right up her alley.

"What's he saying?" she asks over my shoulder.

"I volunteered you to help us with a service project. You, me, Ethan, Jon Sharp, Rich Kawaski, and Leon Stevens are gonna do a trail cleanup at the Halfpenny Creek trail."

"Wait. Did you say Leon Stevens?"

My phone pings again and I look down at the text that's just come through.

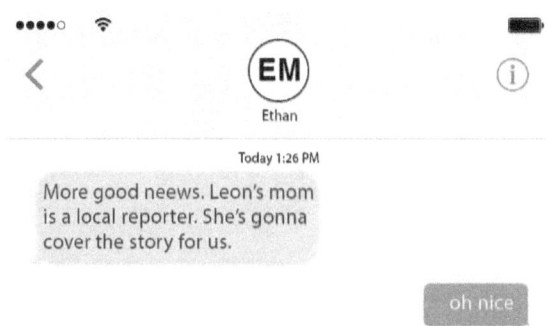

It's all I can type. Leon Stevens, whose reporter-mom must be Angela Stevens, who I just decided I would not be calling back.

I mean, what am I supposed to say? "Sorry, Leon can't be involved, and we definitely cannot have his mom run a story on our cleanup because I'm currently ghosting said reporter."

"What's going on?" Mariana asks. "Lemme see."

I show her the phone.

"*Merda.*"

The only reason I know what she's said is because I know she's not supposed to say it.

"Yeah, deep *merda.*"

"Well, let's just go with it and see what happens. I'll be there, too. If she's running a story on the project, she's got to mention all of us. I can talk enough for you and me both. Okay? I'll run interference so she won't even remember the lake incident."

I'm not convinced, but I nod as I text Ethan.

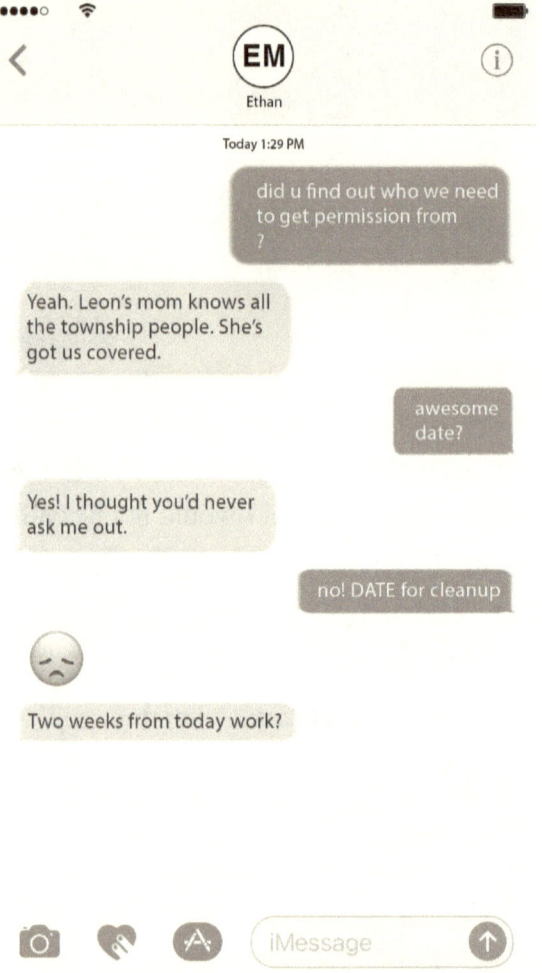

I turn to face Mariana. "You free two weeks from today?"

She considers for a moment, then opens the calendar on her phone to double-check. "That's Halloween weekend," she says. "That works for me, but I need to be home by two. If we start early, it should be fine. You sure you don't want to come over for the trick-or-treaters? Luis and Marco have the whole house decorated and plan to scare as many little kids as possible."

"I'm good, thanks." Halloween is not my thing. Jump scares, in general, are not my thing. For the obvious reason.

"Oh my God!" I fumble my phone, failing to catch it, and it falls to the carpet.

"What now? What's going on?" Mariana has been steadily watching me text back and forth while simultaneously scrolling on her own phone.

"He just asked me out. Like on a real date. Like a planned date."

"YES! Say yes!" She's up on her knees now, giving my bed trampoline treatment, eagerly bouncing on her knees and practically falling over herself.

My heart races. But I…don't feel like I'm going to slip? Like, it just feels kind of like normal excitement. Maybe Mariana is right. Maybe I could get used to Ethan like I'm used to her. Maybe I'll stop slipping around him if he's a part of my everyday life.

"Slip!"

"I know, I know. I'm texting. Give me a minute, okay?"

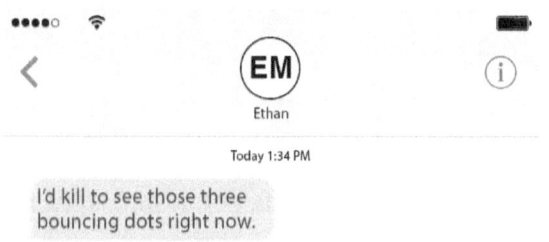

Mariana grabs the phone from me to read. I can only grin like an idiot and hope Ethan is doing the same. If I close my eyes and picture it hard enough, I think I can imagine his dimple. I wish I could stop grinning. It hurts my face.

"Omigod, you are the world's most boring texter."

"What?"

"You don't even sound excited!" Mock disappointment drips from Mariana's words.

I grab my phone back, insulted, and reread my texts.

"What do you mean? I sound plenty excited. I asked where he was taking me."

"There's not even an exclamation point or an emoji there. Girl, you're killing me."

"Fine," I huff. "What should I say?"

She beckons twice with her fingers, then holds out her hand. I plop my phone back into it.

"I need to see it before you hit send. Promise." I don't let go of the phone until she promises.

"Fine," she says, then swipes the phone and starts typing. A minute later, she hands it to me.

"I would never say it like that." I tap back to delete her words, get rid of the praying hands emojis, and reword it so it sounds more like me. Then I hit send.

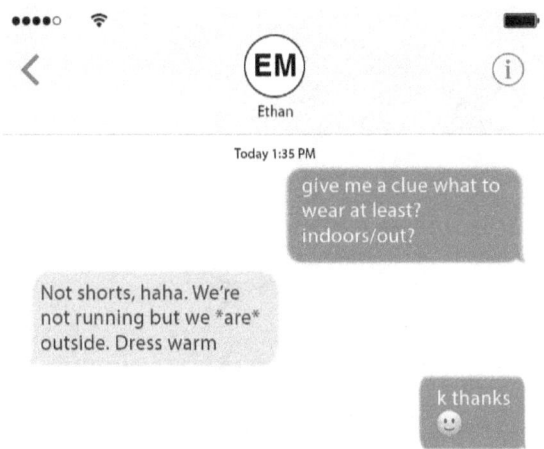

I turn the screen to Mariana.

"Proper emoji use." She gives me two thumbs up. "Okay, so that's all covered. What now?"

I look at my desk.

"Want to help me with my German translation?"

She makes a face. "Pass."

"Some friend." I heave a sigh. Then, I stand. "Come on. Mom and I had tacos for dinner last night. There are leftovers for lunch. Did you eat yet?"

Mariana hops off the bed. "I did, but I'll never say no to second lunch! Then, we can taco 'bout Ethan more."

I throw my head back and groan.

"I surrender. No taco puns, please."

"Wait, wait, wait. How do tacos say grace?"

"Mariana."

"Lettuce pray!"

Now I laugh. Sometimes, I'm really not sure whether I want to hug or strangle Mariana Salvadore. Maybe both.

CHAPTER TEN

Clay class is different now. Ethan doesn't put his earbuds in. He's still quiet, but he smiles at me more, and I smile back. Jenny McGinnis tries to flirt with him almost every day, but he doesn't respond to her and he rolls his eyes a lot whenever she tells him how strong he is and asks him to wedge clay for her.

She asks so she can admire his biceps, I'm sure. I enjoy watching this, too, but her tactic is a tad obvious. And she's annoying. Most of the time, she stands near our table, hovering over Ethan, until Mr. Sandoz reprimands her for not working on her project. I keep hoping she'll fall for the deathtrap chair, but conveniently, she doesn't sit.

I'd love to see her on the floor, pieces of the chair spilling around her in a mandala of splintered wood. Maybe I'm evil for fantasizing about Jenny's bruised tailbone, but the girl doesn't take much of a hint. You'd think by now, she'd get that Ethan isn't interested.

I find myself watching Ethan's hands a lot while he's sculpting. He *is* talented. His hands mold the clay into the head of a lion, realistic in its creation. By contrast, my dragon incense burner is all cartoon.

Watching Ethan's hands, of course, reminds me of their warmth, of the gentle way he took my hand and led me across the street to the field to look at stars…not that any of that actually happened.

But I remember his hands.

And for some stupid reason, I can't stop thinking about them.

So when Friday evening finally rolls around, I'm practically dying for Ethan to take my hand again. I've been thinking—no, obsessing—about how I'm not going to slip this time. I'm going to hold his hand, I'm going to talk about things—maybe close, personal things—and I'm not going to slip. Not tonight.

At Ethan's recommendation, I'm prepared for the outdoors. It's gotten chillier this last week. Definitely no ice cream tonight. It's more hot cider and pumpkin muffin kind of weather. I dress in a heavy burgundy sweater and cream-colored leggings with soft brown leather boots that come mid-calf. The boots have virtually no heel, which is good because I'm pretty sure I'd roll an ankle if I ever tried to walk in heels.

Mariana was dying to wear heels by the time she was fourteen. I think most of the girls in our class felt that way. Not me. I'll stick with flats, preferably sneakers. I sometimes wonder if it's really that I'm intimidated by heels or if I'm just afraid I can't run to avoid a slip like I can in sneakers.

The doorbell rings before I have the chance to get downstairs to watch for Ethan's arrival, and Mom answers it. She suggested the two of us watch a movie tonight, but when I told her I had plans with Ethan, she practically pushed me upstairs to get ready.

I dab a little bit of lip gloss on, snatch my phone and purse off the bed, then jog down the stairs. (See? Can't do *that* in heels.)

Ethan's gotten a haircut. Most of the California golden blond is gone from his hair, and it's a light brown, freshly combed. I think he might have even used a little gel. I smile as I reach the bottom step.

"Hi," I say.

"Hey."

So Ethan of him.

"You look nice," he adds. My smile grows a little wider.

"So do you. Are you wearing a sweater?"

Ethan wears a light blue button-down under a ribbed, navy blue sweater with a pair of dark jeans, and he kind of looks like he's ready for senior portraits or something.

He grins. "I learned my lesson after wearing shorts to eat ice cream in the cold."

Standing beside him, Mom fights back a smile. She's practically beaming. "You two look adorable. Would it be appropriately embarrassing of me if I asked to take a pic?"

I groan. "Oh, Mom, no."

She gives me puppy dog eyes, but Ethan's already answered her by sliding beside me, placing his arm around me to rest on my shoulder. The place where his fingers meet my sweater practically sears my skin. I can smell his aftershave, too. Or maybe it's cologne. Did Ethan put on cologne for our date?

"Say cheese!" Mom holds up her phone and snaps a couple of photos while we plaster smiles to our faces.

I hope I'm not doing that lopsided smile thing I do when I'm feeling awkward. I really wouldn't want the first photos of me and Ethan to be photos I never want to look at again.

"Okay, enough," I say after she's taken at least half a dozen.

"Fine, okay. Have a good time. Home by ten?"

Ethan nods and gives a mock salute. "Yes, ma'am."

Mom groans. "I am *not* old enough to be a ma'am. Stop that now. Get out of here. Drive safely and text me your location when you get there, please."

My shoulders drop. "Mom. Really?"

"Just in case!"

Ethan smiles. "I'll make sure she texts the moment we're there, but you can always give my mom a call, too. She knows where we're headed."

My mom glows. Ethan just scored major points.

Then we're out the door. Ethan opens the car door for me and I let him. No getting out of it this time, but it's not as awkward as I thought it would be to have a boy open the door for me. I slide into the passenger's seat and reach for the seatbelt as he closes the door. It's a beautiful night, clear and crisp. I lean my head against the window to look up, but I can't see any stars with the streetlamps reflecting off the glass.

When he's in the driver's seat and has the car running, I finally ask, "So?"

"You'll see."

I give an exasperated growl. "Come on! I've waited all week. Where are we going?"

Then he laughs and I hate that his dimple is on the cheek I can't see. "Okay, okay. I'm still not going to tell you, but there's a box in the back seat with some supplies that might give you a hint."

"Supplies?" I ask. What kind of date requires supplies?

"Mmhmm."

I turn around and peer into the dark back seat as he pulls onto the street and starts driving, then I give him an uncertain glare.

"That's no help. It's dark back there."

He grins again. He knew I wouldn't be able to see anything. But now I have an idea. I pull my phone from my purse and turn on the flashlight to properly examine the back seat.

"Hey! Cheater!" Ethan cries.

"I'm not cheating. You told me I could look in the back seat!"

"Yeah, but only because I knew it was dark."

I glance at him and bat my eyelashes innocently, not that he can see; his eyes are on the road. Then I turn my gaze back to the box sitting on the seat. A folded blanket at the top covers whatever's in the box, so I *still* can't see.

"You've got a blanket over the whole box anyway. I don't know what I'm expected to see." I sigh, turn off my phone's flashlight, and face forward again.

"Oh well! You'll just have to wait."

I give an exaggerated sigh again and tilt my head to lean against the window. Now that we're out of the development and passing mostly harvested fields, I look up to see if Orion is out yet. I think we're headed in the right direction for me to see my favorite constellation, but instead, I spot the International Space Station low on the horizon, gliding across a wide expanse of sky, and it reminds me all too well of the night I slipped when we were watching the stars.

So far, my heart has been calm, though I'm excited, and I haven't felt even a hit of the rush through my veins that precedes a slip, so I'm hopeful that this date might actually go off without a hitch. My heart does give a small stutter when I think too long about the fact that I'm on an actual date, though.

When we pull off a dirt road with a cornfield on one side and a field of recently mowed grass on the other, I'm perplexed. The car shimmies down the dirt and gravel, bumping along over Pennsylvania potholes, and we seem to be heading directly to a tree line. I shoot Ethan a look.

"You're not taking me to the woods to murder me, are you?"

"Maybe, but that would definitely interfere with your ten p.m. curfew."

"That's true."

"Don't forget to text your mom, though. We're almost there."

Interesting. *There* seems to be the middle of nowhere.

"Almost where?"

"Ah, here!" Ethan sits a little straighter as he takes a right into the grass, and the tires protest as they roll over a few large holes. Probably groundhog burrows.

"Text your mom now."

I do as I'm told, letting her know Ethan and I are in a field somewhere off Barlow Road. I refrain from mentioning the potential murder part of things. Internally, I cringe at the fact that I just told my mom I parked in a field with a boy. It sounds so much worse than it really is. So then I think up the first thing I can to reassure her that her daughter is not, in fact, snogging or getting snogged or whatever it is she might think. Stargazing, I tell her. Ethan has taken me to look at the stars.

I turn to Ethan as he shifts the car into park.

"Okay, I've waited long enough. You've taken me to an empty field in the dark in the middle of October. *What* are we doing?"

He reaches around and pulls the box from the back seat onto his lap, then removes the blanket and holds it up.

"Stargazing," he says.

I swallow.

We really are stargazing. Ethan brought me with him to a dark field to stare into the great, dark unknown. Ethan really *has* taken me to look at the stars.

"Oh no, you're disappointed. This was stupid. This was a dumb idea. I'm sorry. We can go to the movies or something." He looks down as he rambles, then shoves the blanket back on top of the box.

I grab his sleeve to stop him, and he looks at me in the darkness. I almost wish the interior light of the car were on so he could see I'm telling the truth.

"I'm not disappointed. At all."

He seems unconvinced. "You're not just saying that?"

I laugh and shake my head. "I'm not. This is…one of my favorite things to do, actually."

"Okay, now you really *are* just saying that."

"I swear! I'm not. I love the stars. There's just…" I trail off.

"Something about the vastness," he finishes. He takes the words right out of my mouth, and it's eerie because I know he's said them before.

But *he* doesn't know he's said them before, not to me anyway.

"Come on." He opens the car door, then gets out, balancing the box beneath one arm.

As I get out, I catch a brief glimpse of his face before I shut the door, and the car's interior light goes out again, plunging us into darkness. I stay put until my eyes adjust, but the image of Ethan's face is still burned on my retinas.

Oh man, I have it worse than I thought.

"Hang on," Ethan says as he fumbles through the box for a moment from where he stands beside the car. "Just stay put."

"I'm not going anywhere."

As though there were anywhere to go in the dark. I know I said I'm not klutzy, but in this place, I'd probably step in a groundhog hole and twist an ankle.

A flashlight pops on around Ethan's side of the car. The beam bounces as he walks around the front of the vehicle and lights the ground in front of him, one arm still around the box. Then he does the most Ethan thing he knows how to do. He stops in front of me and grins.

"Okay," he says. "Now we can go."

I nod and follow along beside him until he reaches the section of the field he's looking for. He shoves the flashlight into my hands while he goes about setting up a blanket on the grass.

My heart thumps a little harder at the thought of lying on a blanket beside him, but I'm pretty sure Ethan is a perfect gentleman, and I don't *think* we're here for anything other than looking at the stars.

Now that I know we're going to be sitting on the ground, I kind of wish I'd chosen dark leggings, but I suppose I'll stay clean enough. It's not like we're sitting in the dirt. When Ethan has the blanket set the way he wants it, he places the box in one corner and beckons me to join him. As I sit, he bounces up, takes the flashlight from my hands, and stands in front of me. He angles the beam of the light so it illuminates him from below.

"Welcome to the Ethan T. Morrow Memorial Planetarium. Our technology is second to none. In fact, it's so advanced you'll swear your eyes detect nothing but the actual sky above. Now, ladies and gentlemen, I direct you to turn your gaze upward and to the southeast, where you'll locate the constellation Orion just over the trees at the horizon. One of the most recognizable constellations in all the night sky, Orion the Hunter holds his shield and raises his sword to his prey and is most recognizable by the three stars that make up his belt."

I laugh. Ethan is ridiculous. Almost as ridiculous as Mariana. And he is definitely making this up as he goes.

He holds up a hand. "But hunting isn't all Orion is famous for. Every October, thanks to Halley's comet, a meteor shower peaks from Orion's part of the galaxy, and the resulting phenomenon is known as the Orionid meteor shower. It's said that wishes made on these meteors have a thousand times the potency of wishes made on regular shooting stars."

I laugh so hard I snort. I can't help it.

"You're totally making this up," I say through my giggles.

He flops next to me, a grin wide on his face for only a fraction of a second before he flips the flashlight off again.

"Maybe, but the Orionid meteor shower does peak tonight, so I'm glad we're here."

I smile back in the dark.

"Me, too." My voice is barely more than a whisper.

"Thanks for indulging me."

"You know calling it the Ethan T. Morrow Memorial Planetarium means you're dead, right?"

"Uh, did I say memorial? I meant honorary. It's the Ethan T. Morrow

Honorary Planetarium." There's embarrassed laughter in his voice.

I turn my head to the sky in time to catch one of the meteors we came to see. It streaks across the sky in a white blaze before burning out in an utterly spectacular display. Two more meteors flare before I can even process what I've seen.

"Amazing," I breathe, and I make a wish despite myself.

Ethan hesitates a second in the dark, then reaches for my hand. His fingers are warm against my palm, and tingles shoot from my hand through the rest of my body. I'm suddenly hyperaware of everything around me—the sound of the last stubborn crickets refusing to admit fall is here, the subtle whiff of Ethan's cologne that mixes with the fresh scent of grass and damp soil. All of it is magnified a hundredfold as he touches my hand, as though he amplifies everything in me just by being.

"Six. Seven." Even his voice seems closer in the dark outdoors.

I've missed several of the meteors. I've never felt like I wanted to experience everything at once, like I'd miss out if I focused too hard on either Ethan or the meteor shower. It's kind of unfair that the two vie for my attention. Maybe I need to immortalize Ethan in the stars, and then I can watch them both at once.

There's only one problem with my logic. I'm pretty sure there has to be a tragedy involved to get immortalized in the stars, so perhaps I need to keep Ethan here on the ground and learn to split my attention between Ethan's dimple and the sky above.

After a half-hour, we've lost count of the meteors, and the air has grown chilly. I try not to shiver, but I fail miserably, and Ethan laughs as I shudder beside him.

"PJ! You could have told me you were cold."

"Yeah, but I don't want this to end. It's not like we're in the Arctic. I'll be okay."

"You're nuts, you know that?" Then he drops my hand, reaches into the box, and pulls a second blanket out, draping it over both of our shoulders. "I always plan ahead."

The blanket immediately stops the shivers. Warmth is good.

"Huh. What else have you got in that box?"

"Well, funny you should ask. I happen to have"—he pulls out an old-school thermos— "hot cider."

I open my mouth to say the first thing that comes to mind, but the first thing that comes to mind is "I love you," and even though I would say that to anyone who happened to offer me a cup of hot cider, it's different when it's someone you actually maybe kind of *do* have feelings for. Not that I love him. I can't. I'm sixteen. What do I know of love?

I know I can't tell him I love him just for bringing hot cider.

"You're the best!" I say. It's a sad alternative to what I really want to say, but it works so I go with it.

Ethan puffs his chest out a little. "I am, aren't I?"

We share the thermos, sipping, then handing it back again, and the cider is really good, warming my insides to the core. Between that and the blanket *and* Ethan beside me, I'm comfortable. Maybe more than comfortable.

"This is really good," I say after another sip.

"Thanks. My mom makes it every fall."

"Wait, your mom *made* this?"

"Yeah, why?"

"Ethan. This is like the best cider I've ever had. I assumed you went to some gourmet shop or something. She should sell this stuff! Or at the very least, she should give some of it to the neighbors…"

"Hint taken."

"Yesssss."

"Well, since you mentioned a gourmet shop…"

I sit up a little straighter. What else is in that box? I'm beginning to think this boy is a date-planning genius. Not that I have anyone to compare him to, but still…

He pulls out a couple of large, spherical gourmet lollipops and hands one to me.

"Thing is, you're going to need light to appreciate this, so…"

He pops on the flashlight and illuminates his and my lollipop, and I gasp. "There's a planet in my lollipop. How did you do that?"

"Okay, this one I actually didn't have any part in making. I bought them from a shop online. Mine is Neptune. Yours is Jupiter. They were all out of Saturn because, well, Saturn is the coolest, as everyone knows."

"Is that the Ethan T. Morrow Honorary Planetarium stance on planetary rankings?"

"Yes."

I twirl the lollipop over the light, examining the swirls and divots that make it seem like a miniature planet is really stuck inside the sugared sphere.

Then I look up at Ethan. "This is too pretty to eat."

He smiles. "I had a feeling you might say that."

Then he reaches into the box again and pulls out a pink box from a place I recognize all too well.

"You went to The Cookie Crumble?" I can't hide the excitement in my voice. I didn't realize it before now, but it appears sugar is the easiest way to my heart.

Speaking of my heart, it hasn't done any of its weirdness tonight. I'm not sure whether I'm more excited about that or whatever's in that box. It's a toss-up.

He grins wider and opens the lid.

The two enormous vanilla cupcakes he reveals are topped with a galaxy swirl of frosting—a mass of ooey-gooey black goodness airbrushed with pink, purple, and silver stars. Looking at them, I feel like I've just been dropped into the middle of the Milky Way.

"Take one!" he urges.

I do. They're almost too pretty to eat as well, but a girl's gotta do what a girl's gotta do. I rip the bottom of the cupcake off and smash it onto the two-inch-high galaxy frosting to make a cupcake sandwich. It's still messy, but it's a little easier to eat this way.

"Did you just massacre that cupcake? Who does that? You...you... killed it," Ethan says as he watches, aghast.

I shrug and laugh with a mouth full of cake. (It tastes as good as it looks, omg.)

"And you were worried about me murdering you tonight!" he continues, pretending to be appalled. "You should have been more concerned with the poor cupcake you just ripped apart without a thought."

I shove his shoulder, and as soon as I've swallowed the bite, I speak. "It's the cleaner way to eat a cupcake," I inform him. I lick a bit of frosting from the side of the cupcake. "Every civilized member of society knows this."

As if to reassure me that he's a barbarian, Ethan bites into his cupcake, consuming half of it with one mouthful. There's frosting all over his upper lip and even some smashed onto his nose. He makes grunting noises to emphasize his lack of civility.

"Attractive," I say.

But I smile, shake my head, and take another civilized nibble of my cupcake sandwich. And even though it's the neater way to eat a cupcake, I still manage to drop a dollop of black frosting on my cream-colored leggings. Damn. That's not going to come out.

When we finish eating and have wiped our hands (and face, in Ethan's case), Ethan switches off the light again and lies back to stare at the sky.

I take the blanket from my shoulders and put it over him, then scoot next to him beneath the blanket's warmth to watch.

We don't speak.

And for the first time, maybe ever, I'm struck by the fact that I don't feel the need to say anything. This is just…perfect as it is.

Every now and again, the headlights from a car pass on Barlow Road and ruin the dark, but for the most part, it's dark and quiet. Lying beside Ethan, arms barely touching, I'm struck by how natural this feels.

Nothing in my life has *ever* felt natural.

Maybe Mariana's right. Maybe I *can* have this.

CHAPTER ELEVEN

"I can't have this."

The words are not mine. They're Ethan's. It's Monday morning, we're in clay class, and he's talking to his clay lion.

Still.

The words—those specific words—shake me a little.

"This little guy needs to top a box, I think. What the heck else am I going to do with a lion's head?" With that, he gets up and goes to grab another chunk of clay.

Mariana smiles. She's already heard all about the date with Ethan, of course. I texted her the minute I got home, which led to a phone call because I do *not* need text evidence of me swooning over a boy in case my mom ever decides to look at my phone.

Because I *did* swoon. I swooned hard.

After Ethan took me home with promises to deliver more of his mom's cider, he held my hand as he walked me to the door and said good night.

My heart pounded like a hammer, but he didn't kiss me.

Even though I was waiting for a kiss.

Even though I was hoping for a kiss.

Maybe it's for the best.

I mean, I didn't slip after all, and if he'd kissed me, I definitely would have slipped. Which…means I could have gotten to kiss him again? I weigh the pros and cons of this as I work on my sculpture.

"So the creek thing is this weekend, right? And you're sure I can still get home by two?" Mariana says.

I nod. The Halfpenny Creek cleanup has been well-received by everyone we've pitched it to. The township supervisor wants to feature it in the quarterly newsletter, Leon's mom still wants a story for the local section of the paper, and Miss Gilfert, the guidance counselor in charge of officially logging the service hours, is thrilled we've found something that will "enhance the natural beauty of our close-knit community." (Her words, not mine.)

"We start at seven."

Mariana groans. "Are you serious? Can't we start at like nine or something? Seven? Who wants to be up and coherent at seven on a Sunday morning?"

I shrug. The time doesn't bother me so much, at least not when I know I'll get to spend it with Ethan.

"You've got it bad."

"Mariana!" I convey the rest of my words with my eyes. Just because Ethan got up to get more clay doesn't make this class a safe place to talk about him.

I reserve that for Brit Lit.

"Just saying. Anyway, did I tell you Marco's dating someone?"

"No! When? Who?"

"Apparently, a girl whose car broke down while he was on the tow crew."

Way to go, Marco. I'm actually a little proud of my former stalker. Okay, so he never actually stalked me, but his early obsession never quite left the back of my mind. Proud of him. He's gotten considerably less creepy over the years.

Ethan and I don't get to spend a lot of time during the week together. Between his track and my cross-country practice, we're both running (not together) after school, and then I'm in serious homework mode. It seems the teachers have recognized the school year is in full swing and are assigning a new project every other day before the old assignments are even handed in. I swear they don't remember what it was like to have a life.

This leads to a lot of time spent at my desk in my room, staring at the Jupiter lollipop I stuck in my pencil holder. Staring at the lollipop, of course, makes me think of Ethan and the dark and the stars and of all the things that could be. And then I open my phone and stare at the photos Mom took and texted to me. He looks happy. *I* look happy.

Even Mom thinks we're cute. She's mentioned Ethan no fewer than three times this week. I keep telling her to get her own guy, but she still insists she's not interested in dating. She says her time is better spent saving lives than trying to catch the eye of some random guy, to which I keep telling her the guy isn't supposed to be random.

"Are you in the market for a dad or what?" she asked me on Tuesday night. "Maybe someday I'll date again, Pigeon, but I just don't have that kind of energy. Trust me, when you get to my age, you'd rather spend time doing the things you enjoy by yourself than searching for someone else to enjoy them with."

"That doesn't even make any sense," I replied.

But it does. It makes perfect sense. Mom has always seemed like a complete person by herself. When I think about Mariana's mom and dad, they're like one entity in my head. Always together. They might as well be one person. They talk about their plans for house renovations together. They organize their kids' birthdays and graduation parties together. They're even part of the same bowling league on Thursday nights. I rarely think of Mariana's parents as individual people with their own thoughts and dreams. I'm pretty sure they're so in tune with each other that they just have all the same goals.

Maybe that's what happens when two people spend so many years with each other; they grow to have the same life and the same dreams. But Mom has only ever been Mom to me. She has no counterpart. I understand why she feels the way she does, but I have to wonder. Is there a way to do both, to be both—a complete person by yourself *and* the other half to another person?

It's almost too much to think about. I'm not even sure I'm a complete person by myself, but then, I'm sixteen. Am I supposed to be? Or does that come later?

So relationships (and the balance of them) have been on my mind a lot this week. *Ethan* has been on my mind a lot this week. By the time Friday rolls around, I'm more than ready to spend time with him. I may have even thought about kissing him once or twice. I decide to take the initiative and text him first for once.

Entirely too much time passes before I see the three dots finally jump again. When they do, I bite a cuticle, waiting for his response. He's usually quick to say yes. He's usually the one asking *me* to hang out.

Wait.

Is Ethan tired of me? Has he not been thinking of kissing me this week the way I've been thinking about him kissing me?

Why didn't I consider this?

Then my phone pings.

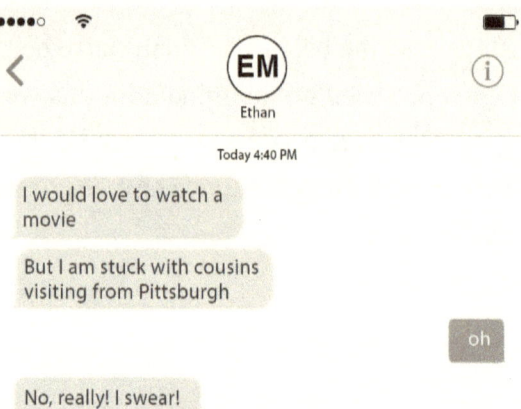

The next thing that comes through is a photo of Ethan with two kids a few years younger than us who sport a vague family resemblance to Ethan. At least he's not tired of me.

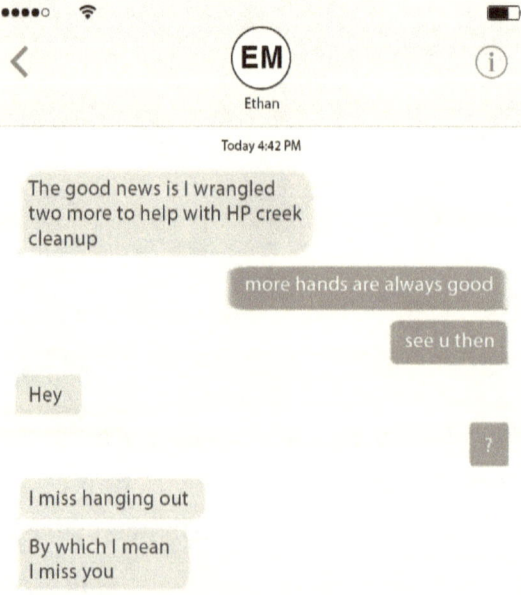

I can't wipe the stupid grin from my face. Ethan misses me. He's not tired of me. He *misses* me.

Then I realize I haven't answered him back, which is really pretty awful of me, so I tap out a smiley emoji and tell him I miss him, too.

I'll never make it to Sunday with nothing else planned. How did I used to spend my weekends before Ethan took them over? My memory is kind of fuzzy on the details.

I call Mariana and see if she wants to sleep over. Mom works until three a.m., covering an extra half-shift, so she'll be home sometime in the middle of the night. She never minds if Mariana stays over anyway.

So Mariana and I spend all of Friday and Saturday numbing our minds on movies from the eighties that somehow people my mom's age and older label "classic." I don't get it. The movies are spectacularly bad, and the soundtracks are incredibly cheesy. But we laugh and stuff our faces with salt and vinegar chips and don't talk about boys at all, even though half the movies are about boys and girls and dating mishaps. (The other half seems to all be about drug addiction. What was *going on* in the nineteen-eighties?)

Even though she didn't get home and to bed until after four, Mom is up when Mariana and I tromp down the stairs at nine on Saturday morning, bleary-eyed and empty-bellied. Still in the t-shirt and sweats that she slept in, she stands at the stove, spatula in hand, flipping pancakes. There's already a giant pile of pancakes keeping warm in a covered dish on the kitchen island. Judging by the smell, they're pumpkin cheesecake.

"*Meu Deus*! Those look amazing!"

Mom turns and smiles at us. She gives Mariana a wink. "Thank you, Mariana. Secret recipe."

Mariana laughs, but then I add, "It really is. She won't tell me how to make them."

"I'll tell you when you need to know, Pigeon."

"Hopefully, before you lose the recipe to dementia," I grumble.

Mariana grabs a seat on one of the island stools as I pull a couple of plates from the cupboard. "Ms. Ellis," she says. "What are you doing up so early? You came in long after we went to bed. How are you even a functioning human being right now? Do you have superpowers you hide from us?"

"Oh, Mariana. I wish. No superpowers. I just slept hard and"—she shrugs— "I guess I got enough sleep. It'll catch up with me later, and I'll probably have to nap. The downside to being old."

"I have three cousins older than you, Mrs. Ellis. You're not old," Mariana says.

"Oh, you sweetheart." Mom tousles Mariana's hair.

"Off today?" I ask. I could look at her schedule, which is always clipped to the side of the fridge, but it changes so often I rarely bother.

She nods as she scoops out the last of the batter onto the griddle, then rinses out the big glass mixing bowl. "What do you girls have planned for the day? Is Mariana spending the afternoon?"

With a mouthful of pancake, Mariana says, "I can't, but I wish I could. With the creek clean up tomorrow, I have to help Avó with laundry today. It's sheets day again."

"Hmm, laundry. *That* sounds like a great idea." Mom gives me a pointed look, making it clear she doesn't appreciate the massive pile of dirty clothing in the corner of my room.

I raise my hands in defense. "Okay, okay. I'll get a load started."

It's not like I don't ever help out. I'm no Mariana, but I always unload the dishwasher. Still, if I'd known how Sunday morning would start, I would have made Mariana stay the night again.

Mariana chronically runs late for anything that isn't school, but if she'd stayed, I could have rolled her out of bed myself to get her out the door on time on Sunday. Instead, it's Sunday morning, she's running behind, and Leon's mom cornered me the minute I arrived. Everyone else arrived a few minutes before I did so they got to witness my extreme discomfort as Leon's mom peppered me with questions.

"Ohhhh! So *this* is the infamous PJ Ellis," she said. "PJ, I'm so glad to finally meet you. I've been trying to get ahold of you, but I wasn't entirely sure I had the right number."

I managed to apologize profusely, once again using the excuse that something's been wonky with my phone, and I'm not always getting messages until days or even weeks later. But there's no getting out of doing a short interview for the Bluestone Lake story she wants to run, not once she sees me standing here. The fact that the temp is thirty-eight degrees is probably the only reason I'm not a sweaty mess of nerves and slipping backwards half a dozen times.

So when Mariana finally shows up, I make sure to fix her with an appropriate glare to express my disappointment. I'm still going to kill her for leaving me to this interview. Or at least throttle her a little. Or maybe just punch her in the arm.

"I'm so sorry I'm late!" she announces to everyone as she reaches the trailhead. "I couldn't find my phone. I looked everywhere, and Luis refused to drop me off until I found it. Go figure. It was in the bathroom."

There's laughter among the boys. The fact that she's announced she left her phone in the bathroom is almost enough to make me forgive her. Almost.

"Thank you for talking with me, PJ," Mrs. Stevens says to me as she grips my freezing fingers in one of her well-manicured hands. "Do you mind if I get a photo so we can run it with the story?"

Before I can say no, she snaps a quick picture with her phone. She turns her screen and flashes the photo at me. It's truly awful.

"You know what?" I say, and I almost can't believe what I'm about to suggest. "I have a photo you can use if you don't mind. What's your number again?"

I text her the picture Ethan took of me. Even though I'm in a ponytail and yoga clothes, at least I'm showered in that photo. Not so today. I mean, we're picking up trash and hauling logs and branches out of the muck.

We've come fully prepared with heavy-duty, black plastic garbage bags and a box of latex gloves. One of the guys even brought a trash-grabber-thingie, but he acts like he's too manly to use it, so he generously donates it to Mariana, who's more than happy to accept it if it means she doesn't have to touch junk on the ground.

Leon's mom takes a bunch of photos of us together before we start. (Ethan manages to brush the backs of his fingers against mine as we pose, which likely means my smile is genuine.) Then she continues to snap photos as we get to work. At least she's off the Bluestone Lake incident.

Talking to her wasn't as bad as I thought it would be. Maybe I should have even done it sooner. But I have to assume my reason for not slipping was due entirely to my annoyance with Mariana for being late and not running interference as she promised.

And yet, I managed to do an entire interview with a *stranger* and somehow didn't slip even though my heart was pounding. First, a date with Ethan, now an interview with a stranger.

Could my days of slipping be behind me? It's almost too much for a girl to hope for.

"Come on, PJ. You duped me into volunteering for this. Get a move on, girl." Mariana yells over one shoulder as she treks ahead, and I force a laugh.

"Sure!" I call back. "You're not bending down every ten seconds while you're walking. The rest of us are up and down! Cheater."

She turns only to stick out her tongue and clap her grabber-thingie a couple of times in response.

The hours pass quickly, and I can't believe how fast two o'clock rolls around. Mariana bugs out, and the rest of us quickly begin to spend more time loitering than cleaning. I didn't think picking up a trail would be quite this exhausting, but it's cold and damp, and the constant motion for hours on end is tiring. We stopped only to scarf down lunch when Leon's mom ran out to get us a bunch of subs from a local deli. Otherwise, we've been hustling all day long.

Not long after Mariana leaves, the rest of us realize this endeavor is not a one-day project. Not even close.

"Hey, it's almost three. Do you guys wanna call it and just make this a weekly thing? We haven't even gotten to the really bad part of the trail yet." Ethan rests on a large rock and I take a moment to lean beside him.

"Nah, man! Let's push through. We can do it!" Jon hops from foot to foot and hits out a bunch of air punches like he's prepping for a boxing match.

Ethan scrunches his face at Jon. "Who are you even fighting right now?"

"I dunno, bruh. I just have energy."

Leon whacks Jon in the arm. "He drank one of those energy shots with lunch."

"Nah! I'm just really hyped about kicking litterbug ass."

"Bro." Leon sends a warning glare to Jon and motions to his mom.

Jon presses his mouth shut, his eyes wide with guilt. Then Jon squeaks out, "Sorry, Mrs. Stevens. I meant I want to kick litterbug butt."

"Mmhmm." Leon's mom has been working from the parking lot and has popped in on us a few times just to check up. Of course, she showed up at this moment.

Rich, who's always been more reserved, finally weighs in. "I'm with

Ethan on this one. It's gonna be dark in, like, three hours. There's no way we're going to get it all done, and I gotta take my little sisters trick-or-treating tonight."

From there, we pull out phones and shoot through a few dates until we find one that works for all of us, which isn't until Thanksgiving week.

"You seem like reasonable young adults here, but I just want to bring to your attention that the weather will come into play shortly, and you *might* want to think about postponing this project until the spring," Mrs. Stevens says.

"Alright. Let's plan to meet the week of Thanksgiving, and then we'll go from there if we have to plan for the spring," Ethan responds.

"We won't be here to help you then. No more family slave labor!" one of his cousins says. I think it's Mike, but it's hard to tell because Mike and Sam are twins, and I can't remember who was who from when Ethan first introduced them.

"Lucky," Leon grumbles in response.

Ethan turns to look at me as everyone makes their way back to the trailhead. "What do you think?"

I shrug and tuck a stray strand of dark hair behind my ear. "Cold weather doesn't bother me too much, and we don't have to have everyone for the cleanup anyway. We can come whenever we want and get some hours in as long as Miss Gilfert signs the forms for us."

Ethan tugs on my hand as I start to follow everyone back to the parking lot, and I turn to face him. His hair is a tousled mess from the wind or maybe from his pillow, but his hazel eyes sparkle in some weird, magical way his eyes always seem to sparkle, and his smile is just as inviting.

I find myself watching his lips.

This sends my heart into a lurching, roaring mess, so I hold tight to the here and now and focus my eyes back on his.

"Hey," he says, his eyes darting to the trail as the last person from our group leaves our sight.

I lick my lips. "Hey, yourself."

He gives a little laugh. "Do you want to hang out later? I couldn't ditch Sam and Mike earlier, but they'll be cool hanging out with my mom and my aunt at home tonight. We could…go see a movie?"

I smile. "Yeah, okay." Then I remember Mariana lamenting my lack of enthusiasm, and I smile a little wider.

"Can I give you a ride home?"

I fully planned on running home after the trail cleanup, but there's no way my shoulders, back, or legs are going to support my original intentions, so right now, Ethan's offer is pure gold.

I nod, and we walk hand in hand back to the parking lot. I like the feel of Ethan's fingers around mine, of our palms against each other. Even if we're both filthy and cold. Somehow, there's something solid in him, something I *want* to trust.

CHAPTER TWELVE

Ethan makes Sam and Mike take the back seat even though they both have longer legs than I do. I didn't plan on riding shotgun, but he gives them one look, and neither offers a complaint.

It's a four-minute drive home anyway. We're there before I have a chance to apologize for hogging the seat with all the legroom.

Before I close the car door, I lean forward to look in the car at Ethan. "See you later?"

He nods. "I'll text you."

Then I sprint into the house and head for the shower as fast as my legs will carry me. I'm counting on scalding water to soothe my bones and wash away the aching muscles in every part of my body. Mostly, it does. Mom says that's the benefit of young bones. They recover quickly.

When I come back downstairs in a pair of worn jeans and a flannel, I find a heart-shaped note from Mom on the refrigerator. No surprise— she picked up an extra shift at the hospital. Beneath the note is a twenty-dollar bill so I can order dinner. Always taking care of me, even when she's not here. She's good people, Mom.

I really should get a job to help with the finances. Nothing in retail, though. I'd slip every ten seconds and end up having to quit before I even accepted a job offer. It'd have to be someplace boring, somewhere quiet. I should see if the library has anything open. I know my way around the library, and I could easily shelve books. I mean, how hard can it be, right? At least then I could offer to pay my own phone bill so mom has one less thing on her plate. Working weekends and evenings would cover a phone bill, wouldn't it? Is it weird I have no idea what my phone costs?

Then I think of all the free time I'd miss out on with Ethan...and my plan to get a job quickly fades into nothingness because how could I possibly give up time with Ethan? And now I'm sitting in the kitchen, alone, smiling like a complete dork.

My phone pings twice in succession.

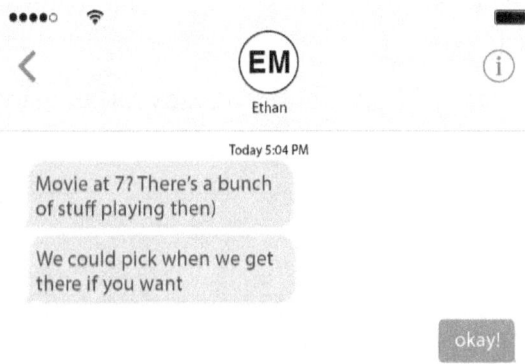

I make sure to add in the exclamation point to show my excitement. Damn you, Mariana. Now I'm paranoid every time I text Ethan.

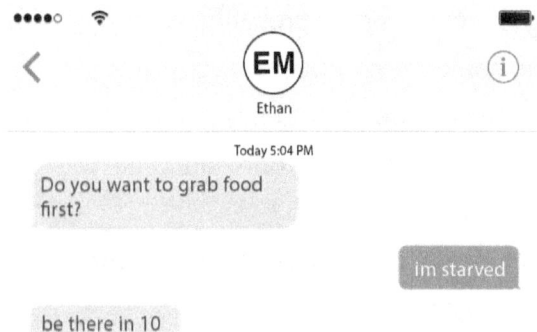

I look down at my clothes and debate changing, but Ethan has seen me sweaty and gross from a run, showered and dressed for a real date, and at school almost every day since the school year started. It'd be kind of silly to change for someone who has already seen me at my grossest.

Still.

A little lip gloss can't hurt, right?

Ten minutes later, I open the door to reveal Ethan holding a squirming orange ball of fluff with large pale blue eyes.

"You…brought your kitten?" I say as I bend down to examine the cutest thing I think I've ever seen in my life. In response, the tiny thing spits at me, but the hiss is so pathetic I have to laugh.

"Not my cat! I thought it was yours," Ethan replies as I usher him into the front hall.

"I don't have a cat," I say, but I'm already reaching to take the kitten into my hands. I hold it to me as if it's been mine forever. It went from spitting to purring in two-point-three seconds.

"You don't?"

I shake my head.

"I swear you told me you had one once. Huh. Maybe I'm thinking of some other cute, dark-haired girl."

The kitten yowls, which gives me the perfect opportunity to glide right over Ethan calling me cute.

"Oh my goodness! You're probably starved, aren't you?" I coo. "Where did you come from, little…er…guy?"

I'm ninety percent sure the kitten is a boy.

"Anyway, I figured he was yours since he was prowling around under the bushes outside."

I don't think kittens are usually alone when they're this little. This guy can't be more than six or eight weeks old. "Where's his family? Are there any more of them out there?"

"I don't think so, but I can double-check, just in case."

"Would you?" I ask as I pull the refrigerator open with my free hand and grab the lactose-free milk. Good thing mom is lactose intolerant. Cats are, too. Or so I've read in my infinite quest to research everything about cats in order to convince Mom we should get one.

As Ethan uses his phone's flashlight to check outside, I put the little fluff on the floor and pour a bit of milk into a plate. He begins lapping it immediately, and within seconds, there are droplets of milk all over his whiskers, his face, the floor, and the cabinets nearby. He's a ravenous little thing.

When Ethan returns empty-handed, I scroll through my phone to try to figure out whatever I can about this little guy. You'd think I would know more about kittens, given how badly I've wanted one for so long.

"No siblings?"

He sits beside me on the kitchen floor. "None that I can see. Or hear. I mean, this guy was pretty loud on his own. Hey, little guy!" He strokes the kitten's back and then turns to me. "We should call him Spots."

I tilt my head and give him a look. "He's an orange tabby. There's not a single spot on his little body."

"I know! That's what would make it great!"

"We are *not* calling him Spots."

The fact that I'm even debating what to call him is thrilling. I've got a cat. In my house. Mom can't even blame me. He literally found his way to us! Now that he's done with his milk, the kitten turns himself to grooming, washing every inch of his paws and face before moving to the rest of his body.

All thoughts of going out to eat or seeing a movie are gone from my head. This cat *is* life. Well, the cat...and Ethan, who smells *really* good. Did he put cologne on again? I feel like I catch just a hint of a whiff every now and again. Can't put my finger on it. (This is a marked change from most of the boys at school, who think wearing cologne is a substitute for showering.)

"Pablo," I say. "His name is Pablo."

"Like Picasso? The guy who cut off his own ear?"

"No! Like the nervous little penguin from a show I used to watch when I was little. I loved that show."

"*The Backyardigans*? The penguin was blue. Shouldn't you at least name him after the orange character? What was it…Austin or something?"

"Austin was the purple kangaroo. Tyrone was the orange moose."

Ethan snaps his fingers. "That's right. I remember."

"I can't believe you remember *The Backyardigans*."

"Hey, I only have a vague memory of it. I'm not the one naming my cat after a character."

I smile, then pick up Pablo and snuggle him in my arms again. He's already purring. "Vague memory! Pshhh. You remembered Pablo was blue."

He shakes his head and changes the subject from children's cartoons to something more important.

Holding up his phone, he asks, "Where am I ordering from? We're obviously *not* going anywhere now."

I flash my most winning smile. "Pizza? If you order, I'll treat."

"Save your money," he says as he pulls up the number for the pizza shop. "You'll need it for cat supplies."

He's right. Mom's twenty-dollar bill has a better use now. "Yeah, probably should at least get a litter pan and a couple of cans of food tonight."

When the pizza arrives, we struggle to keep Pablo off the table and away from it. (Is it the cheese he's after?) After we're done eating, I scoop him up, plop him in a shoulder bag, and we head to the store. Shopping for pet supplies with Ethan feels very domestic. For a moment, it's like I'm twenty-five and living an adult life or something. But only for a moment. Adding up the price of a litter pan, litter, a couple of cat toys, and canned food sends me into sticker shock.

Holy cow! No wonder Mom was reluctant to agree to a cat. And we haven't even taken him to the vet yet. I cringe. I definitely need to apply for a job at the library.

As we head to the checkout line, I'm suddenly a bundle of nerves. Should I have texted Mom first? I probably should have.

"What's that face, Slip?"

I tilt my head and scowl.

He sighs. "Yeah, yeah, I know. PJ. You know, someday you're going to tell me about the nickname. I'm making it my life goal."

"Well, if it's your life goal, then I'll have to keep the suspense for a very long time. Can't have you checking out early just because you've completed your life goal."

"Fine, it's just a high school life goal, then. Anyway, what's on your mind? You've got that face again."

"What face?"

What's wrong with my face? Why can Ethan tell something's up just by looking at my face? It's unnerving.

"The I'm-rethinking-the-wisdom-of-my-decisions face," he says.

We step forward in line. The white-haired lady at the register greets us with a smile and starts ringing up all the items that might be my financial undoing. Mom really is going to kill me.

"Aw," she says. "Someone's getting a new cat!"

Pablo chooses that moment to pop his head from my bag and mew like he's got some kind of radar. He's all ears, the scrawny thing.

"Oh, my word! Aren't you just the cutest?" She presses a few more buttons on the register. "That's fifty-eight twenty-four, hun."

I pull the money from my pocket and hand it to her. That's pretty much half of my life savings. Not that I spend a lot. There's just not much opportunity for me to earn money aside from helping out around the house, but the library is open on Monday afternoons. I'll stop by tomorrow and inquire about a weekend job. Mom might be less likely to murder me if I already have something lined up.

Then Ethan, Pablo, and I head back home. I'm infinitely glad that Ethan drives and has a car at his disposal because I'm not sure how I would have lugged twenty pounds of cat litter and an unwieldy litter pan home with me in the dark, even if the grocery store is just at the other end of the neighborhood.

"So do you think you should maybe say something to your mom?" Ethan says as he pulls into the driveway.

"Um, yeah. Probably, I should."

"You're not going to, are you?"

"Nope."

He laughs as we enter the house, litter pan in one of his hands, twenty pounds of cat litter in the other. Somehow, I ended up cradling Pablo.

"I mean, I will. Obviously, I won't keep him a secret, but trust me on this one. The best way to get my mom to say yes is to put this face"—I hold Pablo up to Ethan's face, and the fluff gives a pathetic mewl— "in front of her. She'll be toast. If I text her now, she'll start searching for someone else who can take him, and my plan will be foiled."

"Foiled, huh? Are you an evil villain? What's that make me?"

"My minion."

Ethan presses his lips together and lifts an eyebrow, unimpressed with my character assignment for him.

"My partner in crime?" I suggest.

"Better."

I get the litter pan set up in the half bath on the main floor and set Pablo gently into the litter. It takes him all of two seconds to figure out what he's supposed to do there.

"Whoa," Ethan says. "Poor little guy really had to go."

No joke. I swear Pablo sighs when he's done. Then he does this little skittering thing in the litter to cover the wet spot he left behind.

After that, I give him a little canned food, which he gobbles up like the gremlin he is, and then I bring him into the living room and plop him on my lap. Ethan sits beside me on the couch, and it's weird how not nervous I am.

Pablo must have a superpower—the ability to instantly make me forget about everything not him. He curls up on my lap, but it isn't quite what he's looking for, so he keeps climbing until he reaches my chest, where he promptly curls up and purrs himself to sleep, his little needle claws poking me through my flannel as he makes mini-biscuits.

"Movie?" Ethan grabs the remote on the coffee table and pulls up a menu.

By the time Mom comes home, we're halfway through an action flick-turned-romcom. Mom seems surprised to see us sitting on the couch. I turn just enough to peer over the back of the sofa to where she's come in the front door.

I hope she doesn't think we were doing anything other than watching a movie. Ethan shifts just an inch or two farther away, which can only make things look worse, like we were snogging right before she came in or something. Oh God, am I never going to be able to think of kissing as anything but snogging ever again?

"Hi, Mom!" I say brightly.

Mom's gaze flits from me to Ethan, then back again. "Hi, PJ. Hi, Ethan. Penelope, can you help me in the kitchen for a moment, please?"

Ouch. She used my full first name. I'm in trouble, and I haven't even gotten to show her Pablo yet.

"Uh, yeah. Sure, but there's something you should probably know." I stand, and Pablo gives a mew of protest as I cradle him in my arms.

"What is this?" Mom's eyes grow wide as she takes in the ball of fur gathered in my arms.

Hold him out. Hold him out. Fluff in the face. Can't say no.

I hold him toward her.

"We found a cat," I say.

She closes her eyes for a moment, then heaves a sigh and rubs her forehead. "So it would seem. Kitchen, please."

"I'm sorry, Mrs. Ellis. I found him. If it's a problem…"

"It's okay, Ethan. I just need to talk to PJ for a moment."

I follow Mom into the kitchen, stroking Pablo's fur as I go.

I sit on the stool at the kitchen island and hold Pablo in my lap. Now that he's awake and his belly is full, he's getting frisky, and he wants to explore. He settles on his back once I pull out a feather wand from the bag on the island and start waving it for him to attack it.

"You're not going to let me keep Pablo, are you?"

I don't look at her. I can't. If I keep my eyes on Pablo, maybe I can keep the tears from welling.

"Pablo?"

I give a lopsided grin and finally look up. Mom looks at Pablo and nods, making the connection.

"PJ, I know we haven't exactly covered this, but I think I've still made it clear that I don't approve of you being alone in the house with a boy."

Wait. What?

I squint my eyes.

"Don't give me that look. I know Ethan Morrow is a perfectly nice kid, but perfectly nice kids have hormones, too."

"Oh my God, Mom!"

"This is not up for debate. No staying here at the house alone. Got it?"

"So, Pablo?" It's the only thing I can think to say. I don't want to think about Ethan's hormones. Or mine. Pablo derailed our date, but given that I'm finally holding a cat of my own in my hands, I'm weirdly not even disappointed.

"Pablo can stay. Maybe now someone will stop texting me pictures of shelter cats and leaving printouts on our fridge every other day."

I grin.

"Really? He can stay? I have a cat?"

"Yes, but you heard what I said, right? The part about—"

"Being alone in the house with a boy," I rush. "Got it."

She presses her lips together, but she can't suppress a smile.

"He's pretty cute."

"I know! I love his fluffy little tail. And his tiny mew. Look at his *toe beans*, Mom! Toe beans!"

"I meant Ethan, but yeah, Pablo's pretty cute, too."

My mouth opens in shock, but she just shrugs.

"Mom."

CHAPTER THIRTEEN

Pablo is the cutest cat in the entire world. And maybe the most expensive. The vet appointment Mom took him to resulted in an astronomical bill. I offered to pay for part of it, but Mom refused to take my money. Seems like Pablo has a bunch of parasites that need treating (Ew! Gross!), and he'll also need to be neutered as soon as possible. They said it's cheaper and healthier to neuter early rather than wait, so little Pablo has an appointment next week, and he has no idea what's in store for him.

"Couldn't you at least have given him a few months with his…you know?" Ethan asks on the phone Tuesday night.

I snort. "It's not like he's aware of his…parts, or anything. Besides, Dr. Petroski assured us it was healthier for him all around. He goes in next Wednesday."

"Poor guy. Put him on the phone. I want to give him some encouragement."

I hold the phone to Pablo's ear, but he's much less interested in Ethan's voice on the phone than he is with one of my shoelaces. Finally, I put the phone back to my own ear just in time to hear the last of Ethan's words to him.

"—still a man, no matter what they say. Okay, little dude?"

I laugh. "Ethan, he'll be fine."

"If you say so. Hey, since the little guy messed up our evening on Sunday, I was wondering if you want to go see a movie this Friday instead. I'm supposed to start the new job on Saturday, so I was thinking it would be good to, you know, hang out or something."

Or something? What's "or something" mean?

"You're getting a job? Where?"

Ethan didn't say anything about a job. And now he's talking about a job and "hanging out or something" as opposed to going on a date. Did I miss something? Did I screw up our star-gazing date? How can he call me a cute, dark-haired girl just two nights ago, and now I'm not even sure he's interested?

"Mariana's brother's garage," he answers, pulling my mind back to my question.

"You're working with Luis?"

"Well, kind of. I mean, he needs someone on the office side of things. What I know about cars can be summed up in one paragraph, and that's probably pushing it. Maybe a full paragraph if I use a lot of adjectives, which is what I do for Mrs. Tortello's class. She hates it, always crosses out words on me, and accuses me of adding fluff. But anyway, I can run a spreadsheet and work the phones and make appointments and stuff, you know?"

I can almost picture his sheepish grin at admitting he knows nothing about cars. I wouldn't expect Ethan to know anything about cars. Art and photography and stars, maybe. Cars? He doesn't seem the type. He was, after all, just giving moral support to a cat over the telephone, for crying out loud.

"Anyway, it's good money. I'll be there Saturdays and then after school on Tuesdays and Thursdays."

"Oh."

I should probably say something more than "oh."

"Well, PJ, is that disappointment I hear in your voice?"

"No. I mean, yeah! Of course, I'm disappointed. Cross-country is finally over for the season, and I thought…" How on earth do I say this without outright admitting I'm totally hooked on him? "I guess I just thought it'd be cool to spend more time together. Or something."

Oh, no. Now I've said "or something." I scrunch my face, suddenly glad we're on the phone, and he can't see me.

"My lady, I am at your disposal anytime you wish. Just say the word. Wanna go out now? I can pick you up in five."

I laugh. "Ethan! It's ten-thirty. On a Tuesday. My mom would have my head."

"Hey, what she doesn't know…"

"Yeah, yeah, won't hurt her. But she's home tonight, so no sneaking out. Besides, I'm not a sneaking out kind of girl anyway."

"I never thought you would be."

"Oh yeah? Well, what kind of girl *do* you think I am?"

I'd actually kind of like to know. This could be fun.

"Hmm." He pauses a moment, though I'm uncertain whether he's just trying to make me wait or if he's actually contemplating. "I think you're a mystery."

My heart thumps.

"A mystery? Please elaborate."

"You're the kind of girl who has a nickname but won't tell me where it comes from."

"I'm klutzy!" I insist.

"Are not, and I *will* find out someday."

"Mm."

"You're the kind of girl who went out of her way to avoid me for a while, but now you can't stay away."

I can't help the laugh that escapes my throat. "Can't stay away?"

I mean, it's true, but that's not the point. He's enjoying this too much. Also, how did he know I used to avoid him? Was I that obvious?

"Yeah. And you're the kind of girl who likes long runs on wooded trails."

"That's true, but that's a given. You ran with me on the Halfpenny Creek trail."

"You're the kind of girl who likes stargazing and contemplating the cosmos with dapper fellows like myself."

"Dapper fellows? Are you ninety-six years old?" It takes everything I have not to laugh-snort, even though my heart is racing a little because Ethan *does* seem to know me, and that's unnerving.

"And you're the kind of girl who can make a guy completely crazy, wondering if you enjoy being with him or not. You're thinking. Always thinking. And sometimes I think the thoughts must be good because you get this spark in your eye, like you've just figured it out—all of it, all of life. And then, there are these other times when I think the thoughts aren't good at all because you look like you want to run away as fast as you can. And it makes a guy lose his mind because…"

My breath sits in my chest, heavy, unmoving.

"Because?" I say, my voice hardly more than a whisper.

"Because sometimes a guy really wants to kiss a girl like you."

Silence fills the line. I can't speak. I don't remember what words are or how to use them. I'm sure he's waiting for a response here, but I don't…know how to give one.

He clears his throat. "So anyway, a mystery. Like I said. There's not a lot of mystery in the world anymore. I mean, other than the Bermuda Triangle. I heard a plane went down last week. One of those tiny prop engine kind of planes, not like a jet or anything. One minute, it was on the radar, the next minute gone. No distress signals or anything. How weird is that?"

Ethan's trying to bury the fact that he just told me he wants to kiss me.

"Pretty weird," I answer, but my voice doesn't sound right.

I hear a voice in the background on Ethan's end, and then everything is muffled, like Ethan's holding the phone to his chest, so I can't hear what's being said.

"Hey," he says when he's done. "My mom's making me get off the phone. Despite the fact that I am getting A's in all my classes, she says I need sleep." He says the part about his grades twice as loud, presumably for his mom's benefit.

"Making sure she's aware of your academic status, I see. Very subtle."

"I do what I must."

I sigh. "She's probably right, and I should go to bed, too."

I roll my eyes at myself. Why did I say *bed*? Why? Now Ethan, who was just thinking of kissing me, will envision me in bed, too.

Why are words so hard? Why do I *suck* at them?

"I'd still rather talk to you. But anyway, see you first period tomorrow?"

"Every day," I say.

I'm smiling when we hang up. It's a stupid kind of smile. I let my phone fall to the bed, then pick up Pablo and hold him to my chest. He begins to purr immediately before swatting at a lock of my hair.

"He wants to kiss me," I whisper.

The week drags on just to spite me, and by the time Friday rolls around, I'm a mess. I've been texting Mariana ever since I got home from school.

And on and on we go. Mariana was *not* a help in figuring out what to wear or what to do. And honestly, why should I expect anything different? She's never kissed a boy, either. Still, I feel like she just knows more about these things in general. Me? I'm clueless.

I end up wearing a deep red mock turtleneck sweater and a camel-colored faux-suede skirt. (With cream leggings underneath, and *no*, that black icing stain from the cupcakes did *not* come out, but it's under the skirt, so…) I pair the outfit with ankle boots that give me an extra inch. I'll top it all with a tan peacoat that belts at the waist.

I look good. I think. I put my hair up in a twist, then pull it down again twice before I finally twist half of it and leave the rest around my shoulders. I'll be warmer that way, anyhow.

So when Ethan picks me up at six to get something to eat before the movie, I'm so nervous I can hardly get a bite of my spicy chicken wrap down. I munch on the chips that came with it instead. Somehow, they're easier.

"You okay?" Ethan asks.

I think I could lose myself in those eyes of his. He must know he has me on edge. He's toying with me. After the conversation we had Tuesday? He's got to know what's going through my head. How could he not? He's been giving me this crazy intense eye contact every morning in first period. It's had my pulse skipping almost all week.

"Yeah, I'm fine."

"Gonna keep me guessing, huh?"

I give a smile, but it feels strained.

"I'm working on my mysterious vibe."

Ethan glances at my lips. My heart bucks wildly.

I breathe. I force the breath to come.

The movie, at least, gives me a moment of reprieve—a hundred and sixteen minutes to pretend I'm not affected by the warm hand that's holding mine, by the subtle scent of cologne (maybe aftershave?) that permeates the air ever so slightly, by the fact that Ethan Freaking Morrow is sitting beside me in a movie theater and that he's planning to kiss me tonight.

If he doesn't, I swear I'll die.

If I'm paying attention to the movie, I can't be distracted by these things, right? I *think* that's the way it's supposed to work. Instead, I've spent a hundred and sixteen minutes blankly watching the screen without comprehending what's going on in the slightest. No, Ethan is *all* I can think about.

And now his thumb is rubbing against my palm. What did I just watch? It started out fantasy but ended up sci-fi. I think it dealt with space, and there was a ship and a planet. Maybe. There may or may not have been a planet. I shake my head to clear it. A swell of cinematic orchestral music accompanies the credits as they start to roll. The lights in the theater brighten, and I can't help but catch Ethan's eye. There's a glint in it. He's torturing me on purpose now. He has to be.

When we leave the theater, we emerge into a hard, cold rain, and Ethan holds his jacket over the two of us as we make a mad dash through the parking lot. Even so, we're drenched by the time we reach the car. He holds the door for me, and I jump in, laughing, soaked from head to toe. Ethan flops into the driver's seat, his jacket spraying water as he throws it onto the back seat.

It takes a few minutes for the car to warm up. The windows fog with our breath, creating a cocoon of privacy in a dark parking lot only sparsely sprinkled with dull yellow overhead lamps. The rain pounds on the roof and the windows. For a moment in time, it truly feels like we are alone in our own small world. And I am very, very aware of Ethan.

Don't do this, heart. Don't. You've got this. You're okay. You're gonna get through this. You haven't slipped with him in a long time. He's safe. You're safe with him.

I tell myself *all* the things, but I'm not sure my heart is buying any of it. It gallops away beneath my ribcage.

"Good movie," Ethan says.

"Yeah. It was."

"What'd you think was the best part?"

My mind reels. I was not expecting conversation. I remember virtually nothing about the movie.

"Oh, uh, I don't know. What did you think?"

He rubs his hands together to warm them. "Well, I thought the space mermaids were pretty badass."

Mermaids? I *really* must have missed a lot.

"I—"

"Joking with you. There were no space mermaids, PJ."

"Oh."

"But I did enjoy the whole wormhole time travel thing."

I think I vaguely remember that being a major plot point of the movie.

"I suppose if you could jump through time and plan where you came out and how you were going to fix things, time travel would be pretty cool," I reply carefully.

I wish my heart would slow, but talking about time travel has me on edge. Sure, it's the time travel talk that has me on edge. Not Ethan's nearness. Not his cologne. Not his eyes. Not the fact that if he doesn't kiss me in the next two minutes, I might slip right here and now.

"So you *did* catch some of the movie."

I furrow my brow. "What do you mean?"

He leans close, his nearness making my breath hitch a little in my throat.

"PJ, you're so distracted tonight. I can't tell if you're worried about something else or…if you're going to tell me we shouldn't…do…this anymore." He motions between me and him.

"What? No!" The words are out of my mouth before I've had time to even contemplate how desperate I sound.

He leans back in his seat and lets out a breath, but now I sit forward, concerned.

"Ethan, is that really what you thought?"

He shrugs. "Yeah. I mean, no, but I was worried about it."

I close my eyes for a moment and force my breath to stay even, my pulse to slow. I cannot slip right now. This is too important.

Before I let the words fall away, I blurt, "You told me you wanted to kiss me. On Tuesday. You said. And I…I've been thinking all week. And waiting and then thinking again."

Now I have his attention. He sits up and leans toward me slowly, his gaze glued to mine. My heart is going to explode. I'm sure of it. My lungs feel as though I'm struggling to breathe underwater. The pressure in my veins threatens to overtake me.

I don't want to lose this moment.

So I do something I never thought I could. I lean in and press my lips to his. I want so badly not to slip, not to lose *this*, whatever it is Ethan and I are building here. I don't know what we have or where it's going, but I know I want to kiss him. I know I want him to kiss me.

And he does. I didn't think words could be spoken without issuing a sound. I couldn't imagine what kinds of words could be said in a kiss. How could I? But there's definitely a conversation happening here, one I couldn't begin to express with any of the words I know in the English language.

Ethan gently places one hand on the side of my neck and the other on my cheek, like he's holding me together, like he might be able to keep me here.

It's almost enough, I think. I could—

Suddenly, I'm stumbling in the rain, trying to keep up with Ethan as we run to the car. I almost fall as I roll an ankle. These boots weren't made for running. Ethan's quick, though. He catches my arm and keeps me from going down.

"Careful!" he says, laughing.

And oh, I wish I could laugh, too. I do. I want to feel this moment the way he feels it. I want to be a normal person. Instead, I've lost our first kiss to an obsolete timeline that will never exist.

He opens the door for me, then dashes around to his side of the car as soon as I'm in. The rain pounds the roof of the car with so much force it almost sounds like someone's running a white noise machine at full volume.

The sound blurs my thoughts. I don't want to think. I want to feel. I want what I was just having, or what I was about to have, or whatever. I want my night with Ethan the way it should have been.

"Good movie," Ethan says after he's thrown his jacket onto the back seat and started the car to warm it up. The windows are already fogging. Again.

"Yeah. It was." I can't help but reply the same way I did before. It's like I'm on autopilot.

"What'd you think was the best part?"

"The wormhole. Time travel." At least I know there were no space mermaids this time.

My heart rate finally begins to slow. Maybe it's because I know where this night will lead, so my body isn't on high alert this time around. I would give anything to get back to where I was before, anything to experience this the first time like Ethan gets to.

"Me, too! But to be honest, I'm kind of surprised you actually gave me an answer."

"Why's that?"

"Well, you're so distracted tonight, I can't tell if you're worried about something else or…if you're going to tell me we shouldn't…do… this anymore." He motions between me and him. Again.

I hold in a sob. Because it's not fair to do this. I *should* break it off now. I *should* tell him we're better off just being friends. I should make any excuse possible because if I slip around Ethan like this, nothing will ever be right between us.

How can you have a relationship with someone when you slip every time your blood runs hot? Every kiss? Every argument? What kind of resentment builds when I experience it all, and he never does, when I remember angry words someday exchanged, but he never actually speaks them?

And yet, I don't break it off. I want this too badly tonight. I want him. I want to be a normal teenager for one godforsaken night.

I meet his gaze evenly when I speak the words I shouldn't. "No. You told me you wanted to kiss me on Tuesday. It's all I've been thinking about ever since."

He sits up, the disappointment and fear clearing from his eyes. He's got the slightest lift to his lips this time when he begins to lean forward, his gaze dipping to my mouth. The rain thundering on the roof overhead, the dim lights of the streetlamps in the parking lot—all of it is exactly as it was the last time.

I lean forward to let him kiss me, and I kiss him back because I've never wanted something so badly in my life. His hands find my cheek and my neck as they did before. This kiss speaks, too, but my end of the conversation is muted this time. There's a sadness in my bones. Excitement, yes, but sadness, too, because I can't help but know this is *not* my first kiss with Ethan, even though it's *his* first kiss with me.

I'm a fraud.

When we finally break apart, he smiles as he leans his forehead to rest against mine. I give a small smile in return, burying the sadness inside somewhere. I'll deal with sadness later.

"I know this sounds crazy," he says. "But I feel like we've done that before. I feel like I already knew what it would be like to kiss you. Somehow."

A small sound escapes my throat. "Crazy."

CHAPTER FOURTEEN

Ethan working at the garage today is probably the best thing I could ask for. Sure, I was upset he got a job because it meant less time he'd spend with me. But right now? Spending time apart is probably good for me. I texted Mariana after I got in last night, requesting immediate assistance first thing in the morning. She demanded more info via text, but I was too tired—and too sad—to say anything more.

I let her five calls go to voicemail. I'm a crappy friend. And yet, when I said I wanted to talk to her first thing in the morning, she doesn't disappoint.

I startle awake when a pillow hits my body, and I open my eyes to a scowling Mariana standing with her hands on her hips. The combination of disappointment and annoyance on her face could rival my mother's when I fail to empty the dishwasher.

"What are you doing?" I moan.

"Hey, you're lucky I didn't aim for your head. The only reason I didn't is that cute piece of fluff beside you."

She's referring to Pablo, of course. I pull my phone off the nightstand, glance at the time, and then groan again.

"It's seven-thirty in the morning. What are you *doing* here?"

"You ignored me last night. You told me we'd talk in the morning. It's morning. So I'm here."

I rub my eyes as I sit up. They're grainy. My throat is parched, too. I didn't sleep well, with memories of both timelines looping through my mind on repeat. All in all, I feel like poop. I flop back onto my pillow, but Mariana means business.

"Did you break into my house?" I ask.

"Your mom was leaving for work just as I got here. She let me in."

I groan again. "She's not supposed to be working day shift."

"Well, be glad she is. Otherwise, I was just going to spam text you until you woke up."

I shoot her a look. "I turn my notifications off at night."

She shrugs. "Then I guess I would have had to resort to throwing rocks at your window."

She would have, too. And I would have deserved it, just like I deserved the pillow she threw at me. I should have messaged her back last night.

She sits at my desk, pulls my Jupiter lollipop from the pencil holder, and twirls it. Pablo rises with interest from his place by my head, stretches with a yawn, and jumps from the bed to the desk to inspect it. He sniffs at the lollipop, bumping his nose on the clear plastic wrapper.

Mariana takes the opportunity to snatch him and snuggle him in her arms. He doesn't resist, instead issuing a purr I can hear from across the room.

I rub my eyes again. "Give me ten minutes."

Then I shuffle to the bathroom. I was just going to brush my teeth, but I look awful. My makeup—the little I had on last night—is smudged all over my face. Shower, it is.

I'm much more awake by the time I emerge from my scalding water. When I return to my bedroom in my fuzzy flamingo-print robe, Mariana is sending Pablo into dizzying spins until he falls over in his attempts to catch the infuriating red dot from the laser pointer.

I flop onto the bed, my barely towel-dried hair splayed out behind me, slowly soaking my pillowcase. I'm not really any more ready to talk than I was ten minutes ago, but Mariana won't tolerate my sealed lips for long.

"Well?" she says.

"He kissed me." I rub a finger along my bottom lip, remembering the feel of Ethan's lips as he pressed them to mine.

Mariana squeals in response.

"Twice," I add.

She drops the laser pointer to the desk and groans. "Dammit, Peej."

"I know."

"How can you do this if you're still slipping? I thought we figured he was okay. Safe. I thought you said you haven't slipped in a while."

"I haven't. Until last night. And I knew it was coming. It was like I could feel it threatening all night long, you know?"

"So what are you going to do now?"

"I don't know." The words are low, like if I don't say them too loudly, maybe I didn't really say them at all. I sit up and fight the tears welling in my eyes.

Mariana tilts her head, the worry on her face saying more than her words ever could.

I look away. "How can I have a relationship like this? Our first kiss. It was...amazing and special and charged with, like, this energy I can't explain. It was the two of us finally, *finally* getting to the same place at the same time. Finally, jumping and taking the same risk. And then..."

I snap my fingers.

"Poof," she says.

"Yes, poof."

Mariana hesitates. "Was it that bad the second time?"

A tear crests my eyelid and falls onto my lap. Damn. I knew the tears were coming, but I hoped to hold them off at least a little longer. Once I start crying, it's that much harder to speak. Ugh. Better get it all out.

"It wasn't bad. It was still good. But it wasn't the *same*. And now I've got memories of a first kiss—of a moment—that Ethan will *never* have. Time overwrote his experience, but I get both copies, and it *sucks*.

How can we have a relationship if things like this happen?

"What happens if we argue? What if he says something awful, and then I slip? Then I resent him for what he said when he never even gets the chance to actually *say* it! Then he's confused and hurt because I'm angry with him, and he has *no* idea why. What kind of a relationship can you build off of that?"

Silence fills the room. Pablo jumps back onto my lap, his loud purr filling the air again as he shoves his face into my hand for cheek scratches. I oblige, scratching him all over.

"And what happens if and when we want to take the relationship further?" I add, somewhat reluctantly. "What happens when our first time together *isn't* my first time? Because if it happened with a kiss, you know it would happen with…something else."

"You do mean sex, right?"

I groan. "Yes, Mariana. That's what I mean. It's not like I'm even remotely thinking about that right now, but if we stay together long enough, that's what people do, right? Like, that's where relationships naturally eventually go."

I fall silent again. Mariana looks down at her hands. I didn't think she'd be able to help. I mean, really, who could in this situation? There *is* no help. There's no one coming to rescue me from myself. I bite my lips to keep the sob in, then lean to grab a tissue from a box on the nightstand and blow my nose.

"Aw, PJ. I wish I had answers for you. I wish I knew. I mean, could you maybe…tell him?"

I give a laugh that's half-laugh, half-cough as I wipe my eyes with another tissue. "The truth?"

"Well, yeah. I mean, wouldn't that relieve a lot of the pressure?"

"Seriously?"

"Yes, seriously. Tell him, Peej."

"I can't."

"Why not?!"

"He'll think I'm crazy. *I* think I'm crazy!"

"PJ, what kind of relationship can you have if you can't be honest? You push people away, keep them from getting close, because you don't want to have to face the truth."

My tears finally taper off. I'd be relieved, but it's not like I've stopped crying for a good reason. No, Mariana's words hit in just the wrong spot. Anger flares hot in my gut.

"What?" I croak.

I can't even comprehend that she's just spoken those words to me.

"It's true."

"*What?* Do you have any freaking clue how hard it is to live like this?" My voice breaks. "Do you have any idea what it's like not to be *able* to tell people what's really going on? To have to hide from my own mother? From my teachers? From my friends? You're the only friend I *have*, and right now, I'm questioning that."

"PJ—"

"NO! You don't get to 'PJ' me in that voice. You have no clue— none—about what it's like to live like this. Do you know…do you know, in middle school, there were times when I thought I should just end it? I had a dozen pills in my hand once. Eighth grade. I thought, I'll go to sleep. It'll be peaceful. I won't have to do this anymore. I won't have to keep slipping. I won't be alone with no one to understand."

Mariana gasps and puts a hand to her stomach, then covers her mouth. She closes her eyes as if in pain. Good. I hope she feels the pain *I* feel. Then maybe she'll have an inkling of what it's like to live the way I do, to be *this*.

"Thank God you didn't," she whispers.

"I did."

I let the words sink in before I continue.

"I did. Six minutes in, I panicked and slipped. And then I was standing there with a handful of pills again. I can't even fucking kill myself, Mariana."

She stands, crosses the room, and sits on my bed beside me, pulling me to her as she cries. Then I cry, too. I cry for real—giant, ugly sobs. Because suddenly, I can't hold it in anymore. She holds me tight and rocks back and forth as I soak her shirt, and she soaks the back of my robe.

Pablo sits on the comforter, watching us with interest. He's probably wondering what kind of home he's found his way into and what kind of crazies he's now living with. He's probably contemplating if he wasn't better off fending for himself in the wild.

When Mariana and I are both spent, I reach for the tissue box and place it on the bed. She grabs one and dabs at her eyes. How nice to cry and just have it affect your eyes. Not me. My nose leaks like someone turned on a faucet. I blow until I'm doubly spent and surrounded by a sea of snot-filled tissues.

"I'm glad you slipped," Mariana says. "I don't know what I'd do without you, PJ."

She reaches to hug me again, throwing her arms around my body and smashing me in a giant, tight hug. I laugh, not necessarily because I want to, but because I don't have a choice. Mariana just does that to me sometimes.

"Now. What are we going to do with you?" She rubs a hand in circles along my back.

"I don't know." It's a miserable answer, but I feel miserable, and it's the truth.

"You won't tell him? You won't even try?"

"If I thought he would believe me for even a minute, I might, but in all the years, you're the only one who's ever accepted my awful truth. I couldn't even convince my mom."

Mariana sighs in response.

"I tried to get her to understand." I sniff. "I tried twice. Mari, if you could have seen the look on her face... It was utter panic. Like she realized she was going to have to institutionalize her only child. Like she had just come to terms that I was completely off the deep end. If I hadn't slipped both of those times and erased the timelines where I tried to tell her, who knows where I would have ended up?"

"But you're older now," Mariana says. "Shouldn't that count for something? Not just a grubby kid making up wild tales? Maybe you should start by telling your mom and *then* tell Ethan. If you have to bear the burden of slipping, other people should be able to deal with knowing about it."

I shake my head. "No. I love Mom. So much. But all talking to her earned me was the threat of multiple therapists, only one of whom I was ever comfortable enough not to slip around—who also didn't understand, by the way, even if she was good to talk to."

Mariana issues a weak "Yeah."

I lean forward and grab my laptop from beneath the bed. I pull up my passcode-encrypted diary. "Remember this? This was thanks to Dr. Edmunds."

"I think I remember you mentioning it. Did it help you slip less when you wrote stuff down?"

"Not really."

She closes the laptop, takes it from me, and places it back under the bed.

"Then all that's important is that you do what's right for *you.* We'll figure this out. You're not alone, PJ. I won't let you go through this alone, and I'm sorry for saying what I did before."

I wave a hand. "If I hadn't told you about my issues when I did, and exactly how I did, I'm not sure you ever would have believed me, either. So there's that. Even if I told Ethan—or Mom, for that matter, I'd have to have enough time to know I was going to slip and to get them to share something that no one else knows in order for them to believe me. What happened with you was a fluke—a good fluke, but a fluke, nonetheless. My slips with Ethan seem to come out of nowhere. One minute, I think I'm okay. The next?"

"Poof," she says, parroting our earlier conversation.

"Yeah. Poof."

"So. What's next, Slip?"

I close my eyes and shake my head.

"I wish I knew."

"Wrong answer. French toast is next." Before I can protest, she grabs my hand and leads me downstairs to the kitchen. "Come on. I'll cook."

Ethan texts me on his lunch break.

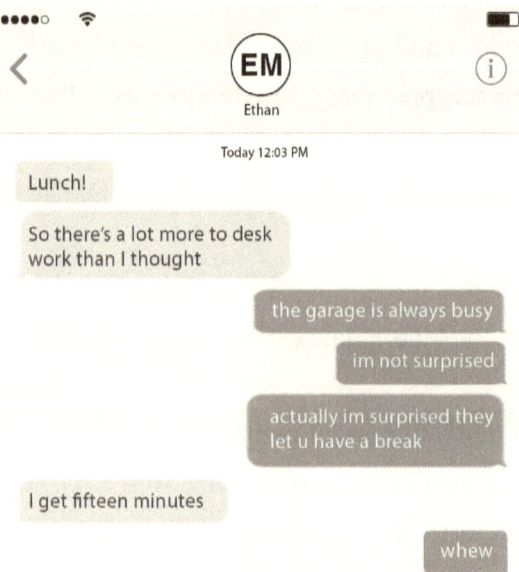

I shouldn't text him back. I know I shouldn't. If I'm going to end this thing, I should end it here and now. Or, at the very least, I should ghost him. But that just feels wrong. The idea of ghosting him, or ghosting anyone, really, leaves an overwhelming ick in my gut.

There's an ache in my chest when I think about no longer having Ethan in my life. And with Thanksgiving around the corner, I'm not even sure how I would go about breaking things off. We're doing the Halfpenny trail cleanup that week. And then we're into the holidays. Who breaks someone's heart between Thanksgiving and Christmas? Maybe he's Jewish. I've never even asked. Who breaks someone's heart right before Hanukkah?

I put my hands to my face and rub my eyes. Is it better to do it before the holidays or pretend everything is fine? Ugh. *This* is why I don't do relationships. This is why avoidance is better. My phone pings three times in succession, and I automatically turn to look at it. I'm hopeless.

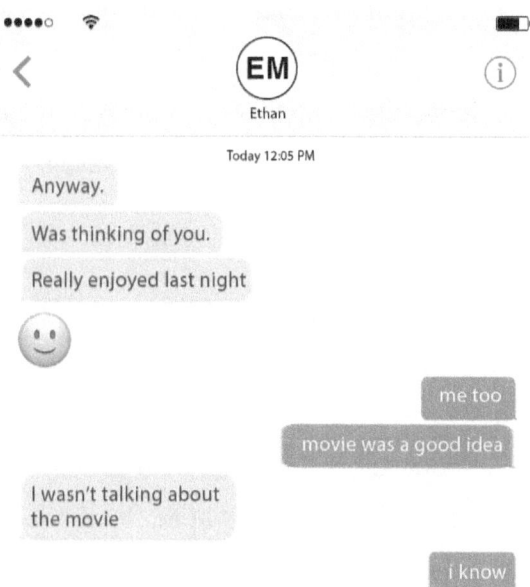

End it, PJ. END IT.

But I don't end it. At least, not yet.

CHAPTER FIFTEEN

It's done in my mind. Finished. This relationship can't happen. I can't have Ethan. I'm beginning to come to terms with it. I only need to let Ethan know. Because that's the right thing to do.

But being across from him in first period for the next month before the end of the semester will make things really awkward. And seeing him for the trail cleanup, too. It's better if I wait at least a few weeks to say anything. At least then we'll be into the spring semester and no longer in clay class. Unless he also has Intro to Watercolor for first period during the second half of the year. Then I'm screwed.

I need a run.

Turns out I need a lot of runs. That's basically how I spend Saturday and most of Sunday coping, and my legs feel it.

Ethan asks to spend time together on Sunday, but I'm trying not to make this worse than it is. The only problem is that I can't think up a believable lie. Mariana? No, she's with her avó today, helping cook for a big event at their church.

I'm hanging with Mom, I tell him. It's not exactly a lie. When she gets home from her shift at seven-thirty tonight, we'll probably watch a movie on television or something. In the meantime, I have a cat to keep me company and about ten metric tons of trig homework I can't put off any longer. But even though I stare at the textbook pages blankly, I remain unable to fathom what I'm supposed to be doing. I finally text Mariana.

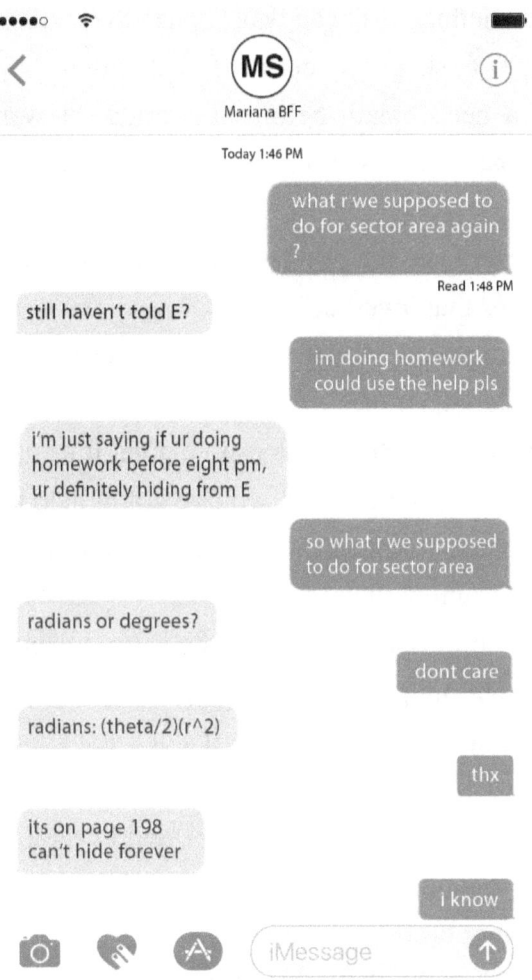

She's right. But I can still try.

The phone rings in my hand—Mariana. I frown.

"I'm busy," I say as I answer the call. "Doing homework."

She laughs. "Yeah, I know. Didn't think anything would have changed since you texted me twenty seconds ago. Take a break. I need an ear."

Hold on. Mariana needs my help? This so rarely happens I don't even know what to make of it. Sometimes I feel like our relationship is so one-sided that she must be sick of my drama. So, yeah. If she needs *my* help with something, trig can wait. I push the textbook aside.

"What's up?" I ask, giving her my full attention.

She takes a deep breath before answering. "I want to apply for the Young Global Scholars Program at Yale. It's a two-week summer course."

"Okay?" I don't see the problem yet. What does she need my help with? "What does that involve?"

"It's like a course on solving global challenges."

How very Mariana of her.

She plows onward. "But that doesn't matter. It's not what the course is. It's how much the course costs. You've got to help me find a way to convince my parents this program is worth the money and that I can skip two weeks of the summer job to attend."

"Are you kidding? Do they know Yale is Ivy League?"

"Have you met my parents?" Mariana deadpans. "Luis didn't go to college. Marco isn't going to college. It's not that they're anti-college, but they believe in hard work. I don't think they believe school counts as hard work." She makes a strangled sound, and I hear a thump.

"Did you just bang your head on the wall?" I ask.

"Yes," she mumbles.

"Okay, tell me more about this program," I say, trying to coax her back from the edge of despair.

"I only have the flyer Mr. Elhab gave me in history today, but Peej, it looks amazing." She reads the details listed on the flyer aloud, but most of it just glosses over the program highlights.

If Mariana's parents think this program isn't work, something is definitely wrong with them. Everything Mariana reads off sounds like a massive amount of unnecessary summer work, like nothing I could be convinced to take part in in a million years. Thank goodness students like Mariana exist. She was clearly made for this program.

I pull up the website on my laptop and locate the financial aid section immediately. Yikes. After one look at the price, I can see why Mariana is terrified to ask her parents. But…

"Mari! Apply for the scholarship."

"There's a scholarship?"

"Yes! Did you even check the website?"

"I guess I…I mean…I planned to. I just…"

"Panicked first," I say. "You pulled a Slip."

"Well, let's not go *that* far. I didn't completely lose my grasp on reality."

I snort. "I'm sending you the link to the application. Get it in before the end of the year. Then, when you're accepted, you can tell your parents all tuition and travel costs are covered, and they don't need to worry about it. Two weeks of lifeguarding at the pool doesn't compare to a worldly experience like this. They'll be so proud of you, they won't even think about saying no."

There's no doubt in my mind the school will offer a full scholarship to Mariana for this program once she applies. She's the kind of student any college could only hope to attract, the kind of student who makes learning and change look easy, the kind of student who gets a full ride to Ivy League schools on academic performance alone.

When she doesn't respond right away, I say, "Hey. You know I'm really proud of you, right?"

"Stop. Don't make me tear up! I told Luis I'd help him straighten up the shop a bit today. He'll know something's up if I show up all red-eyed." As if to emphasize her point, she gives a sniff.

I don't think she really gets what I'm trying to say, so I continue. "I mean it, Mari. You work really hard. I know you think your parents don't value that, that they're more focused on their kids getting reliable jobs and 'making it' in the real world, but I've seen the way they look at you. I watched them the night you were inducted into the National Honor Society.

"If they'd clapped any harder, they would have ended up in my mom's ER for extensive contusions on their palms. Their eyes were *shining* with pride. Your avó might even have been glowing from the inside out. Don't underestimate them. Give them this chance to be proud of you again. Because they will."

"Oh, PJ!" She half-sobs my name. I hear the distinct sound of a nose being blown before she says, "Now you've done it. Why'd you have to keep going? I'm all tears."

"Sorry."

She sighs. "What would I do without you?"

"Probably check the website on your own and read all the same info I just did and figure out you are exceptionally eligible for a scholarship."

"I meant the pep talk."

"Oh. Well, I could give you Maggie Burak's number. I'm sure she could fill in."

She gives a full-throated laugh. "Seriously. You're the best, PJ. Manifesting this now. I'm going to apply for that scholarship. I'm going to get it. And I'm going to Yale. This is happening. Now get that trig homework done already, would you?"

"Well, I *was* working on it until someone interrupted me!"

Her laughter echoes in my brain even after she hangs up. I love the sound of a happy Mariana.

I act as normal as I can on Monday morning and try to remind myself everything with Ethan is temporary, that once we're done with the trail cleanup and once the semester is over, I'm going to let Ethan go. Gently.

I don't want to hurt him. I hurt enough for the both of us.

But Ethan catches up to me and Mariana on our walk home after school.

"Hey!"

I smile at him, though looking at him already makes my heart ache a little. Why is his grin so adorable? Why does he always look so genuine?

"Hey, Ethan." Mariana sounds happy to see him, which instantly makes me suspicious.

"You guys mind if I walk home with you?" He looks at me when he asks the question.

I can't say no (and I don't really want to, even if my brain says I should), so I nod and smile at him.

"I thought you had a car," Mariana says.

"Yeah, like my mom would let me take it to school. It's her car. I just get to use it sometimes."

"Still lucky," Mariana grumbles. "Some of us have parents who won't even let us get our permits despite being sixteen for four months now."

"I don't understand why it's such a big deal. I don't even *want* to drive yet. There are too many crazy people out there," I say. "I don't trust anyone."

"That's because you're afraid of... Well, you're too timid to drive, Slip."

She almost said it.

She almost said out loud that I'm afraid to slip while driving. I stare at her, my jaw clenched in warning, and she gives me a quick apologetic look.

"I dunno. PJ's quiet and all, but I think she'd be okay driving. I'd be more afraid of you on the road than PJ," Ethan quips.

"What?" Mariana holds a hand to her hip, looking truly offended by

Ethan's words.

Ethan laughs and ducks away as Mariana tries to smack him in the arm.

"I'll have you know I am a strict rule-follower. I would count my Mississippis at every stop sign."

"Mmhmm." Ethan takes my hand as we walk, and the conversation moves from one topic to the next as we navigate the neighborhood.

Warm and strong, his hand reminds me of how hopeful I was that he might be able to keep me from slipping again, how much I wanted to rely on his strength to keep me rooted in the present.

But it doesn't work. And my wishing it would work only makes me a fool.

He squeezes my hand lightly, and I tilt my head to look up into his hazel eyes as Mariana talks about Luis's girlfriend, who is undoubtedly his soon-to-be fiancée. Ethan's eyes assess me. Like his kiss, there's a whole conversation there if I look deep enough. I wish I could turn away, but I can't. I'm starting to think he knows already. He suspects I'm going to run from him—metaphorically, if not literally. My heart gives an offbeat thump. I *hate* when it does that.

"You okay?"

"Mmhmm." I nod, completely aware of how unconvincing "mmhmm" sounds.

"Well, this is where I say goodbye," Mariana says as she reaches the street where she turns off.

"See ya, Mariana."

"Don't miss me too much, Ethan."

He puts a hand to his chest while still gripping mine with his other hand. "Every breath without you is a hardship, but I'll try to survive until tomorrow."

She laughs, that husky sound I love, as she turns her back to us and makes her way down the side street. When did Mariana start enjoying Ethan's company enough to tease him? I ponder this.

"So, you free for a while?"

Damn. Now I'm alone with Ethan, and while my heart is thrilled, my mind knows better.

"Actually, I was planning on taking a run."

He laughs. "You're dedicated. Cross-country's over for the season. Take a rest."

I kick a stick off the sidewalk and onto the grass. "I know, but I like it. Keeps me happy."

"Well, we know what happens when PJ's not happy."

I swear the world stops spinning. What does he mean? Suddenly, I question why he and Mariana were so chummy a moment ago. Did she tell him?

No. She wouldn't have.

Would she?

"What happens when PJ's not happy?" I ask.

"Uh, she's...not...happy?" Ethan shrugs, clearly unprepared for me to ask the question.

Okay. So he's just being silly. I breathe. He isn't aware of my penchant for slipping into the past whenever I panic. Good, good.

"I suppose that *is* the definition of not happy," I say.

When we reach my house, Ethan turns to face me. Even now, in November, he's still got a residual tan from so much time spent outdoors, but as his eyes take me in, I can't make out what he's saying with them. He gives my hand another squeeze and grabs my other hand with his, so now we're facing each other, both of my hands in both of his.

"You sure you're okay?" he finally says.

I try to give a breezy response. "Yeah. Why?"

"I don't know." When he stands this close, I feel like my emotions are on display under a microscope. "You just…seem distant."

"You're imagining things. Don't go all paranoid boyfriend on me now."

Oh no.

Why did I use that word?

Boyfriend.

I've convinced myself I'm breaking up with him, but I'm not making this any easier on either of us by continuing the charade.

To make matters worse, he smiles when I say it. Even his eyes smile. Why are his eyes so pretty?

"Boyfriend, huh?"

"I mean, we're not…you're not…" I stammer.

"I like it."

Then he leans in and kisses me—sweet this time. There's a difference between daytime kisses on the sidewalk and night kisses in a car, I suppose. This one is definitely rated PG. And for all that I say I'm going to break things off, I kiss him back.

Worse? I enjoy it.

"Don't suppose you'd like company on your run?" he says as he pulls away.

I'm running from my obsession with you! I want to scream.

"I really need to get out and just clear my head. I can't…do that with you around."

It's a rejection, but he smiles wider.

"Is it wrong that makes me happy?"

I deadpan. "Yes."

Other than first period, it's easy to avoid Ethan on Tuesday. He's working. Thursday, too. Wednesday, of course, is Pablo's surgery, so I use the kitten as an excuse not to get together after school.

Pablo, as it turns out, is not affected by being neutered. At all. He is, however, pretty mad we confine him to a cat carrier for the rest of the evening. I try to keep him occupied by dangling feather toys in front of the bars on the door, and he reacts with far too much energy for a furball who's just been under anesthesia.

Thursday night, my phone pings with a string of texts.

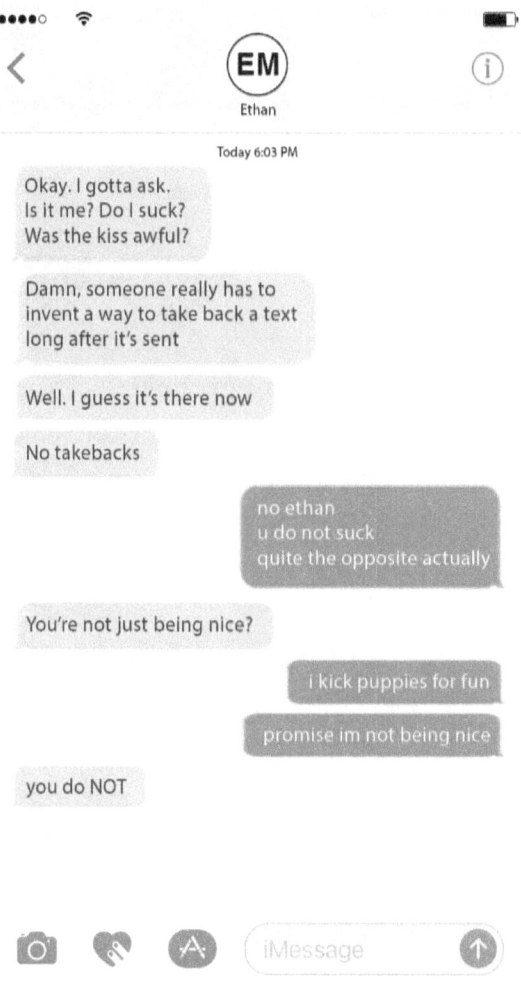

And there it is. I can't avoid him forever. Thanksgiving in two weeks. After that, it's only three weeks until Christmas break. Before or after? Before? Or after? Is it wrong I still enjoy being with him, even knowing I won't be able to keep him? I feel like, somehow, this makes me an evil person.

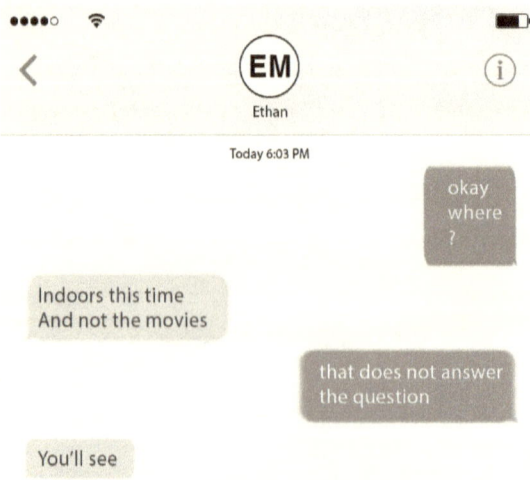

Ethan likes surprises. On one hand, this is fun. On the other, I'd feel a lot more comfortable if he would stop springing surprises on me. I'm already tapping my fingers on my thumb just to avoid thinking about it.

It'll be fine. Just me and Ethan. I've been around him plenty of times without slipping. So yeah, even though I slipped that one time recently, I—

And suddenly, it's nine minutes and fifty-three seconds earlier, and I'm sitting on my bed in my room, my Brit Lit homework spread around me. My phone is going to ping any minute, and I can't even freaking stay in one place long enough to agree to a date tomorrow night.

Tears of frustration build in my eyes. I try not to shed them, but I lose. I always lose. Ping, ping, ping, ping. I don't look right away. I don't want to have to reassure him again that he's a good kisser because, oh my God, he's a good kisser, and those kisses make me melt every time I think about them, and I really should not keep this thing going.

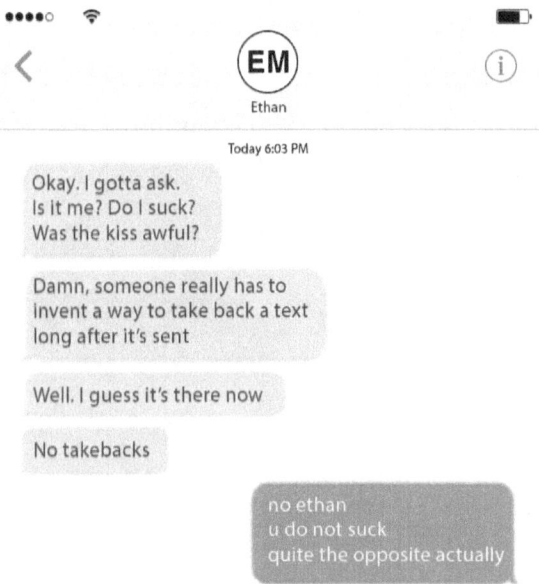

I don't bother asking this time. It's indoors, and that's all he'll tell me. At this point, maybe I'm just going to spite myself. I'm not even sure. I'm tired of slipping. I'm tired of living in fear of slipping. Maybe it's time I just do whatever I want whenever I want to.

I'm going on that date tomorrow, and I'm going to have a good time. And if I slip, I'm going to have extra time on my hands during that date tomorrow. Maybe I'll spend the extra ten minutes snogging the heck out of Ethan Morrow, and that'll teach me to stay in one place.

CHAPTER SIXTEEN

There are entirely too many people at the mall. I haven't been here since shopping for school clothes with Mom when I was twelve. It's a little overwhelming, but Ethan holds my hand as we stroll. His touch grounds me.

For now.

I'm not sure what we're doing here other than shopping. I have yet to stop at the library to inquire about a job, so I'm pretty broke, but there's not much I would buy even if I could afford it.

This doesn't phase Ethan, though.

When I tell him I wish he'd told me so I could have brought some cash, he just waves me off with a hand.

"What kind of date would this be if I invited you out and then let you pay?"

"Uh, Ethan?"

"Yeah?"

"We're in the middle of the mall. What are you paying for? Pretzels and slushies? My new wardrobe?"

He squeezes my hand. "Pretzels and slushies are up for debate later, and I like your clothes just fine. We're here for fun." He pulls me toward a thrift shop that's at the end of an obscure arm of the mall, and we leave the majority of the crowds behind.

"Okay, look. I didn't ask what this date was, but I gotta know. What are we doing?"

Once we're in the store, he stops and looks at me, his face the image of all seriousness. Is he about to make us take a math test or something? What's with him?

"You have fifteen minutes to put together an outfit for me, and I have fifteen minutes to put together an outfit for you. Anything goes. No limits. Ready?"

My mind is spinning. He wants me to what?

"But…why?"

He bounces on his heels, impatient with me. "PJ, where's your sense of adventure? It's for fun. It's a game. Make it a competition."

"I'm sorry, I—"

"No. Trust me on this. It's fun. Now go. Time starts"—he looks at his phone— "now."

Then he races away toward the women's apparel section of the thrift shop, not giving me even a breath to argue.

This is the weirdest date I've ever been on.

Not that I have many of them to compare to.

I sigh. Then I make my way to the men's side of the store, pick up a pink and orange striped shirt with a wide collar and silver buttons that looks straight out of the disco era, and fold it over my arm. I find a pair of pants that match, but they look way too small to fit Ethan.

I consider.

That actually could be funny…

Okay, I'm starting to see the draw of this game. Oh, there's a ridiculously large cowboy hat that will probably dwarf Ethan's head and obscure his beautiful eyes! And terrible maroon polyester pants that *will* fit, I think. This is a good start.

Fifteen minutes pass quicker than I thought, and, in the end, I have an armful of clothing I shove into Ethan's hands in exchange for all the ridiculous things he's picked for me. I laugh as I spot a pair of sparkly purple leggings and a yellow feather boa.

"This isn't fair. You had more time to prepare."

He grins. "Hey, we each had fifteen minutes."

"I mean mentally. You knew what we were doing tonight."

"It's okay. It looks like you got the hang of this pretty quickly. Now we go to the changing rooms. The rule is you have to wear *all* of it unless something is too small to wear in some way or another, though you get extra points for trying."

"Wait, so do I get points if I get all of it on, or do you because you picked it out for me?"

"Ten points to me for every item that fits you. For every item that doesn't, but you manage to fit somehow anyway, ten points to you."

"Got it."

"Meet you back out here in five."

When I reach the women's side of the changing room, I dump the pile of clothing onto the bench seat and start giggling as I get undressed. I don't even know how I'm going to get all this stuff on. I kick my clothes to the side and slide on the leggings first. I twist to watch them shimmer in the mirror. Actually, is it weird I kind of like these? They might be kickass with a pair of black boots. Huh.

Layer after layer, I pile on. In the end, I'm left wearing the purple leggings, fuzzy white leg-warmers, and a gold leotard. To top it all off, I've got a leopard print jacket, a yellow boa, and tortoise shell sunglasses. The horrible Christmas sweater is way too small for me, so I use the arms of the sweater to tie it around my leg.

There are also six pieces of costume jewelry, which I throw on one after the next. Who actually wears this stuff? It's horribly gaudy—three rings with fake rainbow jewels almost the size of my palm; two necklaces, one gold and one of which is a long string of fake pearls; and, of all things, a tiara.

Of course Ethan found a tiara.

When I emerge from the changing room, I burst into laughter. Ethan's already standing outside my door, his back and one foot against the wall. His cowboy hat is tilted downward as though he's trying to mimic something he saw from an old Western movie.

Oddly enough, the hat fits him. Everything else looks pretty awful, though I did a good job of picking clothes that fit. More points for me.

"Oh, those maroon pants." I shake my head. "Priceless."

He looks down. "You like them?"

"No!"

He tugs on my boa. "Hey, look, I might look like a defunct cowboy from nineteen seventy-five, but at least I don't look like I kick puppies for fun."

I freeze. He can't remember. How does he keep doing this? How does he remember words I never said (or texted) in this version of reality?

"I mean, that outfit, it's…something," He continues. "I did good on this one! Okay, time for photos."

The thought of taking pictures snaps me from my moment. "Oh, Ethan, no. We do *not* need photo evidence of this."

"We do, we do!" He pulls me close and snaps a few selfies.

Then I find myself smiling—laughing even—despite the fact that I'd rather not have picture evidence of this moment. I can't help it. We are behaving like toddlers. Or crazy teenagers.

Once I move on from the fact that Ethan somehow remembered my puppy-kicking comment, behaving like crazy teenagers actually feels quite glorious. My body has never felt less anxious.

"Okay, that's a hundred and twenty points for me and one hundred even for you."

"Wait! Don't forget about this!" I point to the ugly sweater tied around my thigh.

"Oh, right. Make that a hundred and ten for you. Alright, ready for round two?"

I give a sly smile. Now that I get the gist of this game, I'm more than ready, and my competitive streak is beginning to shine. We return to the changing rooms for our own clothes and to put all the pieces from the first game aside.

I hold up the purple leggings, then pull them from the pile and hang them on the back of the changing room door. I'll have to consider.

I'm fully prepared for the second round. I see how Ethan played the last round, bulking up on jewelry items that were a sure fit. So I'll do the same.

When our fifteen minutes are up, and we head to the changing rooms, I can hear Ethan groan from the men's side.

"You've got to be kidding!"

I laugh. I wrapped six scarves and nine pieces of costume jewelry in the center of the bundle I handed him.

"If you don't want to lose, you shouldn't have taught me the game!" I call back.

I'm not a good loser.

Come to think of it, I'm not a very good winner, either.

When we emerge, I'm dressed in a fluffy pink prom gown that's about ten inches too long, a pair of orange spandex leggings, a polka dot button-down shirt, a camouflage jacket (very subtle against the pink gown), a silvery wrap, earmuffs, three necklaces, and *another* tiara. How the heck Ethan found two tiaras in a thrift shop is beyond me.

But I've got him beat, and he knows it. He's wearing everything I gave him, and he looks even more absurd than he did the first time. Because not only have I given him scarves and jewelry, but I've also found a formal gown. And it fits.

I burst into a fit of laughter again, but if I'm honest, he's totally rocking the royal blue, floor-length satin gown and all the scarves and jewelry. Plus a pair of men's combat boots. It's a good touch if I say so myself.

"A hundred points for you." Then I tally up everything I made him put on, counting on my fingers to be sure I haven't missed anything. "And a hundred and eighty points for me."

"Rub it in…" He glares at me, but he's smiling.

I mean, all things considered, Ethan's a pretty good sport.

"Photos!" I shout.

He doesn't groan, but I can tell he wants to.

"I'm down with this," he says in between snapping pictures. "But if this goes anywhere beyond you and me, I'm moving back to California, even if it means living with my dad and Lindsay."

"Threat duly noted."

"It's not a threat. I'm just saying."

By the time we change back into our clothes, I've made a decision on the purple leggings. They're going home with me, though I'll have to borrow money from Ethan to buy them today. I kind of feel guilty having tried on a bunch of things without the intention to buy, so it's only fair that I spend money here. I also pluck the tortoise shell sunglasses from the pile. I kind of like the way the frames look on my face, and if I ever *do* get a license, it might be nice not to have the sun in my eyes.

"You're getting the leggings?"

I flash an evil grin. "You have only yourself to blame."

We spend the rest of the evening walking the mall, drinking slushies, and trying to win cheap stuffed animals from claw machine games that are deliberately rigged to make winning as difficult as possible. Ethan insists on paying for everything. I try to argue, but my pleas fall on deaf ears.

"How are things with your mom?" I ask. I watch the concentration on his face as he maneuvers the claw into position. "And your dad, actually. Did you guys talk?"

Ethan gives a frustrated sigh as a plush hamburger slides from the claw's grasp just before it reaches the shoot that would dispense it as the prize. It falls back against the glass and rolls to the bottom of a pile of stuffed toys that have faced a similar fate.

"Yeah. We're okay. Dad and I talked."

"Like I suggested."

He turns his head to glance down at me. "Yes, *Mom*. Like you suggested."

I laugh and smack his arm. "Don't ever call me Mom."

He leans over to kiss me quickly, bites my bottom lip as he pulls away, and says, "Trust me, I don't kiss my mom like that."

Ethan's kiss leaves me with a tingling in my veins. I giggle. "I really hope not."

Then he fishes in his pocket for another two quarters to feed the machine he insists on playing, throwing away more money. Tomorrow, I think. I'll check the library while Ethan's at work. I'll have plenty of time to see if they have anything available. If we're going to make going out a regular thing—

My mind seizes mid-thought. What am I *doing?*

I'm breaking up with Ethan. I already determined this. We're not staying together. Going out is *not* going to be a regular thing. I'm only allowing this through Thanksgiving.

And suddenly, the fact that Ethan has scored a fluffy orange cat that looks like Pablo doesn't seem nearly as exciting as it would have been ten seconds ago.

I smile through it anyway.

Later, on the ride home, Ethan gets philosophical with thoughts of a future I can't even bring myself to think about.

"Do you have a dream college yet?" he asks.

We're almost halfway through junior year. Everyone I know has a plan for where they want to go after high school and what subject they want to major in. I can't think that far ahead. It makes me entirely too anxious.

And we know where that leads.

"I don't know," I finally answer. "You?"

He glances at me. It's just a moment, but I catch the surprise. "Come on. You've got to have some idea."

I bite a lip and stare out the car's window at the dark landscape swiftly passing by. "No. I really…don't know."

The truth is, there's nothing that interests me enough where I can imagine spending the rest of my life doing it. I'm not mechanically inclined, so anything technical is out. I'm okay at math, but I don't love it. Science is fun, but I don't want to work in a lab and couldn't imagine testing on animals. Maybe botany, but beyond playing with plants, I don't really know what that involves. I *could* major in German, but what would I do with a degree in German—work at an airport? Teach? I guess school *is* something I'm familiar with.

"PJ, you're one of the smartest girls I know. What do you mean you don't *know?*"

I shrug. "I just don't feel like there's anything that calls to me, that I'm good enough to do, you know?"

"That's because you're awesome at everything you do. It must be difficult to figure out which path is the right one when you're good at all of them."

My ears warm with the compliment. Whether it's warranted or not, it's a nice thing for him to say. "You're sweet. Wrong, but sweet."

"I'm not wrong!"

In my discomfort, I try to deflect back to him. "Anyway, where are you planning to go? Since, you know, you seem to have it all together and all."

"Mom wants me to go to Boston 'cause that's where she went, but I don't think I want to go far, you know? Like, I don't see the point. I mean, Boston would be a great place to visit, but I don't want to stay there for four years."

"I think you'd probably come home for the summers."

"You know what I mean."

"So where do you want to go?" I push.

"I dunno. Thinking about Penn State. Maybe the local campus."

Huh. I didn't see Ethan as a local kind of kid. I say as much. "I feel like you're the get-out-and-explore type."

He chuckles. "I lived in California for three years. I like it here. Here feels like home."

"And what do you want to major in?"

"Geology, I think."

"Geology!" I couldn't be more surprised if he said he wanted to major in chicken farming. "I thought you'd go for the arts. Photography. That whole thing about building a portfolio and all. Wasn't that why you agreed to take headshots for Jenny?"

"I love photography. I do. I just... I don't know. When I was photographing Jenny, it got me thinking. Is *this* what I want to do with my life? Like, how does photography make a difference in the world? Aside from which, every freaking smartphone has a camera and a million filters and no one needs a real camera—or a real photographer—anymore."

"Okay, I can't argue the 'everyone has a phone with a camera' part of this. But photography is a huge part of making a difference in the world, Ethan! It shows people the parts of the world they'd never know—the effects of climate change in all the remote places, it reveals cultures we'd never know about, and...and...gorgeous landscapes some of us will never see. It's travel. Adventure! I think it's just as important as geology."

He gives me another quick glance.

"It sounds like maybe *you* should pursue photography."

I laugh. "Oh no. Definitely not. If you scroll through my phone, you'll see one-thousand two-hundred eighty-seven photos of Pablo."

"Yeah, but maybe you *need* to get out and explore. It sounds like you want to."

I'm quiet for a long moment. I'd love to explore. I'd love to see the world—the deserts and the canyons, the oceans and the cliffs, and everything in between. But that's...not in my cards. It's not the kind of thing someone with debilitating anxiety does.

"Maybe someday," I say, mostly to end the conversation.

When Ethan drops me off at home, he kisses me again. On the darkened front porch, this time. I don't have time to get nervous. The kiss is everything I want it to be, and my heart isn't even leaping out of my chest. No pressure in my veins. Just a dizzying sensation in my skull that's all part of my recent obsession with Ethan. He tastes like mint gum and a little like the chocolate covered pretzels we ate right before we left the mall.

"Definitely wasn't a fluke," he says as he pulls away. He looks into my eyes, and I smile. "This kiss was just as good for me, but..."

"But?" Now my heart stutters. Oh God, am I bad at this?

"But we should try it one more time, just to make sure."

I close my eyes and melt into him, pressing myself against his warmth, letting him consume me. Because he does. Everything that he is consumes me.

"I really enjoy doing that entirely too much," he says, revealing the dimple I love.

"Can I let you in on a secret?" I whisper.

He nods.

"Me, too."

His eyes flick to my mouth and back up again. "Good. Now get inside before I keep you out here, kissing all night. 'Cause I'm pretty sure I could do that."

Now it's my turn to grin back at him.

"My mom gets off at eleven. She'd put a stop to it."

He groans as I unlock the front door.

"Good night, Ethan."

"Good night, PJ."

I enter the dark house, close the door behind me, and lean against it until I hear Ethan's car start. The headlights flash once in Ethan's date night routine, their light bouncing off the opposite wall. Then, except for the hall clock ticking, all is dark and quiet. I sigh.

Pablo comes trotting from the kitchen, mewing at me as if to scold me for being out so late.

"Hey, buddy, come here."

I drop my bags and sit on the floor to scoop him up. I swear he's put on a pound in the last week.

"Are you my chunky monkey?"

He headbutts me in response, his purr already roaring like a tiny motor.

"I won't judge. What do you think, Pablo? Am I awful for not just telling Ethan now?"

He mews again.

"Yeah, well, that's easy for you to say. *You* don't have to slip whenever you're freakishly anxious."

Now he chirps. Are we having an actual conversation?

"You're right. I *didn't* slip tonight, but it doesn't mean I won't tomorrow, or the next day, or the day after that. And Ethan deserves more. He deserves better than that."

Doesn't he?

CHAPTER SEVENTEEN

"I got a job at the library," I tell Mariana on the phone Saturday afternoon.

"No! I forbid you. You may not further divide your time away from me. You've already been spending a ton of time with Ethan. Now a job? I'm history! I'm going to be forgotten. I'll text you one day, and you're gonna respond with 'who dis?'"

"Oh, don't be so dramatic."

"Don't blame me because I see where this is going."

"Mariana."

"No, for real. You'll have no time for me!" she continues.

"Mariana."

"By Christmas, we'll be estranged."

"Mari—"

"Someone will ask 'Didn't you have a best friend?' and you'll reply with 'There *was* a girl once…I no longer remember her name.'"

"The library job is so I can make breaking up with Ethan easier."

The line goes silent.

After a moment, she recovers. "Oh."

"Yeah."

"But I thought… I mean, you didn't slip last night. You said it was awesome. I believe your exact words were, 'he makes me forget I'm a freak.' I mean, if that's not meant to be, what is?"

I sigh. I did say those words.

When I'm with Ethan, I'm a weird combination of nerves and ease. I feel like I could be with him forever and never slip. And the next moment, I'm slipping.

"It's wrong to keep it going if it can't go anywhere, isn't it?" I ask.

"Personally, I think it's wrong not to give him a chance at knowing the truth."

My gut clenches. "I wish you'd stop saying that. Have you told your parents about the summer program at Yale?"

"No. Not until I hear back about the scholarship. Like *you* suggested. And besides, that's not the same. I'm waiting to tell them until I have more information. You have all the information you need, but Ethan's not even on the same page. He doesn't know all the pieces of you that you keep hidden."

I pause, thinking. "I can't, Mari."

"Listen. I understand. I get it. I do. So whatever you need to do, Peej, I'll support you. You know that."

A small comfort.

"So when do you start at the library?"

"Monday."

"You work Monday, Wednesday, and Friday afternoons, don't you?" By the tone in her voice, I can tell she's on to me.

"However did you guess?"

She snorts. "Because Ethan works Tuesdays, Thursdays, and Saturdays."

"It's only six hours a week, so it's not like I'll avoid him entirely."

"So when are you going to do it, then? Break up with him, I mean."

"After Thanksgiving," I say, pulling at a cuticle on my thumb.

She makes a strangled sound. "You're going to break up with him *before* Christmas?"

"Is that illegal?"

"I suppose if you're the spawn of Satan, it's okay."

I groan. "Mari!"

"I kid, I kid! It's better not to let it go longer than it has to."

"So, after the trail cleanup, then."

"Yeah, that's probably for the best."

It is *not* for the best. There *is* no best in this scenario. My mind is so tied up in knots, I don't know whether I should run to or from Ethan at this point. When I tell him about the library job, he's so genuinely happy for me that I immediately feel like a traitorous boob. I was devastated when he first got a job because it meant less time together, but he's happy for me.

"I'm just so glad you're working somewhere you love, you know?" he says over the phone on Sunday.

I do love the library.

"It's like karma or fate or something. What are the chances the library would have something open just when you needed it?"

"I'm pretty excited."

"Are you? You don't sound excited!"

That's because I'm only getting this job to see less of you, and I don't really want to see less of you, but I have to because...well, because I'm me!

But I don't speak the words that run through my mind.

So when I head directly to the library after school on Monday, Ethan insists on walking me there. I guess avoiding him won't be as easy as I thought.

"Don't be nervous." He takes my hand in his. How are his fingers warm when it's thirty-five degrees out?

"I'm not nervous." I'm lying. Of course I'm nervous. Having job is something I've never done before. What if I suck at it?

"You're tapping your fingers together. You're definitely nervous."

"I'm not—" But I am. I'm tapping so I don't let the pressure build enough in my veins to slip. He noticed.

Ethan grins down at me. "It's gonna be okay. Promise. Your first day can't be any worse than mine."

I furrow my brow. "Wait, what? What happened?"

"Luis told me to block off a half-hour for any check-engine light diagnostic appointments. They use this little scanner thing to read what's wrong with the car, right? So I decide to be super confident because I'm me, and I end up making a mess of the schedule for the entire week."

"The entire week? How?" It seems to me like Ethan's making this up. How could anyone screw up scheduling?

"Because when I went into the computer system to book the times, I set each one for half a day, not half an hour. And by the time Luis realized what I did, he lost two days' worth of appointments that could have been booked in the meantime."

I laugh. "You did not."

"I swear, I did. We're talking what could have been thousands of dollars of lost time."

I think he's serious.

"Why didn't you tell me about this?"

He presses his lips together and gives me a sort of side-eye. "I didn't want you to think I was a complete idiot."

Now we're both laughing.

"Okay," I concede. "You're right. I probably will not have a worse first day than you. I don't think anything I could do, short of burning down the building, could cause the library to lose that much money."

"See? Don't you feel better already?"

Oddly, I do.

"Well, here we are." Ethan squeezes my hand once before letting go.

I look up at the building, taking in all the decorative bricks and windows. It's one of the oldest buildings in town, built when aesthetics were as vital as functionality, so it's got these gorgeous, smooth, tall columns in the front of the building that always seem to feel like they're giving me a hug when I walk through the front door.

Along the top of the building, there's decorative trim that runs the perimeter of the roof. I'm not sure whether it's carved or poured, but it's pretty either way. I'm sure the columns and the trim work all have fancy, highly specific architectural names, but I don't know anything about architecture. I just know I love this building.

"What time is your shift over?"

"Oh, um, six, I think." I shift my book bag on my shoulders.

"I can pick you up in the car if my mom's home. Otherwise, I can come walk you home so you're not alone."

Why does he always make this more difficult?

I sniff, the cold air burning my nose.

"You're sweet, but you don't have to do that."

"Come on, it's dark. I assume your mom won't be home to pick you up. Someone's gotta keep an eye on you. Why not your…boyfriend?"

A knife. He's twisting a knife in my gut.

"Okay. You win."

He grins, then leans in for a quick kiss.

"See you later, Slip."

I give him a look as he walks away.

"Yeah, yeah, I know. PJ. I'm gonna find out eventually."

He will *never* find out.

I fill out the required paperwork as soon as I arrive. (They're taking taxes out of my teeny, tiny paycheck?!) Then the library director, Ms. Hoffman, introduces me to the rest of the regular full-time staff and sets me to work sorting books that have already been checked back in, but need to be shelved. It's mindless work.

I love it already.

There's no way I could be anxious enough to slip here. Why I never thought of spending more time at the library is beyond me. I guess I was doing a lot better with not slipping until Ethan came into my life.

Then he showed up and, well—slip, slip, slip, I live up to my nickname.

It's absurd to want to be with someone who is literally the cause of the very panic attacks that ruin my life. I should *hate* Ethan. I shouldn't even want to look at him. I should want to run in the opposite direction.

So why don't I?

I swap two books on the cart. *I* before *e* except after *c*.

"How are you holding up on day one?" Ms. Hoffman emerges from her office to check in on my progress…or to ensure I'm not ready to run away in total madness—one or the other. "Oh! You're quick," she says. "You've got that cart almost filled already."

"Yeah. It's just about ready for someone to shelve everything, I think."

"Someone! Ha, PJ, you're funny. That someone is *also* you. That's your next task."

"Hoffman!" One of the librarians on the other side of the library holds up a mangled children's book. "What do you want to do with this one?"

"Oh my God! What is that?" Ms. Hoffman squints at the mess.

"Apparently, a kid spilled milk on it, then snuck it into the dishwasher to try to get the milk off because *that's* easier than getting a paper towel. Then Dad didn't realize it. Ran the load. And, well…this."

Ms. Hoffman shakes her head. "Chuck it. They're paying for it, right?"

"They didn't even *try* to argue the replacement fee."

"Dishwasher. That's a new one. Never a dull moment," Ms. Hoffman mumbles, shaking her head, as she turns back to me. "Okay, so when you've got the whole pile sorted alphabetically onto the cart, you'll shelve everything in the main section of the library."

"Oh."

"Do you need me to show you, or do you feel comfortable giving it a try on your own?"

"I'm sure I can figure it out." I think of Ethan messing up on his first day. "I just have a small stack left to add to the cart. Then, I'm good to go. Shouldn't take too long when they're already in order, right?"

"Exactly! That's why we alphabetize it here first. It's easier to push a cart down the aisle as you go. You're good, then?"

I nod. "Sounds easy enough."

"Great. That'll probably take you the rest of your shift, so come see me when you're done, and I'll show you how to clock out."

"Okay."

Mind-numbingly easy, this job.

When I clock out, there are unread messages on my phone, a few from Mom and one from Ethan.

Mom is a saint. My mouth salivates. I swear I can already taste the creamy fudge center of the chocolate cake that only The Cookie Crumble can pull off. I text back my profuse thanks, then switch to my conversation with Ethan.

I grab my coat and backpack from the rack in the break room and shrug into both, still giggling a little as I think about Ethan learning the origin of the word *dork*.

Ethan will never use the word again, guaranteed.

When I step outside into the dark night, my breath fogs in the air. It must have dropped ten degrees since the sun went down. I'm suddenly very, *very* glad for the ride.

"That is *not* cool." Ethan's voice startles me.

He leans against a brightly lit column, so it's not like he's creeping in the dark or anything. I just wasn't expecting him to meet me at the door. He pushes off the column, falling into place beside me, offering to take my book bag. I let him, not necessarily because I want to, but more because I don't think he'd take no for an answer.

"Hey, I'm not the one who used *dorkalicious* as a word."

He coughs. "Can we not?"

I laugh.

"It's not funny!" But he laughs a little, too. He laughs even while he holds the car door open for me.

The ride home only takes a few minutes. When we turn into the neighborhood, Ethan asks, "Do you want to come over to my house for a while? My mom made a quiche for dinner. I'm not a hundred percent sure, but I think it's like an egg pie thing with lots of cheese and weird vegetables mixed in."

"As appetizing as that sounds, I have a ton of homework to get done tonight, plus a history test to study for," I say.

"Oh. Okay. Maybe next time, then."

Ugh. I'm dirt. I'm worse than dirt. I'm the dirt that gets stuck in the treads of your sneakers after you've run three miles through the woods. There's probably dog poo mixed in that dirt.

"But, hey," I say as he pulls into my driveway. "Hang here for a moment, okay?"

I run inside to pack a piece of cake in a plastic container for him, and when he sees what it is, he brightens.

"Is this…"

"The Cookie Crumble, oh, yes." I hand him the container, which he places carefully, almost reverently, on the passenger seat.

Then he turns to me. "You do lo…care about me!"

We stare at each other for half a second. It can't be longer than that. And yet, we both know he almost used the 'L' word. Even jokingly, he still almost used it.

I forge forward with conversation.

"You're my favorite person," I say. It's true, even if being around him does make me slip. "Oh! But my mom says you must eat dinner first, including all the weird veggies."

He gives a mock salute. "Consider it done."

When Ethan drives away, and I'm alone in a quiet house again, I can't get my mind off the fact that he nearly said "love."

I prepare my dinner from a container in the fridge that's covered in heart-shaped sticky notes from Mom and cut a large slice of cheese-filled lasagna for myself. I sit and stare as my lasagna spins in the microwave…and I wonder if the lasagna on the plate is a metaphor for my life.

Spinning. So much spinning. Every time I think I've reoriented myself, I'm spinning again. And the heat is there, too—the sizzling kind—especially when it comes to Ethan.

Pablo startles me when he jumps on the island stool beside me and mews.

I sigh and put a hand to my head. "Pablo. I am either feeling *really* philosophical right now, or I'm just *really* hungry."

The microwave dings—perfect timing. "At least now I can take care of the hungry part."

CHAPTER EIGHTEEN

Thanksgiving week. Finally off school. Finally time for the trail cleanup. Finally.

"You're not going to do it, are you?" Mariana blows on her hands to warm them up. It's about twenty degrees out here. I'm not sure what we were thinking when it came to planning another trail cleanup date. This is insane. I bounce on the balls of my feet just to keep moving.

"I am."

Ethan's cousins didn't come along this time, and Rich had to bail, so it's just Mariana, Ethan, Jon, Leon, and me. This time, Leon's mom didn't stay. The story ran in the local paper last month, as did the story about my rescuing Kayleigh Owens. That story also came with heartfelt thanks from Kayleigh's parents and an engraved crystal award from the mayor that Mom gushed over and displayed prominently beside the framed newspaper article above the fireplace.

Talk about embarrassing.

Thankfully, I was able to avoid the local television news crew and they settled for using the photo that Ethan took as well as a photo of the award on our mantle to run their story. It probably helped that Kayleigh's mom and dad were willing to sit for an interview.

Mariana shakes open a garbage bag—I bought the biodegradable, environmentally friendly kind this time—as I grab a crushed soda can and toss it in. Even halfway through, this trail is a mess. It's going to need springtime work. And maybe by then Ethan will have forgiven me for breaking up with him.

"So today then?" Mariana says.

My pulse hammers at the question, but I'm resolute. "Yes. Today."

"Like, while we're here?"

I heave a sigh. "No. Later. Can we talk about something else?"

She bites her lip. "Sure. Sorry."

Before I can switch topics, a half-deflated volleyball flies through the air between us, narrowly missing Mariana's head. She glares at the direction it came from, with fierce dark eyes and a scowl that could take down a six-foot-two, three-hundred-pound linebacker.

"Sorry!" Leon waves at us from down the path. "I didn't think it would actually go that far!"

Beside him, Ethan shakes his head and makes a face at us as if to say "What *did* he expect?" I pick up the half-deflated ball and toss it in the bag.

"Clean up," I yell back. "Not play time, Leon." Then I grumble to Mariana. "At this rate, this stupid trail is never going to be clean. We can't even see half the junk under all the leaves. What? Why are you looking at me like that?"

"I'm just imagining how much less stressed you'll be this evening."

"I'm not—" But I am. I'm tapping my fingers and didn't even realize I was doing it. "It's more anger than stress. I don't want to hurt him."

"So you're…angry with him?"

"No, Mariana. I'm angry at myself."

"Ah. Well, call me tonight when you've done the thing. Anyway, moving on to other topics. My mom said you can stay over one night this week if you want. Tuesday, maybe?"

I brush leaves aside with my sneaker, then bend and pick up a wad of fishing line. People are such pigs.

"Yeah, but won't your family be busy getting ready for Thanksgiving? Like, doesn't your mom start cooking three days out?"

Mariana's extended family is huge, and her mom almost always does all the cooking on holidays.

"Not gonna lie. That's probably why she wants me to invite you. Another pair of hands to roll and cut the dough. Anyway, thought it'd be better than spending the week alone, nursing a broken heart, and waiting for your mom to get off work."

"I will not be nursing a broken heart."

Much.

I promised myself I wouldn't.

I won't.

I'm definitely going to have a broken heart. First, I'm going to stomp on Ethan's heart. Then, I'm going to smash my own like a ship in a storm against seaside cliffs. My heart will be smithereens after this. I'll be lucky if the pieces are even big enough to glue together.

Actually, this may not happen at all if I don't pull myself together. I mean, I may just slip myself backwards to this morning, where I'll be stuck picking up trash on a half-frozen, half-mud trail all day again and again.

Damn, my pulse is all over the place.

"What's up, PJ? You're not yourself." Ethan and I sit on the steps of the deck in my backyard. Mom said no boys in the house when she's not home, but I don't think the backyard counts. Especially not when it's freezing, and I'm wearing three layers.

"I don't think we should do this," I blurt.

I have no cool. None.

I cannot believe I just said it…like that. My mind spins as I try to take in what my mouth has clearly thrown out there.

Ethan looks as though he's just been shot in the gut. I guess, in a way, that's what I just did.

"You mean…" He tilts his head. He's hoping I don't mean what I mean.

"Yes, that's what I mean."

His eyes go wide with surprise. Then he recovers, blinks a few times, and runs his hands through his hair. His cheeks puff as he blows out a breath.

"Wow."

"It's not you." What is wrong with me? Why am I one big walking cliché?

He stands, walks the deck, then leans on the railing, looking at the frigid, sad grass. "Wow."

I scrunch my face as my eyes begin to well with tears. "Ethan, please say something else."

"Uh. Sorry. I'm not…really sure…uh…"

Oh no oh no ohno ohno ohno—

We're in my driveway getting out of Ethan's car when I slam back into my body this time. It's a shock, even knowing I was going to slip while breaking up with him, even fully expecting it. I cough as the cold air of the outside hits my lungs after the warmth of the car for the second time.

"You okay?" Ethan's concern is practically palpable.

I hold the car door as I bend over, struggling to breathe, trying desperately to keep my breath even. My fingers tap madly. I'm spiraling. I can feel it.

Ethan gets out and jogs to my side of the car. "PJ, are you okay? What's going on?"

His hand is on my back, rubbing, soothing, but there's panic on his face. If only I could tell—

Then I'm in the passenger seat as we're dropping Mariana off at her house. She's just getting out of the car. I don't even think. I fling my door open and get out and grab her hand. I need Mariana to anchor me.

Startled, she turns to face me, but she doesn't have to ask, and I don't need to say anything. If my eyes relay the frenzy I feel, it's enough. She grips my hand, holding me tight. "It's gonna be okay. Slip, you hear me? It's going to be okay."

Ethan, still sitting in the driver's seat, is utterly confused. My back is to him, so he can't see the panic. I hear the passenger side window roll down. "PJ, you okay? Am I…still dropping you off at home?"

I can't talk. I'll slip if I try.

Mariana covers. "Hey, Ethan, she's okay. She's just having a panic attack. It happens sometimes. I'm going to take her inside, stick some meditation music in her ears, and feed her a couple of queijadas."

Ethan turns off the car's engine.

No, no, no. I squeeze Mariana's fingers in a death grip.

"A panic attack? Oh my God, PJ. Why didn't you say something?" I hear the click of the metal latch as the car door opens behind me.

"Ethan." Mariana is firm. She holds out the hand that isn't gripping mine. "She's okay. Trust me on this one. It has nothing to do with you. Just give her time. I promise I'll have her call you later."

"But I—"

She shakes her head in warning, and Ethan gives in. I want to turn and look at him. I want to see him, but the hurt and confusion on his face will send me slipping again. I can't.

I can't.

Then the car door shuts again, and he turns over the engine, but he doesn't leave right away. I rock on my heels, trying to focus, trying to breathe.

"Just hang in there, Peej. He's pulling out of the driveway now, turning back on the street." Mariana narrates as though I can't hear what's going on behind me, but the sound of her voice is comforting anyway, and behind my closed eyelids, I need all the comfort I can get.

She rubs my arm.

"Okay? You here with me? You going to stay?"

I swallow and nod, barely opening my eyes, letting her lead me inside to the warmth of her bedroom and a plate of freshly made queijadas I cannot possibly choke down at the moment.

She takes my phone from my hand and pulls up Susan, but I can't listen to Susan. Not really. Susan doesn't have the answers. Susan doesn't know a thing about love. If that's even what this is. Susan doesn't slip.

I open my mouth to begin relaying the story to Mariana, but she stops me with a finger in the air. She shakes her head, her dark curls shifting around her face like a lion's mane.

She is a lion. She's a lion, and I'm a mouse, and if she'd been given the curse of slipping backwards nine minutes and fifty-three seconds, she'd probably use it for good just about every day.

Then I realize she's timing this. She's making me wait to start talking.

"You're—"

"Shh. Not yet. You've got two more minutes to sit before we talk."

It's almost enough to make me smile. She's making sure if I slip while telling her what happened, I'll still be here. In her room. Safe.

I want to hug her.

Instead, I sit on her carpet, close my eyes, and try to let Susan breathe the desire to live into me. When two minutes have passed, Mariana nods, and I begin talking. I tell her everything. All of it. How I slipped before I even got past Ethan's "wow." How I couldn't stick around long enough to have a decent conversation. That I couldn't even give him the breakup he deserved. How I slipped a second time because I was so out of control.

"I'm going to have to ghost him." My words are barely more than a whisper.

I'm about to become the kind of person I hate most.

"Or—and hear me out—you could stay together?" Mariana's entire face conveys a false hope.

I hang my head. "You know I can't."

She grabs my hand and squeezes.

"I'll keep slipping even if I stay with him. This is a no-win situation. I think the only way I could make this better is to slip all the way back to before I agreed to hang out with him at all."

"That'd take…a lot of slipping."

I try to do the math. About ten minutes a slip. A month's worth of slipping. A hundred forty-four slips for a full day. It'd be…a number I can't do in my head.

"It's like four-thousand something. I've never done more than sixteen."

Mariana whistles, then grabs a *queijada* off the plate and bites into it. "I don't know what I'd do if Avó didn't live with us," she says around the custardy crumbles.

I finally take one and nibble at it. It's still a little warm from the oven. The entire house smells good, like Mariana's home, like half a dozen foods being prepared at once. I love Mom, but with just the two of us, she doesn't need to cook every day because there are always leftovers. Even then, she usually prepares something simple, like lasagna or tacos.

Sometimes, I wonder if I'd be more grounded in a home like the Salvadore house, where there's always something on the stove, family and friends coming and going, and there's really no chance to hear your own thoughts. Or maybe I'd just be twice as anxious.

"Alright. How about this? What if you write him a letter, and I deliver it, but I don't tell you when?"

Her proposal has some merit. If I wrote a letter and handed it to her, I'd have no idea when exactly Ethan would read the words. There'd be a chance to convey everything I need to without spiraling into multiple slips. But—

"Ugh. A letter." I wrinkle my nose.

She throws her hands into the air. "I know. It stinks! But what's the alternative? How are you ever going to get to tell him in person if you slip as soon as he hears the news?"

I take another bite of the queijada. "I'll think about it."

She doesn't push me further.

My phone pings with a text message. I dread looking at it, but it could be Mom, so I can't ignore it.

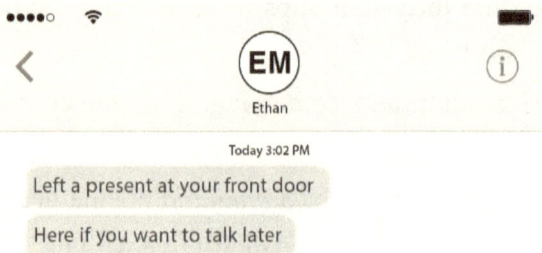

I groan and show the screen to Mariana.

She pouts. "He's really kind of sweet."

"I knooooow," I wail.

"Okay, time for something else."

"Huh?"

She pulls me up by my arm. "Avó and mom need help in the kitchen. Come shell some walnuts with me."

"Walnuts?"

"It's that or potatoes."

So I spend the next hour in the kitchen, shelling walnuts with

Mariana. Her dad won't be home from work until six, and Luis and Marco are both at the garage. The sight of this kitchen filled with women and counters piled high with ingredients that will soon be turned into all manner of mouth-watering treats is almost too much to take. It feels... simple. Cozy. And Mariana's mom doesn't stop asking questions for a second, leaving me little time to think of anything but the answers to her questions. School, clubs, grades, sports, my mom, holiday plans, and on and on.

Of course, that was probably Mariana's plan all along.

When we're finally released from our kitchen work, Mariana offers to walk home with me, but I think I'd rather get in a run before heading home.

"Then you're on your own because Mariana doesn't run," she says, speaking about herself in third person.

I smile and lean in to hug her. I knew she would bail as soon as I said I needed a run, and while I cherish her company, now that I'm going to be on my own for a few hours, I definitely need a run.

She holds me tighter than normal. "Love you, *garota*. No more slips today, okay?"

I nod into her hair. "That's the plan."

"Go. Run your heart out. Text me later?"

"Later." Smiling takes energy, but I do. For Mariana, I do.

Then I'm off, my feet hitting the ground in a soothing rhythm, my pulse hammering in my ears in a refreshing way, my breath puffing into the cold air. I run for miles. I run past sunset. I run until I'm dripping with sweat.

When I finally reach my house, the porch is dark. I slip my phone from my jacket. It's after six-thirty. Mom's not home yet, but she shouldn't be too much longer. I have an hour to clean myself up, wash my sweat-soaked jacket, and pretend that everything is normal.

My sneaker brushes against something solid on the porch. I look down in the darkness at a cylindrical object between the brick of the house and the door.

A jar. I unlock the front door, and flip the switch for the front porch light to reveal a mason jar filled with…

I lean to pick it up and the aroma hits my nose without even unscrewing the lid. Cider. It's Ethan's mom's cider.

The boy is going to be the death of me.

CHAPTER NINETEEN

I don't text Ethan back right away. I'm so spent from trying to break up with him and from slipping that I don't have the energy. It's only later, while Mom is at the kitchen island handling bills and I head to my room with a mug of reheated cider, Pablo bouncing up the stairs behind me, that I realize I should probably get back to him.

I set the mug on my desk and close my bedroom door. Pablo jumps onto the desk, his kitten paws sliding across a few of my papers with his overexcited leap, and sniffs at the steam rising from the mug. He paws at it tentatively. I ruffle his furry head.

"Can't catch that, silly. It's even more elusive than that scary red dot you like to chase. Also, please don't knock over my mug."

He looks up at me and gives a full-throated, hearty mew.

"You want the red dot, huh?"

I pull out the laser pointer and run him in circles around my room until he's panting from the exertion and falls on the floor in surrender. His little, pink tongue hangs out, and he looks at me begrudgingly as though I *made* him run somehow. I laugh.

"I know the feeling, Pablo. But it's good to be tired sometimes, isn't it?"

That feeling saves me, running myself into exhaustion. My muscles ache in fatigue from my run today, and yet, I'll do it again tomorrow. And the day after that, and the day after that.

At least I have some hours at the library tomorrow. That should help.

I sigh. I can't put this off any longer.

I snap a photo of my mug and send it to Ethan, only noticing the Jupiter lollipop in the background afterwards. Damn. How did Ethan slide into my life so quickly? It's like everywhere I look, there's a reminder of his existence.

I pause. Am I okay? No, of course I'm not okay. I'm a mess. And I can't even tell him I'm a mess without becoming more of a mess.

I bite my thumbnail until it hurts. Tears begin to well in my eyes. I wish I *could* talk to Ethan.

I can't help it. I laugh a little, even with tears in my eyes. I wish I could call him. I wish I could hear his voice on the other end of the line. But that's not a good idea. Hearing him will lead me to slip, and I've had enough slipping for one day.

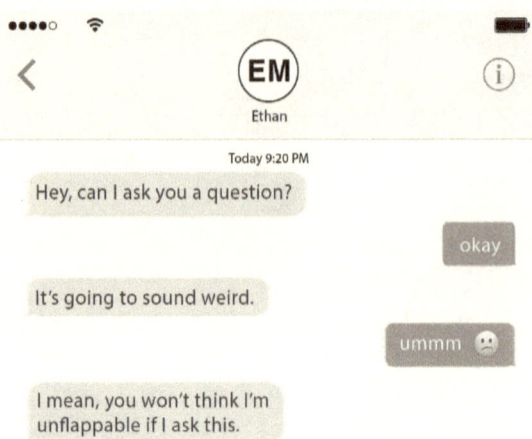

My heart starts to thud a little harder in my chest. What's Ethan about to ask? My mind races through the possibilities. He wants to talk about Christmas gifts. (He's not Jewish, btw.) He's leaving for California again, after all. He's breaking up with me.

At that last thought, a bark of a laugh escapes my throat.

What's wrong with me? How could I panic about him wanting to break up with me when it would make *all* of this so much easier? I wait as the three bouncing dots finally give way to a message.

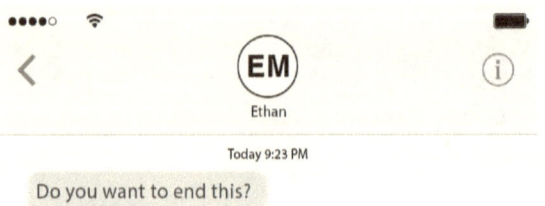

If I say *yes* right now, will I slip? Would it lead to a conversation where I'll slip again? Or could I get through this via text without dooming myself? My legs ache. I want to run, but I don't think my muscles would hold up. So I play dumb.

Ethan

Today 9:24 PM

do i want to...end this?

Alright. Listen. I —
Hey, can I call?

Now my heart *slams* into my ribs.

no. cant talk. mom's in bed
early shift in am

dont want to wake her
w talking

what's going on
?

It's hard to explain

try?

There's a distinct possibility
you'll think I'm crazy.

id never

I just...feel like you want to
end things. And I don't want
to hold you up if that's what
you really want. I guess I just
felt like maybe your panic
attack today had to do with
me. And then I started
thinking. Do I want to be
someone who causes that
kind of negativity? Hell, no!
I don't want to bring that
kind of crap into anyone's
life. So I guess what I'm
saying is if you don't actually
want to be together, you can
tell me and we can end this.
And omg, please tell me I'm
just crazy. Bc I think hearing
that I'm crazy would be
better than hearing I'm
someone you don't want to
be with

wow

I can't believe I just used Ethan's own words against him. Well, word. What is *wrong* with me? This is it. This is my opportunity. My way out.

And—oh, God—I don't want out. Horrified, I drop my phone to the desk. I'm trapped.

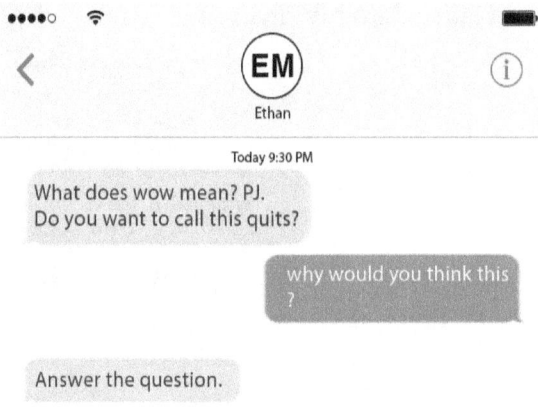

This is it. My out. What am I doing?

of course not!

I groan and lay my head on the desk, pressing my forehead against the cool wood.

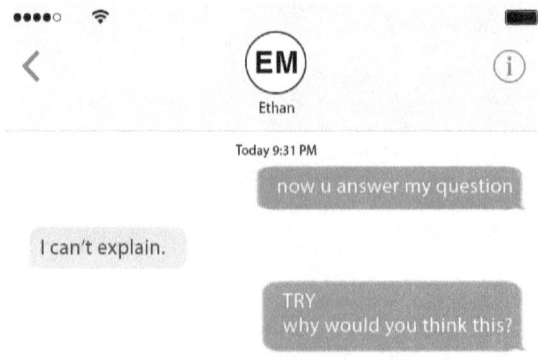

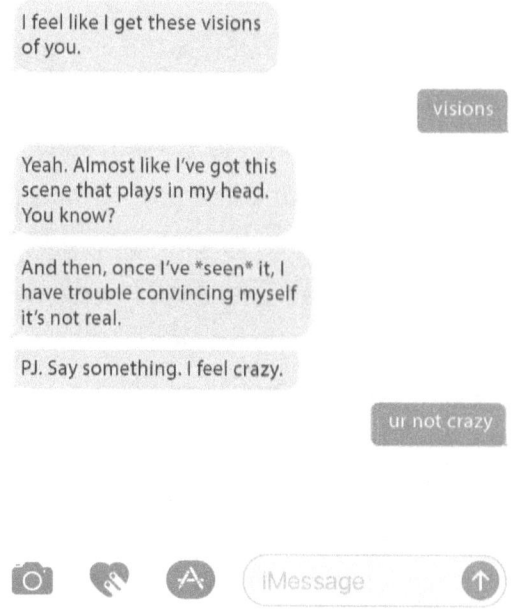

Then *I* do something crazy. I call him.

He picks up before I even hear the line ring. "Hey."

"Hey." I force myself to talk through the pulse that's hammering in my ears while I tap my fingers. I will *not* slip.

"Do you think I need a therapist again?" he asks weakly.

"No." My voice is low, filled with emotion. I'll let him think it's because my mom is sleeping.

"I'll go if you go. You can go for your panic attacks, and I'll go for these crazy thoughts." Then he gives a pathetic laugh, sounding so unlike my Ethan. Where is the confident, easygoing, funny boy I know? He sniffs.

Oh God. Is he crying?

"Ethan, maybe…"

"Don't say it. Don't you dare."

"Maybe it'd be better if we took a break." I rush forward, letting the words tumble from my mouth, not giving myself time to think about their meaning.

If I tell Ethan I want to stay together, we'll stay together, and I'll be forced to face the same predicament day after day, week after week. I think I could fall in love with him if I let myself, and I've gotten used to slipping, used to my own brand of crazy, but...I can't deal with driving someone else crazy. And if Ethan remembers every time I slip, what would that eventually do to him? Who would he eventually become? If he knew I was the culprit, would he resent me?

"Why did I know you were going to say it?"

I sigh, fighting back my own tears. "I don't want to, but I... Well, maybe we just step back for a little, yeah?"

"I don't want to step back, PJ."

After a long silence, I answer, "I don't want to either."

"Then—"

"It's temporary," I tell him.

Liar.

"Temporary?"

"Yeah. There's so much going on, Ethan. Your job, my job, the trail cleanup stuff, school, the holidays. Let's just breathe until after the New Year. It doesn't...have to be weird between us."

It will be.

But if I can get through the New Year, I have a chance at keeping him at a distance, and that's good for him *and* good for me.

Even if my heart feels like it's twisting into a knot inside my chest. I never imagined "heartache" meant my heart would physically ache. I mean, I knew the word existed, but I always thought it was a metaphor.

"How would it not be weird? I feel like we've just opened up this box and spilled everything out. You can't just...pick it all up and shove it back in. The stuff doesn't want to go back in the box, PJ. You can't force it."

I wipe a tear. "I know. But this isn't Pandora's Box. It's *our* box." I don't know what I'm saying anymore. I'm not even making sense. "Let's just…put the box on a shelf for a month. We can leave the lid open so it doesn't all have to fit."

"A month."

"I think it would help."

"Is that what you want?"

I close my eyes.

"Yeah," I whisper. "Just for a little while."

"Then that's what we do." Ethan's voice sounds stronger now, like somehow hearing me confirm his worst fear is better than him imagining it.

He's already healing. He's moving on. At least, that's what I'll tell myself.

"No Christmas gifts," I say. Because somehow I can see Ethan buying a gift for me even if we aren't dating.

"What if I already—"

"No."

"How do we handle school?"

"Like we always have. I make my mediocre clay sculptures. You listen to music and create masterpieces."

He's silent a long while.

"Ethan?"

"Yeah."

"I have to go."

If I stay on the line any longer, I'm either going to slip or going to go back on my words, and I can't afford to do either.

"'Kay."

This is really awful. How do I hang up now? How do we end this conversation?

"Don't be a stranger," he says, attempting to sound more like himself.

Now I sniff. "Bye, Ethan," I whisper.

I end the call and let my phone drop to the carpet as though it might explode in my hand. Then I pull my knees up, wrap my arms around them, and sob quietly to myself.

It's done.

At least it's done.

CHAPTER TWENTY

It is *not* done. Because everywhere I go, Ethan is there. And not just everywhere I go, but everywhere I don't go, too.

I've fallen into a cycle I don't know how to break.

I stay over at Mariana's on Tuesday night, as planned, but Marco brings Ethan home for a couple of hours. Mariana and I don't realize it right away, of course. We're hanging out in her room, gabbing, listening to music, and pretending I've never known Ethan Morrow.

It's only when the two of us are standing in the kitchen, debating if we might get away with stealing a couple of slices of warm bread slathered in homemade *jaboticaba* jam specifically set aside for their Thanksgiving meal, when Ethan and Marco walk in from the driveway, a basketball under Marco's arm.

"Hey, PJ!" Marco says. "Long time, no see!"

I swallow, and my gaze darts to Mariana, who's fixated on Ethan.

"Yeah," I force out. "Good to see you, Marco."

But I look at Ethan when I speak.

Seeing him is a shock. I wasn't expecting to see him so soon after… well, I figured I'd have at least until school starts again next week. He looks just as surprised to see me.

"I didn't know you'd be here," he said.

"It's okay," Mariana intervenes. "We were just heading back upstairs."

She grabs my arm and the two of us return to her room, my heart racing, the pressure in my veins building even as I'm taking the stairs.

I hardly make it to the bedroom when I feel it happening. I can't—

We're in Mariana's room again. Still? Again? I don't even know anymore.

"Hey, I'm starved. I think Avó made fresh jaboticaba for Thanksgiving. You wanna go pilfer some from the kitchen? It's so good on warm bread," she says. Again.

I stare at Mariana, my eyes wide with the knowledge of who's bouncing the basketball I hear echoing in the driveway, of just how close Ethan is without my even suspecting.

"What? It is!"

I shake my head and draw a ragged breath.

"Dammit, you just slipped, didn't you?" She curses again. "In *my* house? Why are you anxious here, Peej? You don't slip here. You don't!"

"Ethan's outside."

She stands so quickly she drags her leg against the nightstand at an awkward angle.

"Ow! Ow, ow, ow!" She hops around the room, holding her thigh. "That's going to leave a huge bruise. Ugh! What do you mean Ethan's outside?"

"He and Marco are playing basketball in the driveway." I close my eyes, slow my heart.

"What?" She sounds unconvinced but limps to the window to peer out the blinds.

I can see the floodlight from where I sit, though I can't see the figures of the two people I know are playing ball below.

"Damn," she breathes. "Since when do he and Marco hang out?"

"Probably since they started working together at the garage."

She turns to me. "Does he know you're here?"

I shake my head. "No."

She presses her lips together. "Let's keep it that way."

And we would have.

Except that twenty minutes later, Marco busts into Mariana's room. "Hey, troll, where's Avó stashing the jaboticaba jam? I know she made some today. The whole kitchen still smells like it."

Ethan stands behind Marco in the hall, the look of shock on his face probably mirroring mine. He wasn't supposed to learn I was here. That's why we didn't go to the kitchen for a snack.

Mariana throws a pillow at Marco. "Get out, cretin! You can't just barge into my room whenever you want."

"I just did," Marco retorts.

"Yeah, well, maybe I'll extend the same courtesy to you when you're not expecting it and see how you like it. Go ask Avó where the jam is if you need it so badly." She motions him from the room, pointing a finger at the door.

He makes a face at her. Then he gives me a smile and a quick head bob. "Hey, PJ! Long time, no see."

"Hi, Marco. Hi, Ethan."

"Hey." Ethan's "hey" is missing its usual enthusiasm, sending a physical ache spiraling through my chest.

Then Marco makes another face at Mariana and closes the door.

She rushes to my side and sits next to me, grabbing my hand. "Slip, I'm so sorry. Are you okay? I should have locked the door."

"I'm okay."

I'm not okay. I may never again be okay.

But I'm going to have to be okay with not being okay.

Thanksgiving itself is a brief respite. Mom is home. She almost always has to work on holidays, but the hospital is fully staffed, which means she's making a ridiculously large turkey for the two of us. I'm in charge of sweet potatoes, but she's given me the kind from a can with loads of sugar and butter, so I don't have to attempt to cook raw tubers pulled from the ground. At least there's that.

Yes, Thanksgiving Day is good.

Except for the parts where I feel like poop because I'm thinking of Ethan.

Which is a lot, actually.

Mostly when Mom asks how Ethan is doing. Or how Ethan is enjoying his new job. Or how I'm ever going to spend time with Ethan when I'm working now, too. Or where Ethan plans to go to college. Or how Ethan's mom is doing. I carefully steer the conversation clear of Ethan again and again.

But over pumpkin pie, there's no escaping it. I finally have to come clean.

"What are Ethan and his mom doing today?" My mom cuts another sliver of pumpkin pie and puts it on her plate.

I don't know why she took such a tiny piece to begin with. She was definitely going back for seconds. She always does. I reach to cut myself a second slice, too. I cut mine significantly larger than hers.

"Uh, I don't know. I think it's just him and his mom."

"Oh, PJ! Why didn't you say something? We could have invited them over. It's just the two of us and the two of them! They aren't visiting with family or anything?"

Suddenly, the whipped cream I'm spooning on top of my pie doesn't appeal to me nearly as much as it did a few seconds ago. There doesn't seem to be a better way to say it, so I just…say it.

"Ethan and I broke up," I blurt.

Mom puts her fork down on her plate, clears her throat, and looks at me. She looks at me in a way that makes it impossible for me to look back. I can't. I keep my gaze on my plate instead. Pressure builds behind my eyes again, threatening a storm of tears, my pumpkin pie suddenly wavering in my vision. I don't want to cry. It's Thanksgiving!

Then a tear plops onto my dessert plate, a fat droplet impossible to miss.

"Oh, sweetie. I'm so sorry." She puts a hand to my shoulder and squeezes.

I shake my head, my voice too untrustworthy right now.

"Did he end it? Want to go egg his car together?"

I can't help it. I laugh through the tears. Only Mom would suggest such a thing.

"God, Mom, no." And she's broken the spell. I talk. Even though I'm still sad, somehow, my voice is free. "I broke it off. I just... I don't know. I feel like it was getting serious too fast, and, like, I didn't... Like, I couldn't offer a hundred percent, you know?"

It's weird talking about this with Mom, but Mom has always understood everything. We're mother and daughter, sure, but we're also friends. We've only got the two of us. Mom's parents live in Florida, and she never had a great relationship with them to begin with, so it's always just been me and her, her and me.

"Did he...pressure you?" she prompts. It takes me a moment to get what she means.

"Are you talking about sex? Mom, we were dating for, like, three weeks!"

And I thought Mom understood everything. Internally, I cringe.

"Okay, okay. I just had to ask. Is he at least a good kisser? Or is he, like, slobbery? Nothing is worse than a slobbery kisser." She makes a face.

I groan and put a bite of pumpkin pie into my mouth to avoid answering. Then, I try to avoid remembering. Ethan is a very good kisser.

Was.

Ethan was *a very good kisser.*

There will be no more kissing now. No more feeling my fingers and toes tingle with anticipation of his lips on mine.

"I'm not answering that question, so you can stop looking at me like that," I finally say.

"Alright, so what happened?"

I sigh. "I just need to step back. School, the library, you know. It's just too much, too fast."

"College," she reminds me.

My gut clenches.

"Have you thought about where you'd like to go yet? I know you like the job at the library, and it's fine that you work six hours a week, but it's really important you start thinking about what you want to do after high school, PJ. SATs are coming up in the spring. We should probably arrange a few college tours sometime soon. I feel like I'm already late on planning those for you."

"I know."

At least we're off the topic of Ethan now. I should be grateful.

"Anyway, there's time enough for it. Don't get overwhelmed, and I'm here if you want to talk. Now finish that pie, and help me with the dishes."

And that's that.

The library is open the day after Thanksgiving, but it's quiet. Most people are probably out Christmas shopping. Sorting and shelving books is calming. I'm finally coming to terms with the fact that Ethan and I are over. Really over. I still wish I hadn't seen him (twice) on Tuesday, but he hasn't texted me at all this week.

Maybe he's healing, too.

Then Ethan opens the door to the library as I'm leaving work, and I nearly run face-first into his chest. I register his scent before I tilt my head to meet the gaze of the boy standing in front of me. It's achingly familiar, that scent, and before I've thought about what I'm doing, I inhale the intoxicating smell of Ethan/Ethan's cologne/Ethan's deodorant. Then, I *remember*.

And it hurts. Oh, how it hurts.

"Sorry!" he says. "I didn't think you were still working this late. I didn't..." He motions with his hands, making it known he never intended to run into me.

"It's okay," I say. But it's not. I'm already aching inside, and the pressure is building in my veins.

"How are you?" I ask because it seems like the right thing to do.

"Uh, you know. Good."

He looks good. I mean, he looks upset but good. His hair is a little tousled like he was just running his hands through it a moment ago, and his normally bright, hazel eyes don't glitter the way they usually do in the lamplight.

He's hurting.

Oh, God, he's hurting, and it's my—

—fault. It's my fault, but it never happens because I'm thrown back into my body almost ten minutes earlier, standing in front of the W-Z section of the adult fiction with a cart I've nearly finished shelving.

I close my eyes, clutch the book I'm holding to my chest, and slide down the shelf until I'm sitting on the floor. Then I rest my head on my knees and breathe the musty smell of the books to calm my racing heart.

It's okay. It's going to be okay.

I'll avoid Ethan. I'll hang out in the break room for an extra twenty minutes until I'm sure he's already in the library and then I'll sneak out the back entrance.

So that's what I do.

I sit in the break room and scroll Instagram, sharing another photo of Pablo being his cute self. I don't share much else online. Now I'm doubly glad I never posted any photos of me and Ethan. I'd have to delete them, and then people would notice. All twenty-four of my followers... who are mostly kids from school who will find out eventually anyway. If they ever noticed we were a thing to begin with.

Huh.

Ethan posted a photo fifty-six minutes ago.

I shouldn't do it, but I click. He'll never know I looked, right?

A close-up image of a Neptune lollipop fills my screen. The caption below it reads *Some days don't feel real. #WellAlwaysHaveTheNightSky #SpacePops #EatYourPlanets*

Ugh. Ethan. What are you doing to me? I close out Instagram. I can't.

I glance at the clock on the wall. It should be safe now. Ethan should be somewhere inside the building so I can slip out the back entrance.

I pull my jacket on, then peek my head into Ms. Hoffman's office.

"Heading out now," I say.

Only the top of her head is visible from behind a wall of books on her desk. She stretches over them, and I see the hint of her eyes and the tip of her nose. "Oh, PJ! I thought your shift ended twenty minutes ago. What are you still doing here?"

"I got distracted by the pumpkin donuts in the break room," I tell her with a grin. I didn't eat any of the donuts, but she doesn't need to know that.

"Don't remind me! Between that and the leftover pie at home, ugh!

So much sugar! Have a good weekend. I'll see you Monday afternoon."

"Sounds good. Bye, Ms. Hoffman!" I wave, then head down the back hallway.

I halt, defeated, when I get to the back door. It's hooked up to the fire alarm. I won't be leaving this way.

Still, Ethan should already be in the library doing... Wait, what *is* he doing here anyway?

I shake my head. He's probably working on a school project due in the last couple weeks of the semester. Or returning books he borrowed.

It doesn't matter. He's allowed to use the *public* library.

I head to the lobby and to the front entrance...and run directly into Ethan. Again.

"Ethan, hi."

What is he doing here? Why is he only entering the library now? He should have gotten here twenty-five minutes ago.

"Oh, hey!" He drags a hand through his hair. "Sorry, I...thought you'd already be home by now."

I narrow my eyes. Why is he coming in just as I'm leaving...again?

"Were you waiting for me to leave?" I ask, my tone just a little more accusatory than I'd like.

"What? No! There's an accident on Carson Boulevard. Traffic is backed up for half a mile. I got stuck in it. I didn't mean to get here just as you were leaving, though. I swear. I thought your shift ended a half-hour ago."

His face is open, honest. He's telling the truth, which only makes me seem even more like a paranoid lunatic.

"Oh." There's really nothing more I can say.

Why does Ethan still smell so good?

"Anyway, uh, I'll see you." He gives a nod of his head and heads into the library.

"See you," I say in return.

Running into Ethan after a slip. Twice in one week.

I can't help it. I look over my shoulder as he passes through the lobby and into the main library, his walk so familiar I almost ache to be walking beside him.

What is it about this boy? Why doesn't he want to let go? Why does he keep showing up again, even when I slip, even when I make a point to avoid him?

I furrow my brow. I don't want to be mean to him, but if life or fate or destiny or whatever wild force this is keeps shoving him in my face, I might have to—for my sake *and* his. It'd be better for both of us.

I shake my head as I start my walk home.

If only I could figure out how to slip four thousand times in a row, life would be so much easier.

CHAPTER TWENTY-ONE

Once I'm back at school on Monday, Operation Snub Ethan is fully underway. Clay class is unavoidable, but at least it's first period, so I can get it over with. Ethan does exactly as I recommended and keeps his earbuds in. I strongly suspect there's no music in them, but I guess I can't exactly grab his phone and verify he's got tunes playing.

But the rest of the day should be easy. Except for passing in the hallways between classes, I almost never run into him. Easy-peasy.

"PJ!" Miss Fulton waves me over in the middle of gym class as she hangs up the old black rotary phone attached to the wall.

We're sprinting back and forth across the gymnasium to warm up for indoor soccer, so I'm grateful for the break, whatever it is she wants from me.

I reach the corner of the gym where she stands. "Can you head down to the office? They've got a cart with a shipment of new equipment. They don't want it sitting there through the end of the day. Apparently, it's blocking the seating area." She rolls her eyes to show what she thinks of the necessity of the seating area in the office.

"Sure, Miss Fulton."

"Somehow, I don't think our cross-country star is in need of sprints. You've got plenty of miles under your belt. Am I right?"

If only she knew how many miles I run when it's breakup season.

I nod, then turn to head to the office. The gym is on the other side of the building, pretty much as far from the office as you can get, so if I time this right, I can probably miss the first half of indoor soccer. Nice.

They're expecting me when I show up at the office a few minutes later.

"Oh, hi, PJ," Ms. Harmon says from behind her desk. She's got the phone to her ear, but she covers the receiver. "It's the big cart right over there. Can you handle it? Do you want me to have Miss Fulton send one of the boys down instead?"

I wave her off with a smile. "No, it's fine. It's got wheels. I'll just take my time getting back to the gym. It'll be okay."

A boy. Of course she would ask if I need a boy. Really, Ms. Harmon.

I almost want to ask what decade she's living in, but that might get interpreted as the attitude it is, and I'd almost certainly end up with detention. She means well. I just have to remind myself she means well.

I get the first set of wheels over the threshold of the door before the cart gets stuck, and I have to give it a heave to get the second set of wheels over.

And then I crash directly into Ethan Morrow in the hall directly outside.

"Whoa!" He jumps out of the way, but between my pushing the cart and then my steering to avoid him, the boxes of equipment tip, and a box of soccer balls and volleyballs spills open, sending balls rolling down the main hallway.

"Oh my goodness!" Ms. Harmon jumps from her seat as she watches the commotion unfold. "Hang on, I'll give you a hand." She turns back to the phone. "I'm so sorry. Can I call you right back?"

But Ethan waves her off. "Don't worry about Ms. Harmon. I'll help. We'll take care of it."

She looks doubtful as she nods to us, but she's grateful not to have to end an important call, I'm sure. I, on the other hand, would rather spend the next five minutes being lectured by Ms. Harmon on how I should be careful than cleaning up this mess with the one boy in the entire universe I'm deliberately trying to avoid.

"What are you doing here?" I ask.

"Copies." He holds up a paper. "Mr. Whirl sent me to the office to make photocopies."

Now's my chance. If I'm really going to snub Ethan, I need to do it before I slip in his presence. Then he'll remember whatever weird, awkward, horrible thing happens, and even though it never happened in the new version, he'll be afraid of it happening, and he'll want to stay away.

The very thought of making a scene sends my pulse skittering. What if I make a scene, and then I *don't* slip?

It has to be done.

Ethan sets the paper down on one of the office chairs, then returns to the hall to start gathering volleyballs, tossing them into the open, righted box one by one.

"Are you following me?" I yell. My words echo off the empty hallway walls. I grab a volleyball and throw it at him. He wasn't expecting the move, so it bounces off his shoulder. "Are you deliberately trying to make my life miserable?"

Ethan looks as though I've just landed a punch. He stumbles back a step, his gaze darting to the office, to Ms. Harmon—to anyone—for help.

My pulse hammers, the pressure in my veins building quickly. I would *never* dream about doing this for real. If I thought there was even a chance I wouldn't slip, I'd never contemplate this, but there's no getting away from it. A small consolation, at least.

"Wh-what?" Ethan stammers.

"I thought I made it clear I don't want to see you again! I specifically said that you and I, this? We can't do this! And then you show up at the office because you knew I was going to be here? That's ridiculous, Ethan. It's desperate! *You're* desperate." I kick a soccer ball as hard as I can off the wall. It ricochets into Ethan, who blocks it with the back of an arm.

Ms. Harmon drops the phone and races to the doorway of the office, her heels clacking on the linoleum floor the whole way. I'm sure she thinks she's dealing with a head case. *A student who's lost her mind, oh no! Call the police. Call social services.*

It's okay. She won't remember any of this in a moment. I kick the three closest balls to me down the hall without a care how far they might go.

"PJ!" she says, her eyes wide with incredulity. "What is going *on* out here?"

"Nothing, just that Ethan Morrow's stalking me because I won't go out with him." Her head whips around to face Ethan, the attention suddenly on him instead of me.

Ethan's brows draw downward—a mix of anger and confusion I've never seen on his face before. "PJ, are you—"

Then I'm back in the gym, stumbling a little as I fall into a body that's currently in the middle of changing directions mid-sprint. My sneakers squeak on the gym floor.

Thank God. I don't want to hear what Ethan was about to say. I don't want to know. But the possibilities echo in my mind anyway. I stifle a sob that's caught in my throat.

PJ, are you on drugs?

PJ, are you out of your mind?

PJ, are you crazy?

Yes, Ethan. I'm very, very crazy right now.

"PJ!" Miss Fulton waves at me from the wall phone.

I stop sprinting and take a moment to breathe as I walk to where she stands, reminding myself that I didn't say those awful things to Ethan, that it never happened, that I'm not the awful, horrible person I just behaved as in the first version of these events.

"Can you head down to the office? They've got a cart with a shipment of new equipment. They don't want it sitting there through the end of the day. Apparently, it's blocking the seating area."

"Sure, Miss Fulton."

"Somehow, I don't think our cross-country star is in need of sprints. You've got plenty of miles under your belt. Am I right?"

"Mmhmm."

I head to the office, this time fully aware of what—or rather who—I'll encounter.

"Oh, hi, PJ," Ms. Harmon says from behind her desk. Again. "It's the big cart right over there. Can you handle it? Do you want me to have Miss Fulton send one of the boys down instead?"

"No, it's fine. Ethan Morrow's in the hallway. I'll get him to help me wheel it out."

With perfect timing, Ethan walks into the office, holding a paper Mr. Whirl handed him to photocopy. On the phone, Ms. Harmon hardly notices.

"Hey," Ethan says, his eyes darting back and forth from me to Ms. Harmon. No doubt he's wondering what I just signed him up for.

And he's probably on edge from having some sort of premonition of how he thinks this is going to go.

"Hey," I say. "Can you just give me a hand getting the cart through the door? I can take it after that."

He blinks and sets the paper down on one of the chairs. "Oh, sure."

After he helps me wheel it into the hallway without incident, he stops and gives me a funny look.

"What?"

He licks his lips, his brows drawing together as he looks at me entirely too close for comfort. "You ever get a weird sort of déjà vu?"

I press my lips together and give him my most bored look. "No."

He makes a "hmph," but continues to help wheel the cart down the main hallway.

"I got it from here," I tell him. "Just needed help getting it through the doorway."

"Oh, yeah. Sure. Okay."

He still seems preoccupied. Hopefully, he's remembering all the awful things I said and did in version 1.1, and he'll have one less reason to want to be anywhere near me.

My heart hurts.

He lets go of the cart and steps back so I can take it to the gym. I try not to inhale as I walk past him, but it's useless. My body is trained to sniff Ethan like a drug.

As a result, I give him an extra-grumpy "Thanks."

"Sure." He stands with his hands at his side, watching me guide the cart down the hallway. I don't look back to see how long he stands there.

I encounter a similar scenario on Wednesday. Mariana volunteers to tutor again, so I'm by myself for my walk home. No big deal. I've done it dozens of times before. Of course, the last time I did it, Ethan showed up no matter which route I took.

So I decided to get creative. I figure I'll wait and make sure he leaves the building ahead of me before I start the walk home. I know which hall his locker is in, and it's no big deal to be sure he's visited and gone from it before I stop at my own locker and pack up for the day. That way, he can't sneak up behind me this time.

I'm five minutes into my walk home when I see Ethan coming down a cross street. How this is even possible, I'm not sure, but the pressure in my veins is already building, so I might as well do something stupid before I slip. Let Operation Snub Ethan continue full speed ahead.

I wait until he sees me before I do an obvious about-face and walk in the complete opposite direction. Then I look over my shoulder to make sure he *knows* he's the reason I'm running away…and immediately wish I hadn't.

Ethan looks crushed. The hurt on his face is visible even from this distance. I force myself to keep walking. I'm doing him a favor. I have to remember that. In the long run, this is better for him.

I didn't plan on slipping this time. This shouldn't be enough to make me slip. I'm sad, sure, but I'm not panicking, not exactly—

Nine minutes and fifty-three seconds earlier, I was just leaving the school.

Which is what I'm doing now. Again.

I don't want to see Ethan. It hurts too much, and it's not just him I'm hurting. There's a physical pain beneath my ribcage. I slump and sit on the wall of the raven fountain. I wish there were a better solution to this whole thing, but I can't think of anything.

Instead of leaving school to head home, I scour the hallways to find where Mariana's tutoring. I might as well just sit and do my homework and wait for her. I don't want to run into Ethan right now. I just—

—smack directly into Ethan as I'm turning the corner into the main hallway.

Why am I always literally running into him?

"What are you still doing here?" I blurt, sounding every bit the snot I've decided I have to be when I see him.

"I'm meeting Rich for a Spanish project. What are *you* doing here?

Aren't you supposed to be at the library?"

Damn! I have a job. At the library. I can't wait for Mariana. I'm supposed to start at four.

I can't believe I forgot. Ethan has me so unsettled that I've completely forgotten my own schedule.

"I'm just leaving," I say.

He turns and watches as I pass, like he wants to say something. *Please don't*, I pray. I can't be mean again right now. I'm completely out of my head. I need my routine. In fact, maybe I'll run home, even with the book bag.

At least as I walk past Ethan this time, I manage not to make it obvious that I'm inhaling. It doesn't help. I still catch a hint of his scent after I'm down the hall. It's still so pleasant that I hold onto every last atom, like the Ethan-druggie I seem to be these days.

I'm halfway home (jogging, not really running) when I think about the fact that Ethan shouldn't have been at school. I saw him leave. I watched him close his locker and leave the school.

So how did I run into him in version 1.2, and why wasn't he walking home in that version? Why was he still at school?

Nothing makes sense.

Unless he and Rich only made the plans to get together in version 1.2 after I saw him at his locker in version 1.1, but...

I thought I was the only one who could change and make different decisions in my repeat time of nine minutes and fifty-three seconds. Everyone else always seems to be on a set path. It's always been that way before. So why not now? Why is Ethan different?

Later, I'm just finishing up at the library when I text him. I need to know. Did Rich make plans with Ethan, or did Ethan make plans with Rich? It shouldn't make a difference to me, but it does.

I wait for him to reply. Will he? I don't know if I would reply if someone were as mean to me as I was to him. Not that it was in this version of reality, but still.

My mind runs in circles. Even two hours of alphabetizing and shelving books hasn't stopped my dizzy brain from spinning. If Rich asked Ethan to work on their Spanish project after school today, it means *anyone* can change their minds and make things different in version 1.2, which I didn't think was possible, but at least it would mean there's nothing special about Ethan.

But if Ethan asked Rich, it means Ethan changed the course of events from version 1.1, not Rich. And he changed more than just the course of a conversation. Ethan changed *where* he was supposed to be and when. And he's the only person I've ever known who can do that, aside from me.

My mind drifts back to the first time he caught up with me when I was walking home and how when I slipped and decided to take another route home, he was still there. How could he have done that? At the time, Mariana said it was no big deal. But clearly, it is.

I glance at my phone.

I groan. He read it right away. It's been six minutes. He's not going to respond.

I trek home in a miserable mood, texting Mariana as I go. Damn, it's cold. I need a pair of gloves. Or a driver's license and a car. I blow on my free hand to warm my fingers enough to type.

The phone rings in my hand. I answer it and put the phone to my ear.

"Thank goodness. It's freezing out here. I can't text."

"I could come give you a ride. If you need." Ethan's voice is soft in my ear and so utterly unexpected that I drop my phone. It bounces off the concrete slab of the sidewalk and into the frozen grass.

I fumble in the dark, praying I didn't just break my phone or crack the screen.

Why is Ethan calling?

When my fingers close around the phone, I shove it to my ear without even inspecting it first.

"I'm sorry," I say. "I just dropped the phone."

"Really *is* freezing, I guess. Do you want me to pick you up?"

I don't answer his question. "I thought you were Mariana."

As if Mariana hears me, the other line rings. It's Mariana, but there's no way I can hang up on Ethan after I just dropped the phone on him.

"I'm definitely not Mariana. Too tall. Too white. Wrong gender."

I laugh. I don't want to but damn him. He's still got it. It almost makes me wish...

"So, what's up?" I ask as I start walking again. I shove my free hand in my pocket. I'll be home in five more minutes. Four, if I walk fast.

"You texted me. I figured it'd be easier to talk instead, and I...miss your voice."

I'm silent. I don't know how to respond to that.

"So, what's your question?"

"Huh?"

"You asked if you could ask me a question."

"Oh, yeah. It's stupid. I was just wondering if Rich asked you to work on the Spanish project today or if you asked him."

"You were...wondering if—"

"I know. It's dumb. That's why I texted. It's not phone-call-worthy."

"It's always worth talking to you." There's a soft honesty in his voice.

My heart. It hurts.

The other line beeps again.

"Anyway, Mariana's calling me a second time, so I have to run. But you and Rich?"

"That is definitely one of the weirdest questions anyone has ever asked me out of absolutely nowhere. I'll need to know why you need this information."

"Ethan. I know it's weird, but please?"

"I was planning to head home but ran into him and asked if he wanted to stick around and work on it."

And there's my answer. Ethan can alter his course of action in the nine minutes and fifty-three seconds of repeat time. Ethan. Is. Different.

"Thank you," I force out. "Have to go. I'll text you later."

I hang up and answer Mariana's call.

Then I groan.

"Good to talk to you, too," she says.

"I just told Ethan I'd text him later."

"Oh."

"I am *horrible* at Operation Snub Ethan."

"Or really good at Operation Save the Relationship."

I groan again.

CHAPTER TWENTY-TWO

When I've finished telling Mariana everything (from the warmth of my bedroom, with a cup of hot tea in my hands, from a phone that's inexplicably still in one piece), she's quiet—unusually quiet for Mariana.

"What?"

I can hear the hesitation when she finally starts to speak. "Peej, this is big. I mean, no one in your life has ever remembered any hint of version one, right? Not even me. And no one else has ever done anything other than what they were *supposed* to do, right? So, why? Why Ethan?"

"That's what I'm asking you," I reply.

"Yeah, well, I don't think you'll like my answer."

"You are—once again for the thousandth time—going to say I have to tell him, aren't you?"

She does.

She says it multiple times. Our conversation runs in circles until Pablo grows bored and falls asleep at the foot of my bed. I don't get my homework done. I don't even care. Between slipping, talking to Ethan unexpectedly, and talking to Mariana, I sleep hard.

And dream hard.

Dreams where I'm slipping day in and day out, where I slip so far that I finally *do* manage to avoid Ethan entirely. I'm free of my time with him. Free to leave him behind without ever texting him, or talking to him, or kissing him, or hurting him.

And it's horrible.

I wake drenched in sweat. It's so dark that I reach for my phone. Five a.m. There's no point in going back to bed now. I'll never fall asleep, and after that dream, I don't think I want to.

So I get up early and go for a run just as the sky turns that weird predawn color that makes everything seem like it's filtered blue.

Running is good. Really good. I need this.

I need this right up to the point where I reach the Halfpenny Creek trailhead and spot Ethan just coming off the trail.

You have got to be kidding me.

Before I can seriously contemplate changing directions, he spots me. He raises a hand, then turns and heads in the opposite direction off the trail, almost as though he's clearing the area, yielding so I can run. Grateful, I breathe a sigh of relief and make for the trail and the trees.

Ethan.

At six-thirty a.m.

It's too much to process.

The early run means I'm tired for most of the school day. I'm not used to getting up so early. And I completely forgot about my chemistry test. Mom's going to kill me. I'll be lucky if I've gotten a C.

And yet, weeks pass the same way. I mean, there are the holidays, and there are joyful moments, but I slip more often than not whenever I see Ethan, and it's getting hard not to be mean to him just out of spite. By the second semester of junior year, I can hardly keep my eyes open during classes because I spend all night dreaming and waking, then dreaming and waking again.

To make it worse, Ethan has Intro to Watercolor, so I still see him first period. Every. Single. Day. Mariana pulls me aside one frigid afternoon in mid-January. I'm not sure what day it is. I don't *think* I work at the library today.

"Slip." She adjusts her book bag on her shoulders as we leave the school behind. "I'm worried about you."

I shrug. I'd be worried about me too, but I'm so tired, I don't have the energy to worry at this point. I slipped today. I ran into Ethan after lunch. I screamed awful things, made a scene in front of hundreds of our classmates, and threw a banana at him. Who throws a banana? Crazy people, that's who.

Then I slipped, and none of it ever happened.

"What are you worried about?"

"*You*. And Ethan, too. You've been slipping, haven't you? And not telling me."

I suck in a breath. I haven't been telling Mariana when I slip. Mostly because I don't want to hear about how Ethan and I obviously cosmically connected somehow. And I'm tired. I'm tired of experiencing it every day. I'm tired of talking about it. I'm. So. Tired.

"Yeah." It would be stupid to try to lie to Mariana. She'd sense it coming from a million miles away.

"PJ! You promised. You swore you'd always tell me."

My eyes prick with tears, but an icy wind dries them before they can even crest the rim of my eye. I shove my hands deeper into my pockets and tuck my chin into my scarf, using my breath to warm my face.

"I know." My words are muffled by the chunky gray knit. "I'm sorry."

"How much?"

"How much what?" I ask.

"How many times have you slipped and not told me about it?"

I hesitate. Here's where she yells at me. I take a breath.

"Almost every day."

"Peej!"

"I know."

"Every day? Since when?" Her eyes are filled with concern. Worry. For me.

I try to calculate in my head. "Like, late November, maybe? Ever since I broke up with Ethan. I threw a banana at him today."

The words just slip out. I didn't mean to tell her about the banana.

"A banana! *November?*"

"Yeah." Yeah, times two.

"You aren't sleeping." She peers closer at me as we walk, as though she's just noticed I look like trash.

I shake my head.

"Are you slipping in your sleep?"

"I might be."

It wouldn't be the first time, and it *would* explain my extra fatigue.

"PJ, what are we going to do with you?"

I shrug again.

"There's nothing that can be done."

"Pardon my French, but that's bullshit."

"I'm pretty sure that's not French."

She shoves me in the shoulder. Not ready for it, I stumble off the curb. Ugh, I am tired. Normally, I'd have anticipated her shove.

"I'm serious. You need to move past this. It's been two months. It's time to tell Ethan. Whether or not you guys are together, he's haunting you, and you're clearly haunting him. He might be sleeping better than you, but not by much. Have you seen him lately?"

"Every damn day," I mutter.

"Yeah. He looks terrible. What are you *doing* to him in the versions that get erased? Other than throwing bananas, I mean."

My ears warm, despite the air temperature.

"Um. Well. I've called him a stalker. And told him he's a terrible kisser. I might have done that last one in front of a cafeteria full of people."

"Oh. My. God."

"I also dumped a cup of paint-water on him in art class. Right on his head. Then I knew I would slip a second time because I could still feel it in my veins, so in version two, I squeezed an entire tube of red paint onto his white shirt."

"PJ!"

I swallow.

"And I told him I never wanted to see him again."

"Okay, stop."

My throat closes. It's hard not to feel terrible about being terrible, regardless of the fact that it "never happened."

"That's pretty much the worst of it," I tell her.

"No, I mean STOP stop."

We're quickly approaching the corner where Mariana goes her way, and I go mine. I stare at the ground.

"This has to stop. *You* have to stop. You can't keep living like this, and you can't keep doing this to him, either."

I stand at the corner of the sidewalk and shift my weight to one foot.

"Enough. You're going to end up hurting him for real. Or hurting yourself."

"I know." My words are quiet. "But I don't know how to end this, how to stop it from happening. It's like...a runaway train, Mariana. I keep slipping, and he keeps showing up anyway."

She grabs my arms and makes me look at her. Her dark eyes are serious as they bore into mine. "Okay, listen. Here's what's going to happen. I want you to go home. Straight home. Call out sick from the library."

Huh. I guess it's Friday, after all.

"Then I want you to soak in a hot bath and listen to meditation music on your phone. I want *zero* thoughts in your head. Then, a nap. You're exhausted. I'll call you at eight, and we'll talk. And Peej? Get your mom to call Dr. Edmunds. This has gone too far."

I nod. There's no way I'll be able to nap, but I'm not about to tell that to Mariana. She'd probably escort me to my house, serve me warm milk, and try to tuck me into bed. And I don't really want to talk to Dr. Edmunds, but Mariana is right that I should probably start seeing her again, even if I don't talk about slipping. I can still unload about Ethan, and it might help to do that with someone who doesn't know him.

When I get home, I contemplate a bath for about three whole seconds. While the warmth would be *really* good after the walk home, I'm just not ready to sit. In fact, I feel entirely too close to slipping again, and Ethan's not even around. I'm practically living on the edge these days—always—and I hate it.

A run.

I can breathe when I run, and if I stay home and get in the bath, there's no saying I won't just slip right back to walking home in the cold with Mariana. I'd rather skip straight to running in it.

So I throw on a pair of leggings, a t-shirt, and a sweatshirt, then pull my hair into a ponytail, grab a headband to keep my ears warm, and lace up my sneakers. I leave Mom a note on the fridge in case she's home before I am. I think she said she was covering someone else's regular first shift today, but I don't want her to worry if she finds me out of the house. I'm not bringing my phone. I don't want to deal with texts right now. I don't want to hear that ping. Today, it's just my sneakers and the trail.

After a long, anxious day (or, you know, after many long, anxious weeks), hitting my stride feels almost cathartic. Before long, I'm past Bluestone Park, leaving the frozen lake behind me. It's been forever since I ran more than two or three miles in a day, and I'm shocked by how good it feels and how much my muscles need this release despite my fatigue.

I head to the Halfpenny Creek trail, knowing it's still a bit of a mess, but it's not like I plan to run the whole length of it anyway. I just want to smell the pine in the woods for a bit. The dirt on the trail is frozen solid, but there's no snow or ice, so at least it's not slick.

We did a pretty good job on the majority of this trail, truth be told. At a mile and a half in, I wonder if maybe other people started picking up the trail as well. It's cleaner than I remember it being when we left it Thanksgiving week.

The thought of that week sends my pulse leaping a little. I'll have to spend time with Ethan again when the ground thaws out and we get back to the cleanup. There's no way around it, and no matter how mean I am to him in the first version of events, he always seems to come back. I can't get him not to care.

It's infuriating, really. If he would just stop trying to talk to me, or help me, or smile at me or, or…if he would just stop existing, it would really help me to stop slipping. And if I could stop slipping daily, I might regain a chance to sleep normally again. And if I could sleep normally, I could stop having horrible nightmares, and if—

My foot catches a root, and I go sprawling. There's not even time to cushion myself with a roll. There's a sickening pop in my ankle as the root keeps me from falling cleanly, holding my foot in place like some vicious predator. Physics is not my friend. I hit the ground with my full weight and bounce, my head grazing a rock along the side of the trail.

Dazed, I stay down for a long moment and stare at the sticks and pine needles on the ground next to my face. Could be seconds, could be minutes. I'm not sure what happened, actually. One minute, I was running, and the next…I wasn't. The frozen ground feels a lot harder when you hit it the way I just did.

I roll onto my side and put a hand to my head. It comes away covered in blood. Automatically, I reach for my phone so I can assess the damage, but I don't have my armband for my phone. It's…at home. Because my phone is also at home.

Oh no.

My phone is at home.

I dab my hairline a few more times with my fingers. It's still bleeding, but I don't think it's outright gushing blood, so if I can just sit for a few moments and let it dry, it'll probably scab over.

The Halfpenny Creek trail was a stupid idea. I should have just stuck with my original plan to head around the lake and go home. I give a shiver as I blow on my scraped hands. Of all the times I decide to leave my phone at home…

When I'm relatively sure I'm not going to pass out from blood loss, I finally start to stand. I lean on a nearby tree trunk, but a screaming pain on the outside of my ankle as soon as I put weight on it halts me in my tracks. I lift my foot immediately, holding it up and cursing under my breath. I did *not* screw up my ankle. I refuse to believe it's possible.

But when I gently attempt to put weight on it a second time, it hurts so badly I think I *might* pass out. I'm forced to sit again. There's no way I can put weight on it.

I close my eyes and bite my lip in frustration. I tore a tendon. That was the pop I felt; it had to be. I swear, if I screwed up my chances at next season's cross-country—

Pausing mid-thought, I look at the frozen trail all around me, reality crashing in on my misplaced anger. Cross-country is the last thing I need to worry about right now.

I need to get home, but home is over three miles away. Why, oh why, oh why, oh why did I not just go home after the lake? Tears well in my eyes, but I push them away.

Look for a walking stick. Make a crutch for yourself. Get home.

I give myself orders to follow, but I'm already fighting the shivers as I root around the forest floor for a long, heavy stick to act as a crutch. I will *not* freeze to death because I was stupid enough to run outdoors in mid-January in eastern Pennsylvania. I will *not* give Leon's mom a reason to have to write about the dead girl found in the woods.

Wait. Leon's mom. The girl I saved.

If I slip, I can erase my dumb misstep. I *need* to slip. How am I not close enough to a panic attack to slip? My heart is absolutely thundering in my chest.

I still.

Wait.

Nothing.

I try to think about Ethan, about our next interaction, about how much I hate seeing him and not having him, about how much I despise making his life miserable, and how I'm doing it anyway.

With every passing minute, my chances of slipping with enough time to stop myself from falling grow slimmer. But there is absolutely *no* abnormal pressure in my veins right now. No matter how hard I wish it. There's nothing but adrenaline.

Dammit. I start my search for a walking stick again as my teeth begin to chatter. Gotta keep moving. If I keep moving, I can't freeze. My fingers are painfully stiff in the cold as I push aside forest floor debris.

The problem with this part of the trail is that it's mostly pine trees. Glorious-smelling pine trees that drop exactly zero large branches for me to lean on in order to get out of here. If I want to find a stick large enough to use as a crutch, I'm going to have to hobble off the trail and into the woods. I don't like the idea, but how far can I go if I'm crawling anyway? I'll just keep the trail directly behind me.

I don't know how long it takes to find a suitable crutch. Not having my phone also means I have no realistic sense of time. In the woods, on a cloudy day like today, everything looks the same, everything sounds the same, and it's only when it starts getting dark that you really have any notion time is passing at all.

I eventually find a stick I can use after I've more or less scraped up every part of my body hop-crawling around the forest. At least I can get myself out of the woods now…which requires actually finding the trail again. I'm not an idiot. I've watched plenty of movies, and I know it's not *ever* a good idea to leave the trail, but I didn't exactly have much of a choice given the condition of my ruined ankle.

I can't begin to guess how long it takes me to find the trail again. I finally locate it, but by the time I start back, I'm shivering almost violently. It doesn't help that I have to stop to catch my breath every fifty feet or so. Dragging myself along with one good leg and a makeshift walking-stick-turned-crutch requires more exertion than I would have imagined. The healthy sweat I worked up while running has long since dried, and I'm desperately trying not to work up a new sweat as I go. Freezing in your own sweat isn't a great idea.

I keep hoping I'll see someone on the trail who can help me, but January isn't a popular time for hiking. Unless there's snow on the ground, being out in the frigid weather is something rational people generally avoid around here. Still, a girl can hope.

This is okay, though. My ankle hurts. My head hurts. But it's okay. I'm going to get home. And I repeat that to myself right up until it starts getting dark. At least now I know what time it is.

I keep hobbling until sunset becomes twilight, and twilight becomes dusk. That's when I finally let myself have a good cry. I recognize where I am on the trail when I give in and sit down, but I sob because I'm still over a mile from the trailhead, it's dark, it's below freezing, I'm in leggings and a sweatshirt, and there is *no* way I'm getting home on my own two feet tonight.

Leon's mom is going to write a story about the local hero of last autumn who froze to death in the woods less than three months after saving a drowning girl. I try to calculate when someone will realize I'm missing and when they might finally think to search for me. Will they even search the trail? It's not my regular running spot.

Oh my God. Mom won't get home until six or seven. She'll see my note and assume I'm out running. It'll take her an hour at least to realize something is wrong. Mariana said she'd call at eight, but my phone is in my bedroom. Mom won't realize Mariana's calling me. Mariana will think I'm avoiding her.

And no one will know I'm in the dark woods with a screwed-up ankle.

I'm going to freeze to death.

I shove my hands inside the single pocket of my sweatshirt, my icy fingers meeting in the middle beneath the fabric. I'm so stupid.

I have nothing to start a fire, nothing to keep me warm, no food, no water, and—as the forest grows dark and quiet around me—no light except for the moon.

It can't be fully dark for more than an hour when I swear I see a bouncing light far down the trail. My heart leaps into my throat in hope, but whatever the light was, it's gone now, or maybe I imagined it, and it was never there at all.

I pull my knees to my chest, tuck them into my sweatshirt, then pull my arms from the sleeves so I can wrap them around my knees in an attempt to keep myself from shivering to death.

I put the lower half of my face into the neckline of the sweatshirt and blow warm air from my lungs into my makeshift sweatshirt-tent in an attempt to warm my body. I will never take for granted a hot bath again, I swear. In fact, if I'd taken a hot bath and a nap like Mariana instructed, I wouldn't be in this situation at all. But focusing on that won't get me home.

Okay. So I need to survive at least until nine. That'll be about the time Mom starts to realize I'm not home for real. Hopefully, she'll head to my room and see my phone. With any luck, she'll put two and two together and figure out I went for a run and never came back. If she calls Mariana, Mariana can tell her my usual running spots. The Halfpenny Creek trail isn't at the top of that list, but it *should* occur to her. Which means, I probably won't see anyone until ten or eleven o'clock tonight.

Four to six hours, probably.

I need to find a way to not freeze to death for the next six hours. I'm sure I can do this…until my teeth start chattering so hard my jaw aches.

"PJ!"

I pull my head out of my sweatshirt so fast I nearly pull a muscle in my neck. My muscles are so stiff, my body so cold.

The voice was so far away, I'm not even sure I heard it at first, but the forest is dead quiet otherwise. I couldn't have been imagining it unless I dozed off.

"PJ!"

I almost jump to my feet in the dark, ankle be damned.

"Here! I'm here!"

"PJ!"

I strain louder. "I'm here. I'm on the trail!"

Then I sob because the voice does not belong to my mom or to Mariana. The voice belongs to Ethan, and I have never wanted to see anyone so badly in my entire life as I want to see Ethan at this very moment.

When he reaches my side, I hop-fall into him, sobbing, sure I'm somehow going to slip backwards and once again be alone in the deep of the woods.

"Oh my God, PJ. Thank God."

He holds me and somehow manages to unzip his jacket while he continues to keep me in his arms. He wraps both sides of the jacket around me, pressing me to him, holding me in the warm envelope of his coat, his body heat bringing life to my body again. And he lets me cry.

When I stop sobbing like a four-year-old, Ethan gives me his jacket. I relish the warmth as I shove my hands in the flannel-lined pockets.

He calls Mariana as soon as he's sure I'm not going to fall apart if he lets go.

"Yeah, I found her," he says as he uses one hand to pull dried leaves from my hair. His eyes don't leave me as he speaks to her.

There's a pause. I can't hear what Mariana might be saying on the other end, but I can imagine.

"It's okay...No, really...No, it's fine. She's okay....No, I'll bring her home....You don't need to do that...Look, she's freezing, she's got a gash across her head, she's covered in dirt, and her foot's pretty messed up, but she's okay. Yeah. Just let me get her back to the car, okay? I told you I'd call when I found her. I did. Now, I'm gonna get her home."

He doesn't wait for her to reply again. He hangs up. Then he holds the flashlight low, illuminating the two of us. There's nowhere to hide from Ethan this time.

And I don't want to.

Ethan looks at me with an emotion in his eyes I can't interpret, a gaze that's speaking a language I don't understand. I swallow.

Does he hate me? After all this? Can I blame him?

Then he sighs and shakes his head like he's disappointed in me. When he finally speaks, I'm not sure I've heard his words correctly at all.

"Not going to slip on me this time, are you?"

CHAPTER TWENTY-THREE

"What?" The word comes out in a half-frozen whisper.

Time screeches to a grinding halt. Ethan purses his mouth and gives me a small nod as shrewd eyes assess my reaction, but he doesn't give me a chance to ask questions.

"What did you just—"

"Later," he says before he steps close and turns his back to me. "Hop on, and here, you get the flashlight. Try to keep it pointed straight so I can see where we're going."

There's no way Ethan can piggyback me down this whole trail, but I don't argue. I wrap my arms and legs around him as instructed and hold on. My fingers aren't even close to being thawed, but I don't complain. I point the flashlight straight along the trail in front of us so he can see where he steps.

"Watch for killer tree roots," I mutter in his ear. Not exactly sweet nothings.

My head spins as he carries me down the length of the trail. Did he really say what he said? About slipping? Did he figure it out? How? Is this what it's like to be tall? Each of his steps is easily two of mine, even in the dark, even with me on his back. How much faster could I run if I had legs as long as his? Ethan smells good. I probably smell like dirt and dried sweat.

None of my thoughts make sense, but I'm just so relieved to no longer be alone.

When we reach the trailhead parking lot, Ethan carries me the last twenty feet to the car, opens the passenger side door, then spins around to deposit me directly into the seat. I switch off the flashlight and drop it beside me. Then I swing myself to sit forward, careful to keep my throbbing ankle from bumping into anything, and wrap Ethan's jacket tighter around me. I close my eyes, lean my head against the headrest, and inhale. The car, the jacket, it all smells like Ethan. It's like one giant Ethan-hug.

In the time it takes for him to close the door and walk to his side of the car, I'm hit with half a dozen flashbacks of time spent in this car, of driving to get ice cream, of stargazing, of our first (and second first) kiss. I pat the upholstery on the door. Somehow, this car feels like an old friend. It's comfort right when I need it the most.

That should tell me everything I need to know about my current mental state. I'm happy to see a car.

Ethan gets in and starts the engine. Then he rubs his hands together and blows on them.

"Just give it a couple of minutes to warm up, and I'll get the heat blowing."

The clock on the dashboard tells me it's six twenty-eight. Mom's not even home yet. All this time, I've been thinking about how she was going to freak out, and she's probably still driving home.

"How did you know to look for me?" I croak.

"Mariana. You have her listed as an emergency contact at the library." Ethan leans towards me and reaches for my filthy hands, then takes them in his and starts rubbing. He cups them and blows again. I let him. It's painful but so welcome.

I did list her. Mom works so much I figured Mariana would be my better contact in case of an emergency.

"I forgot to call out."

For once, being irresponsible has paid off. If I'd called off sick, no one would have come looking for me for hours yet.

I stare at Ethan, at this boy I pushed and pushed away who's warming my hands in his, and my heart breaks into a thousand jagged pieces inside my chest, each shard stabbing deep. I'm going to bleed out from a thousand tiny cuts inside. When the tears start this time, I can't stop them.

"Hey." Ethan touches my chin to tilt my face upwards so I can no longer hide the emotion streaming down my face.

I don't know what I expected to see in his expression. I don't know if I expected hurt or anger or judgment, but I'm met with kindness and understanding. It's enough to send fresh streams of tears spilling over my cheeks.

"Hey, for real, PJ, it's okay. You're okay." He brushes stray hair behind my ear as he speaks, still holding both my hands in one of his much larger ones. He removes his hand only to turn the heat in the car on full blast.

"I was so awful to you!" The words tumble from my mouth. Once they start, I can't seem to stop them. I sniff. "I was horrible, Ethan. I tried to push you away because I thought it would be easier. I thought it was kinder in the long run, even if it meant being terrible. I said things I didn't mean, things I hoped would hurt so you'd stop caring. And then I...I...threw a banana at you, and you—you *literally* saved my life."

At that, the corners of his lips tug upward in what could be a smile.

"What?" I ask. The knowing look in his eyes sends an unnerving jolt down my spine.

"You did throw a banana at me, didn't you?"

I drop my head. "I'm sorry!"

"But then you didn't...throw a banana, I mean."

"*How* do you know?" Slowly, I raise my eyes to meet his.

"Mariana."

She told him.

Mariana...told Ethan. And I'm not even mad.

"She called me after school today. Told me everything. She was so damn worried about you."

"And you...believed her?" I can't fight my doubts. How's it possible he just accepted at face value the wild and crazy notion of a girl he knows panicking and slipping through time?

"It's kind of hard not to when she told me all the things I thought I imagined in my head were real when she described things I never told anyone about—*crazy* things I considered my deepest fears."

"I'm sorry," I whisper.

"I thought I was going insane, PJ. I thought...well, I thought I was losing my mind. I haven't been able to sleep in weeks. I just...keep having these dreams. Dreams where you—"

"Squeezed a tube of paint on your shirt?"

"Yes!"

"And threw soccer balls at you?"

"You really did all those things, didn't you?"

"I'm awful."

"No! You're not. What you did was awful, but what you've been going through is...so much worse." He searches my eyes in the dark as he rubs my hands. The expression on his face is difficult to read. Finally, he says, "You really slip? Through time, I mean. You really lose your place?"

I chew the inside of my cheek, taking a moment to think about how to answer. Ethan knows. Ethan *really* knows, and he hasn't called me crazy or made me feel like dirt. Ethan. Knows. I think that feeling in my chest is relief.

"Losing my place," I say. "That's a good way to phrase it. It's like someone stole a bookmark from my book and returned it to an earlier chapter, so a chapter I already read ends up being overwritten somehow. And no one around me knows. No one around me has ever understood that anything was wrong." I look down at my lap, screwing up my face in confusion, and add, "Until you."

I wait for Ethan to speak, but he doesn't, so I continue.

"You're different, Ethan. I don't know why. I don't know what makes you different. I just… Every time I slipped around you, you showed up again in the next version of events, even when I tried to avoid you."

I look back at him just in time to see his eyes narrow as he smirks. "You tried to avoid me?"

I nod. "Desperately."

"Desperately?!"

The heat in the car is finally helping my muscles to relax. My body almost feels like a body again and not a block of ice.

"At first, it was because I wanted to avoid your attention and the anxiety that came with it. Then, when I realized you remembered some of what happened in version one, it was because I wanted to avoid hurting you. And then, well, then it was because I wanted you to want to avoid *me* because I thought we'd both be better off."

"I could never stay away, PJ." The conviction in his words leaves no room for argument.

I give a weak laugh. "I know. Not even throwing bananas or dumping paint water on your head could get you to leave."

"I wish… I wish you'd told me," he says. "I wish you'd given me a chance."

"Would you have believed me? No one but Mariana ever has, not even my own mom." Saying that part out loud hurts, like somehow I blame Mom for my condition. "It sounds crazy, Ethan."

"I hate that you were alone—always, I mean. Not just now in the woods, although that, too. I hate that you *felt* alone. I don't know if I could have lasted as long as you without anyone knowing, honestly. I'm not"—he wrinkles his nose, an unreadable expression crosses his face—

"sure how you're still here."

I close my eyes and swallow. "Did Mariana tell you I tried to end it once?"

He sucks in a breath, silent for a moment.

"No," he finally says, his voice raw.

"I…slipped, so it never happened."

He reaches over the center console and grabs me in a bear hug. When he speaks next, his voice is thick with emotion, warm in my ear.

"PJ, you're the most incredible girl I've ever met. You're funny and athletic and smart and gorgeous inside and out and…and…not a day goes by where I'm not glad to know you, where I'm not happy to have spent even a short time as your lucky boyfriend. Because that time was the best time of my life, the first time where I felt like someone understood me, like someone else got it, you know?

"You're that someone. If you'd…succeeded in ending your life, I'd still be wandering around, feeling alone and wondering if anyone in the world was worth connecting with because you are, PJ. A thousand times over, you are worth it."

The heat blowing from the vents in the floorboard and dashboard has begun to thaw my fingers and toes, but the thaw that's going on in my heart right now is all Ethan.

"I didn't think we could *have* a happy ending." I hate how raw my voice sounds right now. I pull back from his hug and wipe a tear from my eye. Every time I manage to stop crying, I start again.

"How about we just start with a happy beginning and save the endings for later?"

"What kind of a relationship can two people have if one of them slips every time she's anxious? What happens when we have a fight and you say something, and I slip, and you've never actually said it, but I resent the fact that you said it the first time, and…and…"

"PJ."

"What?"

"How about you let me decide? How about you give me the benefit of the doubt and do what real people in real relationships do and *talk* to me about it?"

"I didn't know how. In all this time, Mariana's the only person who's ever believed."

"Wait. If I'm the only one you say can remember events from the first version, how does Mariana know about all of this? How does she believe you?" he asks.

"That's a long story, but in a string of slips freshman year, I managed to get information from her that she'd never told anyone else. I would have done the same with you if I thought I could have. But I couldn't anticipate my slips with you, Ethan. I never knew when I was going to go until I was gone!"

"But you're not slipping now," he says.

I blink.

He's…right.

Why am I not slipping? My anxiety is going full steam ahead. I'm exhausted and anxious and overwhelmed with everything that's happened since I came home from school. My ankle throbs with pain as feeling creeps back in, and this conversation with Ethan should be more than enough to put me over the edge.

He narrows his eyes at me, questioning. "You haven't slipped, right? Because I haven't gotten any weird déjà vu so far."

I shake my head slowly.

"I haven't slipped."

Ethan stares at me, then tugs the collar of his coat tighter around me with a noise that could be a sigh or a frustrated huff. "You're not alone anymore."

I nod. "Now you know."

"Now I know. So what are we going to do about it?"

I hesitate, the words on the tip of my tongue. I don't know if it's fair of me to ask. "Can you forgive me?"

He pretends to contemplate, shoving his bottom lip upward, shifting his eyes. I know he's teasing, but I hold my breath, waiting for an answer anyway.

Finally, he squints at me and opens his mouth. "Forgiveness is a good place to start. Yeah, I can forgive you."

I let out my breath. The weight of the last two months lifts from my chest, and I can breathe again.

"Can you forgive me?" Ethan asks.

I almost choke. "For what?"

"For not being there for you sooner."

"Ethan! You had *no* way of knowing. You…have been…everything I could have asked for. More than I deserved!"

"No, PJ," he says. "You deserve so much more. You deserve a friend, a boyfriend, a better kisser—"

I groan. "It wasn't true. You're not a horrible kisser. I didn't mean it when I shouted that in the cafeteria. I just wanted you to move on so you could forget about me. I love your kisses. I crave your kisses. You make my fingers and toes tingle, and you make me forget about the world, Ethan."

He smiles knowingly as he leans in. "I just wanted to hear you say it."

Then he kisses me, and I forget there is anything wrong with the world, with my life, with the universe. I forget that I thought I would spend the next several hours alone, freezing to death in the woods three miles from home.

"Close your eyes," Ethan says.

"They *are* closed!"

For good measure, he stretches his arms around me and puts his hands over my already closed eyes. Ethan drove me home from work today, for which I am an incredibly grateful girlfriend. February in eastern Pennsylvania is *cold*—maybe not as cold as February in Maine, but colder than January here, and I'm so ready for spring, even if it means we'll soon be cleaning the Frigid Death trail—er, I'm sorry, the Halfpenny Creek trail. Plus, although it's considerably better, the tendon in my ankle isn't quite fully healed, so I'm not up for much walking these days.

But when we pull into my driveway, Ethan insists on coming inside to show me a "surprise." I'm not sure what kind of surprise he has in store or why he couldn't have just handed it to me in the car.

He guides me through the house, the two of us shuffling in an awkward dance across the floor as he keeps his hands over my eyes. We go past the living room, and I know we hit the kitchen as soon as Pablo starts howling for me to feed him. But we keep walking. Where is Ethan taking me?

This is so weird.

At the threshold of the sunroom that leads to the back deck, we stop.

"Okay. Are you ready?"

"I don't know what I'm supposed to be ready for, but yes?"

He takes his hands off my eyes and leaps to my side, one arm outstretched into the sunroom, at the center of which sits a treadmill.

"Tada!"

My lips part in shock. There's a treadmill in my sunroom.

I turn to him. "What's this?"

His gaze shifts from me to the treadmill and back again. "I would think that's fairly obvious."

"Ethan, this is a *treadmill*."

"Ah! So you *do* know what it is."

"Where did this come from?"

He gives a sheepish grin, and the dimple I love so much in his left cheek reveals itself. "I've been saving up from the garage."

"You...bought me a treadmill."

"Okay, but it's not brand new. I knew someone who had one they were getting rid of because they didn't use it like they thought they would, and it's not like I paid full price—"

"You bought me a treadmill," I say again, a little more forcefully.

Ethan quiets, looking adorably nervous. "Yeah, I thought...well, I figured if you weren't running from me so much, you might slip less, and"—he waves his hands helplessly— "I sort of have more of a chance of catching you on the treadmill than I do on the trail. Plus, you can run all year long in any kind of weather, and there are no murdering tree roots and..."

I throw myself at him, my arms reaching for his neck, hugging him maybe tighter than I've ever hugged anyone in my life.

"I won't run from you," I tell him. "Not ever again."

He hugs me back, then pulls away and places a quick kiss on my lips. His eyes light with a playful glint.

"What?" I tilt my head to look at him.

"Told you I'd find out where 'Slip' came from," he says with a grin. "Turns out you really *are* a klutz."

EPILOGUE

In case you're wondering, Mariana got into the summer program at Yale. Ever since she was accepted, she's talked about nothing but what she plans to do there and how she's going to change the world.

Predictably, her parents were thrilled. In fact, they were so proud when they read her acceptance letter that they threw an impromptu party the very night she received it. Not that they ever need a reason to celebrate, as the Salvadore family likes any excuse to throw a family party, but this was a good one. There were a lot of people there that night, but even more fresh queijadas. I couldn't be prouder of my friend. Mariana deserves all the celebrations.

Will Ethan and I be together forever? It's hard to know. We're teenagers. It helps that we're planning to go to the same college. I finally figured out my path—I'm going to major in Child Psychology, and I think I'll be good at it. I certainly have the personal experience invested in this career choice, and if I can help other anxious kids, it'll be worth it.

Or maybe I'll write an autobiography and pitch it as fiction. Really, who can say?

But even knowing where I'm headed and what I'll be doing in the next few years, I can't know what the future will hold. I want to believe Ethan and I are strong enough to make it through anything, but I've seen strong relationships break, so I'm not naive to the hardship that comes with navigating relationships, even if this *is* my first.

But Ethan's shown me what it means to fight for something you believe in, to stand your ground instead of running away. So all things considered? I'd say Mariana's not the only one with a reason to celebrate. Happy beginnings are a great place to start. They might even be better than happy endings.

ACKNOWLEDGMENTS

How to thank all the people who made this book possible? That task might actually be *impossible*, but I'll give it a try. First and foremost, my family always comes first. Cae Storms, you were my inspiration for PJ from the very start. I was an anxious young adult who often felt alone in my struggles and like there was no one who could possibly understand the true physical misery of being anxious all the time. The intense stomach pain, the inability to eat while simultaneously feeling ravenous because you haven't eaten in days, the running to the bathroom when you *do* finally eat because your body refuses to digest anything properly, the racing heart, the breathless dizziness, all while trying to hide every symptom because you're in the middle of sitting through a college lecture and can't show it. That time in my life was one of my personal hardest.

But nothing—nothing—is worse than watching your own child go through the same thing. I would take the anxiety from you a hundred times over, Cae, if it meant you didn't have to live with it. And the same goes for Chris Storms, my dear, sweet, second anxious child. I've somehow managed to give the two of you all my lousy, anxious genes. I apologize. But on the flip side, you both feel so deeply, love so strongly, and follow your dreams with the kind of passion that can only be felt by someone so incredibly anxious. So maybe those genes weren't a complete bust after all. (Sorry about the extreme emetophobia, though. That's on me.)

A thanks to my husband, Nathan Storms, who was there for me during my panic attacks long before we brought two anxious kids into this world who had to deal with their own panic attacks. Nate, who even today looks at my harebrained travel itineraries with uncertainty, shrugs, and then says, "Let's do it." I love this life with you, even if my chemical imbalances sometimes make it seem otherwise.

Perhaps the biggest thank you goes to Mom and Dad. You've dealt with an anxious kid for far longer than I have. But it was the 90s and we didn't talk about those things then... Even so, you've always been my safe space, my support, and the reason why I've never been afraid to try new things. Knowing home was always just a phone call away gave me the comfort I needed to keep trying even on the days when things got hard.

To my beta readers and critique partners, thank you a thousand times over for lending me your heart and your own anxious minds for the duration of this book. Erin Fletcher, Mallory Hoffman, Jean Grant, Allison Longo, Barbara Longo, Joe Martin, Cindy Mock, Leann Quire, Jess Rancatore, Vanita Shastry, Cae Storms, Chris Storms, and Angela Westerman, thank you for your invaluable insight on this one.

Another thank you to Sorchia DuBois, for editing yet another book for me, for finding the flaws and pointing them out so my readers aren't upset, but especially for correcting my chronic comma over- and under-usage. And to my dear cover artist, Angela Westerman, a heartfelt thank you for a magical cover that captures the essence of PJ and Ethan so perfectly.

Perhaps most importantly, a thank you to *you*, Reader. Because you make writing books possible. But also because if you picked up this book, you've likely had some measure of anxiety in your life, too. And I know how that feels. You are not alone.

In fact, in 2022, 59.3 million adult Americans were living with mental illnesses ranging in severity from mild to moderate to severe.[1] But in the two and half decades I've been dealing with an anxiety disorder, there's one thing I've learned. Talking about it, making light of it, and laughing at it eliminates its power over you. So talk about your anxieties, fears, and worries with friends, family, or a licensed counselor. Help destigmatize mental illness.

If you, or someone you know, is experiencing mental health-related distress, call or text 988 for crisis support. Or visit 988lifeline.org to chat.

1. National Institute of Mental Health, https://www.nimh.nih.gov/health/statistics/mental-illness

A SPECIAL THANKS TO MY
KICKSTARTER BACKERS
You made this possible. Thank you!

*Derek Ashauer
*Joan & Peter Coombs
*Kim & Jason Coleman
*Sierra Clothier
*Janette Davis
*Ron Delaney
*Mari Shelley: Dream big! Jamie &
Derek DeRewal
*Jamie Diamond
*Mary Ann Drosnock
*John Dunn
*Quenby Eisenacher
*Taylor Epperson
*Melissa Faro
*Stephen Fertig
*Abigail and Julia: Wishing you all
the best as you follow your dreams,
Michele Fragnito
*Gail Gilmore
*Stephen Gorbos
*Janet Graden
*Jean Grant
*Morgan Grogean
*Maria Hahn
*Alisa Harris-Norico
*Melissa Harris
*DL Hammons
*Corinne Hauk
*Jay Heltzer
*Margaret Herrick
*Melanie Hooyenga
*Tanya Hopkins
*Tamara Icenogle
*Virginia Jacobs
*Amy Johnson
*Jenn Johnson-Hamer
*Nancy & David Kershner

*Allyson Larese
*Kay Lawson
*Chrys Lewis
*Mariah Ligas
*Heather Long
*Barbara & Frank Longo
*Jennifer & Daniel Longo
*Joe Martin
*Fernando & Kate Martinez
*Jessica & Brent Metzgar
*Catherine Miller
*Jennifer Miller
*Suzanne Miller
*Cindy Mock
*Maggie M.
*Roderick Nevin
*Adrienne Oakley
*Jessica & Shawn Rancatore
*Vasavi Reddy
*Elizabeth Richards
*Holly Rigg
*A. Michael Roberts
*Wendy Ryan
*Maki Saito-Varadi
*Janet Selman
*Vanita Shastry
*Rachel Simpson
*Andrea Sipple
*Sara Smith
*Heather Spencer
*Jean Sitkei
*Beverly Szymborski
*Barb Triscari
*Katelyn Botsford Tucker
*Denise Varadi
*Ralph Walker
*Angela Westerman

ABOUT THE AUTHOR

L. Ryan Storms is a writer, photographer, traveler, and dreamer. She's a member of the Eastern Pennsylvania chapter of SCBWI, the Alliance of Independent Authors, and the Independent Book Publishers Association. She has written articles featured on the front page of local newspapers, but mostly she writes novels near and dear to her heart. She holds a B.S. in Marine Science from Kutztown University of Pennsylvania and a Master's in Business Administration from Marist College, but writing young adult fantasy has always been her true passion.

Her first young adult novel, *A Thousand Years to Wait,* placed first in the Young Adult category in the 2021 Royal Dragonfly Book Awards and was an award-winning finalist in American Book Fest's 2019 Best Book Awards. Most recently, *Temper the Dark* was a finalist in both the 2023 Chanticleer International Book Awards OZMA division for Fantasy Fiction and the Young Adult Category of the 2024 Next Generation Indie Book Awards.

Storms lives in Pennsylvania with her cancer-survivor husband, two children, and a "rescue zoo" of ever-changing furry and feathered animals. When she's not writing, reading, or keeping her teens in line, she enjoys hiking, photography, and planning the next big adventure.

L. RYAN STORMS
(Photo credit: Laslo Varadi)

Find out what L. Ryan Storms is working on
& visit her blog at www.lryanstorms.com.

By L. Ryan Storms:

THE TARROWBURN PROPHECIES
A Thousand Years to Wait
The Heart of Death
Chaos Bound

Temper the Dark
Marit Unsanctioned

www.ingramcontent.com/pod-product-compliance
Lightning Source LLC
Chambersburg PA
CBHW050033120726
47903CB00006B/2025